THE OFFICER'S AFFAIR

SAMANTHA GROSSER

THE OFFICER'S AFFAIR

First published in 2018 by Sam Grosser Books

ISBN: 978-0-6483052-1-7

Cover Design by ArtMishel

For Steve, as always

My rock, my light, my friend.

The Anzio Experience has remained with me,
mainly because I never expected to live through it.

Alan Whicker

Prologue

Danny came home the day that Monte Cassino finally fell to the Allies. Since the telegram, Rachel had been first to the post every morning, waiting for a letter that might explain. All she knew for certain was that he was seriously wounded. No mention of where or when, not a word about what or how, so that all her thoughts were filled with the endless possibilities.

She wrote to him without the usual pretence at calm, too desperate for news to care if he thought her hysterical, and though she knew her letter might take weeks to reach him, it gave her the comfort of at least doing something towards finding out. It was the sense of helpless suspense she could not stand.

Then a letter came from Captain Andrews and she was too afraid to open it straight away, hiding instead in the best front living room away from the rest of the family, standing by the open window with the flimsy envelope clutched between her fingers. Next door, the postman was in the drive, passing the time of day with the neighbour, and she watched them without interest while she struggled for the courage to tear the letter open.

The postman said goodbye and moved on along the road, his cheery tuneless whistle filtering back to her in snatches. *Wish me luck as you wave me goodbye* she thought she heard, though she couldn't be sure, and the song stuck in her head as an accompaniment for the news she was about to read.

Looking down at the letter, she turned it over in her hands, and saw the small neat handwriting, the same return address as she had used to write to Danny. Fingers trembling, she coaxed open the seal and took out the slip of paper. Her eyes skimmed down across the page.

"*Your husband stood on a mine at Anzio,*" she read, "*His legs were badly damaged … in hospital in Algiers, recovering …*"

She stopped reading, let her hand drop to her side, still holding the half-read letter. He was in hospital now in a faraway place she could not imagine. Then, remembering that Algiers was in North Africa somewhere, the name familiar from the news, she wondered why they had sent him there: it seemed to her to be a long way away from Italy.

She lifted the letter and let her eyes drift over the words again.

He was recovering. He was not going to die and in time he would get better. In time they would send him back to England. He was coming home after all, and they would be together again.

Smiling for the first time in days, she slipped the letter into her pocket and hurried through to the kitchen to tell her parents.

Book One

Chapter One

From the grimy window of the ambulance the house was the same as he remembered it, looming self-assured and solid above the driveway, one of a long row of 1920s semi-detacheds that stretched away down the hill. His father had told him once that he had played in fields here as a boy, but the memory of how it used to be had died with him, and now it was hard to imagine anything here but this middle-class suburban street, as yet untouched by the war.

He ran his eyes across the shabby rendering, and his blood seemed to shrink inside him. Those walls contained his future – his wife's parents' place, no home of his own to come back to any more, and no chance to make a life for himself. This was not what he dreamt of all those nights in Italy.

'You'll be all right now then?' The orderly moved out from behind the wheelchair.

'I'll be all right,' Danny answered. 'Ta.'

'Good luck, then,' the orderly said, and slammed the ambulance doors. The noise reverberated in the quiet street. Danny lingered by the open gate, only half aware of the grind of old gears and the belch of fuel behind him. Fingering the rims of the wheels on the chair, he was afraid to go in, caught in the moment between lives: he was not the same man his wife had said goodbye to, and not yet sure of who he had become.

A shadow at the window of the front room caught his eye. Rachel, he guessed, alerted by the noise, anxious and waiting these two years or more. He forced himself to action, spinning the wheels easily, his upper body still strong, and as he moved himself towards the door she flung it open and stood before him.

'Danny!'

He smiled, touched by her delight, and tears warmed the corners of his eyes.

'Rachel,' he whispered back.

She was just as he remembered her, with her soft curves and kind face, and a cardigan drawn tight across her chest with nervous hands. In the sun her hair seemed lighter, burnished and blond. She was beautiful and for a moment he forgot that he was half a man, that she would no longer want him.

She ran forward two paces, arms stretched out to embrace him, before she slowed, hesitant before the reality of the wheelchair, and the man with no legs that was her husband. Danny lifted his own arms, beckoning, pleading with his eyes for her to come to him. Then with one movement she was there, crouching awkwardly beside the chair, holding him, her head against his shoulder. Slowly, with a sense that the moment could not be real, he put his arms around her and felt the warmth of her body in his embrace. Images of other embraces, men held wounded, struggling, dying, cut across his thoughts. He closed his eyes, forcing his mind away from a world that still seemed more real to him than the loving touch of the woman in his arms. She was crying gently, stifling the sobs against his jacket as he held her and inhaled the familiar sweet scent of her hair, trying to draw himself into her world again.

'It's all right,' he murmured. 'I'm here. It's over. It's going to be all right now.'

Rachel lifted her face to look at him, her eyelashes sleek with tears. She had barely changed. The sweet round face and soft white skin, flushed now from crying, the impossible perfection of her lips. She was smiling but in her eyes was a light of uncertainty and something else it took him a moment to recognise as pity. He looked away from her, swallowing hard, then forced himself to smile as he cupped her face in his hands. She nuzzled against his palms, an old gesture recovered from the past, before he lifted her head and kissed her, the lips just as soft as he remembered.

'I've missed you,' Rachel said, drawing back, shifting her legs against the awkwardness of having to squat by the chair. 'I'm so glad you're home.'

'Even like this?' His hands gestured to the space where his legs used to be, the trouser-legs cut and pinned back neatly over the stumps.

Rachel drew herself up to standing. He squinted up at her, a black outline against the afternoon sun. She nodded. 'Even like that. Shall we go in? We can go in the back way – there's no step there.'

'All right.'

She moved behind the chair, took the handles in her hands.

'I can manage,' he said quickly. 'I'm used to it now.'

She walked beside him up the drive, struggling with the heavy kit bag, and stopped to let him go before her through the gate that led into the garden. Then she stood back and held open the back door and the wheelchair's tyres swished on the linoleum on his way in through the kitchen.

In the living room the wheelchair seemed large and cumbersome though he could see they had pushed the table farther back along the wall and moved the armchairs closer in by the unlit fire to accommodate him. Sunlight fell through the open window, a rectangle of light on the carpet, dust motes floating and restless. Already he felt in the way; this house would never feel like home to him.

'Where are the kids?' he asked.

'At school,' she told him. 'They wanted to stay at home and wait for you, but I didn't know what time you'd be here, or how you'd be. I thought you might want time to get settled before you saw them…'

He nodded, aware of the kindness behind the decision, still the same sweet thoughtful Rachel he had married, but he was disappointed and knew that she saw it.

'I'm sorry,' she said, turning away. 'I thought it was for the best, but perhaps I should have let them stay.' She stared down at her hands, clutched in front of her, and he wished he had hidden his feelings better, that he had not upset her.

'Shall I make some tea?' Rachel said then. She smiled brightly and smoothed nervous hands across her skirt.

'That'd be nice,' he replied.

She nodded and smiled again, eager to please, then hurried out through to the kitchen, the door swinging closed with a click behind her.

In the narrow kitchen Rachel breathed deeply to calm herself and steady her shaking nerves. She had not been prepared for the tension between them, supposing their love for each other would cross the gulf between the two people they had become. The sudden realisation she was wrong caught at the breath in her throat. Twice, in her agitation, she dropped the match to light the stove, and when the gas ignited at last it caught with a whoosh that startled her. Annoyed with her jumpiness she scowled, and prepared the tea with slow deliberation.

When she took the tray through to the living room Danny had his back to her, fiddling with the wireless set on the sideboard. Voices ebbed and waned through the static. Finally he found music, soft American jazz she did not recognise, and she was glad of the distraction from the awkwardness.

Manoeuvring the chair towards the table, he took a mouthful of the tea she had set before him. 'Lovely,' he said, 'the same as you used to make.' Then he lit up a Woodbine, almost flinching as the heat of it touched his lungs. Smoke curled upwards and he lifted his face to watch it drift and eddy above them. Rachel watched too, every movement so familiar, and for an instant the years of separation slipped away.

'What are you smiling about?' he asked.

'I like watching you smoke,' she said.

He half smiled. 'You always did.'

They drank their tea in silence for a while and there was so much that Rachel wanted to say, so much she had planned, but now that Danny was in front of her she could find no words to say anything at all. She sipped at her tea distractedly, frustrated by her inability to break the silence, and flicked quick glances at her husband.

He was still good looking, she thought, the same strong dark features, the same glossy mop of dark wavy hair, but the mischief had gone out of his eyes, and the light that had replaced it made her uneasy and a little afraid. He smoked incessantly; something to occupy his attention she supposed, but his mind seemed to her to be elsewhere, and she could think of no way to call him back.

'How was the trip from the hospital?' she asked.

'It was all right. Took a couple of hours.'

'Will you have to go back at all? For check ups or anything?'

Danny shook his head, and drew back on another cigarette.

'There's nothing left for them to check up on. You can see for yourself.'

He gestured to his legs and she followed the movement with her eyes, drawn against her will to look, to see the missing part of him. She could think of nothing else to say and in the silence all the hoped-for joy of his homecoming faded into the air around them.

Once or twice they risked small smiles at each other, gestures of good will, of hope, but they had been too long apart and too much had changed to find the ease of how they used to be.

The light of the afternoon began to grow dim, heavy clouds full of rain closing in outside, and as the room darkened the distance between them grew. Rachel got up to draw the heavy curtains at the window, adjusting them carefully to let no light escape, the blackout second nature now. When she turned on the lamp on the sideboard it seemed like winter in the room in that light, and cold suddenly, although summer had barely begun. She drew her cardigan tighter round her and sat down again at the table.

'The children should be home soon,' she said.

'I've got presents for them. Not much, but I've been carrying them around since Syria.'

'I'm sure they'll be pleased with them whatever they are. Charlie's been crossing the days off the calendar ever since we heard when you were coming. He's grown up so much, you'll hardly recognise him.'

Danny nodded, and they fell to silence again until the clatter of the children running past the window and through the kitchen, interrupted. Charlie stood in the door to the living room, breathing hard, cheeks red, school satchel hanging in one hand. He stared at the man in the wheelchair, trying to match him to the image of the father he remembered, tall and laughing and strong enough to throw a five-year-old above his head. Behind him Jean was hiding, peering round her brother's arm at this stranger who had left when she was two, a man she could barely remember, a figure in her mother's stories.

'Hello Charlie,' Danny said, 'How was school?'

Charlie shrugged. 'It was boring.'

Danny smiled and flicked a glance to his wife. 'Chip off the old block, eh?'

The boy said nothing, still uncertain.

'Come here,' Danny coaxed with a tilt of his head. 'I've got a present for you.'

Charlie's smile was instant. 'A present? What is it?'

'Well, you'll have to come here and see.'

The boy dropped the satchel and stepped forward, shrugging his arm free of his sister's grip. Both children moved toward the wheelchair as Rachel brought the kit bag and Danny rummaged for the presents.

The gifts were wrapped up in strips of fine cotton – an embroidered doll for Jean and a toy plane for Charlie, skilfully wrought from scrap metal. Both children were delighted and Charlie stood by his father proudly, turning the plane over and over, asking about the mechanics of it, where it had come from. Danny explained as best he could, pointing out the detail, telling him about the Souk in Damascus where he had haggled with the trader over the price, but he was distracted by Jean who still would not go to him, and who took the doll with a shy whispered thank you before retreating behind her mother.

'She'll come round,' Rachel said.

'She looks just like me,' Danny murmured, with a shake of his head. 'No mistaking she's mine.'

Rachel laughed and, squatting down, she chivvied the child from behind her legs towards her father. 'Go on, love. Go and show your dad the doll.'

Jean hesitated, afraid but curious, already jealous of her

brother, confident with his hip against the wheel of the chair, the plane swooping around her father's head.

'Come on, Jeanie.' Danny reached out his hand and she moved forward with a backward glance at her mother for approval. Rachel nodded and the girl stopped at arm's length from her father, holding out the doll for him to see.

'What're you going to call her?' Danny asked.

Jean drew the doll back towards her and stroked the cotton face, considering. 'Delilah,' she said after a moment. 'I'll call her Delilah.'

'That's a stupid name,' Charlie said, interrupting his steady thrum of engine noise. The room seemed very quiet in the pause. 'Who calls a doll Delilah ...?'

'That's enough,' Danny hissed, and Charlie stepped back from the unexpected anger. 'You be nice to your sister.'

Charlie nodded, terrified, and ran out of the room through the kitchen, out into the garden. Danny rubbed his palms across his face, as though he were trying to erase the image of his son's expression, wanting to take back the moment and do it differently. The anger had risen so fast, so uncontrolled, and Rachel swallowed, frightened by this new rage in him. He looked across to his wife, his own fear plain in his eyes.

'He'll be all right,' she said quickly. 'He'll get over it.'

Danny nodded and turned his attention to his daughter, but they both knew it would not be so easy.

Chapter Two

His first evening home, Danny sat at the table in the living room playing cards with his son. Jean was lolling against the wheelchair, cuddling the new doll, as close as she could get to her dad without sitting on his lap. He kept showing her the cards in his hand and winking, but he was still contriving to let Charlie win. Rachel watched the scene with pleasure – it made her smile to see them all together: perhaps everything would be all right after all.

Then the large frame of her father emerged through the door and there was an immediate awkwardness in the room; even the children felt it, falling silent in uneasy expectation.

'Daniel,' George Kirby said. 'It's good to have you back at last.' He stepped forward and bent to offer Danny his hand.

Danny shook it without smiling.

'Ta. But you know I'd prefer to still be over there fighting,' he said. 'Instead of here in this.' He withdrew his hand from the other man's and touched the arm of the wheelchair.

Bewildered, George's smile froze, and he lifted the newly released hand to smooth the corners of his moustache. Then he turned to Rachel in a silent appeal for help and she half smiled and gave a slight shrug. There was nothing she could say.

'Well, yes, I suppose so,' George muttered. 'But it must be nice to see Rachel again. And the children?'

Danny nodded and winked again at Jean, who squirmed. George backed away from the wheelchair and almost tripped on the armchair behind him, unused to its new position in the room, the chairs crowded now closer to the fire. He swore beneath his breath and felt his way around it with his hand before he sank into the cushions. Then he stared at the mantelpiece and the clock there ticked loudly in the silence. Next to it was a photograph of Danny in uniform, smiling and full of hope before he went away.

George's lips twitched into the semblance of a smile at his son-in-law. 'Well, it's good to have you back anyway.'

'Thank you,' Danny answered. He tousled Charlie's hair, and the boy wriggled in mock irritation. His father smiled. 'It's good to be here.'

There was a silence.

'So how was work, Dad?' Rachel said.

'Fine. Same as always.' He was not an easy conversationalist. 'What's for dinner?'

'Shepherd's pie.' One of Danny's favourites for his first meal at home, a choice made after long deliberation. 'Is that all right?'

'It'll do.' He shook the newspaper straight and settled back to read it. Danny and the children resumed their game of cards and Rachel went out to the kitchen, the door swinging shut behind her.

Her mother looked up from the stovetop where she had laid the plates to warm. 'Are they all right?' she asked.

'So far so good,' Rachel replied. 'Fingers crossed it lasts.'

'As long as Danny doesn't goad him.'

Rachel was silent, aware the peace was fragile. Years of

animosity between her husband and her father had conditioned her to expect the worst, and while her mother always laid the blame on Danny, to Rachel it had never been so black and white. They worked in silence then, nothing more to say about it. Rachel counted out the cutlery from the dresser drawer and took it to the living room. Her father had laid the paper to one side and was fiddling with the wireless, muttering under his breath.

'Did you change the channel?' he demanded, turning briefly to look at his daughter.

'No.'

'Then it must have been Kate. I'd wish she'd leave it alone.'

'I'll tell her,' Rachel said with a sideways glance at her husband, who pretended not to see. 'You'll have to stop playing now,' she said. 'Dinner's almost ready.'

Obediently they withdrew their cards for her to open out the table and she left the knives and forks for Charlie to set before she went to collect the plates. They took their places with difficulty, unused to fitting so many people at the table, and the unspoken tension between the two men was heavy.

'Home cooked food at last,' Rachel's mother said. 'Must be nice after all that army food.'

'The hospital food was worse, Rose,' Danny replied. He ate quickly, hunched over the plate without looking up.

'Well, you've got Rachel to cook for you now, so that's something.' Rose's determined cheerfulness seemed only to heighten the awkwardness. No one answered her.

'So, Daniel,' George began, when he had eaten enough to take the edge off his hunger. 'Have you thought about the future at all yet? What you're going to do with yourself now you're back?' He looked across at his son-in-law, fork poised, and waited for an answer.

Danny swallowed his mouthful and Rachel saw the struggle in the tension of his jaw, the tightening of his fingers on the knife and fork. She waited, holding her breath, praying he was not going to start a fight. Not yet. Not already. Let them get through one meal in peace. Danny lifted his gaze to meet the older man's eye.

'There's not much I can do, George, is there. What future do you see for me in this?'

'There must be something you can do?'

'Dad, not now,' Rachel murmured. 'Give him a chance.'

Danny turned on her, shadows of the same rage he let fly at Charlie. 'I don't need you to stick up for me, Rachel. I can fight my own bloody battles.'

Rachel sank in her chair, and wiped at her eyes with impatient, furtive fingers.

'I'm not suggesting he should go out to work tomorrow, but he needs to think about the future, make plans,' her father said. 'He's got to do something. He can't sit around the house all day doing nothing. It's not good for a man to be idle. It isn't good for his self-respect.' He turned to face Danny. 'You'll settle back in much quicker if you're busy, and in a routine. And that's what you want, isn't it? To settle back in?'

Danny laid his knife and fork side by side on the empty plate before he spoke. 'You still up at the BAC, are you? Still a senior engineer?'

George nodded.

'Perhaps you can get me a job up there then. And arrange some transport for me while you're at it. I'll need a car that can take the chair of course, and a strong driver to lift me in and out. Shouldn't be too hard for a great man like yourself to organise. Or shall I just get the bloody bus?'

There was a silence. No one was eating and Jean began to cry.

'Charlie,' Rose said, 'take your sister and go up to your room.'

'Do I have to?'

'He can stay here,' Danny said quickly, before the boy could get up. 'He's old enough to know what goes on in this family. It does no good to hide it from him.'

'He's eight years old,' George said.

'Like I said, he's old enough.'

'And Jean?'

Charlie stared at his father, waiting, confused and afraid but wanting only to please. Danny felt the child's gaze and turned to him. 'Take your sister upstairs, Charlie,' he said softly, and the boy hurried to obey. 'Good lad.'

The children's footsteps faded half way up the stairs and Rachel knew that they had stopped there to listen to the rest.

'Now, Daniel,' George began. His voice was even and controlled, but underneath the anger simmered. 'I know you're upset at what's happened to you. We all are. That's only natural. But you're not in the army any more. You're living here, part of this family, in my house. So you'll keep a civil tongue in your head and we'll get along just fine. Is that understood?'

Danny laughed then, and it seemed to Rachel like old times. 'Yes sir.'

George lifted a warning finger.

'I can't help meself, George,' Danny said.

'Well, you'd better start trying or…'

'Or what?'

'That's enough,' Rose scolded. 'Both of you.'

The two men were silent and the women cleared the plates and took them to the kitchen.

'I'm sorry,' Rachel said.

'It isn't your fault,' her mother answered. 'He hasn't changed at all.'

Rachel said nothing but knew her mother was wrong. He had changed almost beyond recognition.

LATER THAT NIGHT George fumed to his wife in their bedroom upstairs.

'He hasn't changed a bit.'

Rose followed his movements in the dressing table mirror as he paced behind her.

'Still as rude as ever.'

'Don't be too hard on him. He has been through a lot.'

'Bah!' George lifted a hand in dismissal of her words, as if to say his son-in-law's insolence was nothing to do with the war, it was just the way he was made: the impertinence of his class. Danny had as much as admitted it at dinner: he just couldn't help himself.

'Perhaps you should give him some time,' Rose suggested softly. 'You know, to adjust.'

'But that's what I'm talking about. He'll adjust much quicker if he's doing something. He needs to be busy, get himself sorted out. No good is going to come of him sitting about dwelling on the past. I know it sounds hard but really it's the best thing for him. No question.'

Rose hesitated. In thirty years of marriage she had learned her husband did not take criticism well but it needed to be said. She took a deep breath.

'I think he's going to need some time to come to terms with what's happened to him. It can't be easy.'

'We never should have let her marry him.'

'We didn't have much choice,' Rose said, gently.

George stopped pacing and moved to stand behind his wife. She lowered the brush from her hair, still watching his reflection, and he took it from her, began brushing out the curls with gentle, even strokes.

'Remember when we were younger, before the girls were born?' she said. 'You used to do this for me every night.'

George was silent, the only sound the swish of the bristles in her hair, but it was a comfortable silence, bound by memories of the years they had shared. He stopped brushing, then laid the brush on the dressing table. Rose took it and placed it neatly next to the comb as her husband sat down on the bed, stiffly, and regarded his wife in the mirror.

'I remember,' he said. 'A hundred strokes of the brush.'

Then it had been a dark silky mass, soft and heavy on her shoulders. It was greying now, the texture grown coarser across the years, and the face in the mirror was careworn with lines around the eyes, the cheeks no longer smooth and plump. They were growing old, she reflected, and life would offer them no more chances.

He sighed. 'Perhaps you're right,' he said. 'I didn't mean to be unsympathetic. I just think it would be the best thing for him. You know, to get out and do something with himself. No good ever came of brooding.'

Rose smiled at his reflection and her face was lit with echoes of the prettiness of her youth. 'I know you meant well. But you two just rub each other up the wrong way. You always have.'

She stood up and slipped off her dressing gown and he watched her as she slid under the covers of the bed and settled herself down. They had done all right, she supposed, over the years: she could have done a lot worse than marry George Kirby.

'Come to bed,' she said, patting the covers beside her. 'Come on.'

He smiled, and reached across to turn out the lamp.

On their own at last in the soft double bed in the front room downstairs that they had converted at the last minute to a bedroom, Danny told Rachel to pass him the kit bag.

'I got you a present too,' he said. 'But it didn't seem like the right time to give it to you earlier.'

He handed her a small packet with a shrug, as though he was embarrassed at showing her kindness. 'I got it in the Souk in Damascus. You'd have liked it there, Rache. All the pretty fabrics and silverware and jewellery, and everything so cheap.'

'Thank you,' she whispered, and held the package carefully in her hands. He had written to her about the Souks, promised to take her back there one day after the war. She was almost afraid to unwrap it and bring the moment to an end.

'Open it,' Danny said.

She nodded and carefully unfolded the flimsy tissue paper. Inside there was a bracelet, silver inlaid with copper in the most beautiful design she had ever seen. 'It's gorgeous.'

He helped her with the clasp around her wrist and she turned towards the bedside lamp to see it better in the light, shifting her wrist backwards and forwards so that the silver caught and shimmered.

'It's beautiful.' She turned over to face him. 'Thank you so much.'

Danny shrugged and she was filled with love for him, desperate to kiss and to hold him, but there was a defensiveness in the way he held himself, a warning in his eyes that kept her back. Instead she said thank you again, and fell to caressing the bracelet on her wrist.

'Your dad hasn't changed,' he said. 'Still a bastard.'

'But he's been good to us since your dad died. They both have.'

'He still hates me. Probably wishes I'd got killed.'

'Don't say that,' Rachel whispered, horrified.

'It's only the truth. And you know what?' Danny asked. 'For once I agree with him.' He turned away from his wife and reached out to turn off the lamp on the bedside table. When he turned back towards her his face was dark and in shadow, and Rachel could not say what she saw there.

'I would have been better off dead, Rache, and I mean that,' he said softly. 'I can't be a husband to you. You know it's not just my legs that are gone, don't you?' He turned his head briefly towards her and she nodded. 'So I can't be a proper husband to you. Do you understand what I'm saying?

'Yes,' Rachel whispered.

'And I can't be a proper father to the kids. Having to live off your father's charity. I'm just a bloody waste of space. You'd have been better off if I'd never come back and that's a fact.'

Rachel stared, the heat of tears behind her eyes. 'Don't say that,' she pleaded. 'Don't even think it.' She reached out to touch his shoulder, trailed her fingers across the muscle, desperate to be close after so long, but with her touch she felt him stiffen and quiver with the tension.

'Don't,' he whispered. 'There's no point.'

Slowly she withdrew her hand and was aware of the weight of the bracelet on her wrist.

'I'm sorry,' she murmured.

He kept his head averted, and the desire to reach out to him again was almost overwhelming. So long she had waited for this night. So long she had dreamt of it. But in her dreams it had never been like this. They settled themselves down beneath the covers, not touching, and the silence pounded in her head.

'Are you in very much pain?' she asked.

He hesitated before he turned his head towards her. Their faces were close on the pillows and in the half-light she could almost imagine it was how it used to be.

'Some,' he answered. 'But mostly it's up here.' He tapped fingers against his temple. 'That's where it hurts the most.'

'Was it awful?'

'Yes.'

'Can you tell me?' She was afraid to ask, terrified of what he might tell her. 'Please?'

'I don't want to talk about it,' he hissed. 'I don't even want to fucking think about it. Ever. Can you understand that?' The anger went out of him. 'No of course you bloody can't,' he murmured, more to himself than to her. 'How could you? How could anyone understand who wasn't there?'

'I'm sorry,' she said. 'I won't ask again. I just thought …' She wanted to talk more, to reach out and take his pain away, understand his world and lighten his burden by sharing it, but he was silent and did not want her to touch him so there was nothing she could do.

'Good night then, Danny,' she said, settling down, turning out the lamp. 'I'm glad you're back.' She lay as close as she could get without touching him so that she could sense his warmth, the familiar male smell of him that was still the same as she remembered.

'Night Rachel,' he replied. Then, with effort, he shifted further onto his side of the bed, away from her, and slept.

Chapter Three

It was still dark when she woke in the morning and it took a moment to remember. She was used to sleeping upstairs and the sounds of the house were different in her new room, and unfamiliar. Turning, she could make out Danny's shape in the gloom, sleeping peacefully now, the nightmares over for the night, but it was strange to see his form beside her and she had a headache from the broken sleep. Rain still beat hard against the window behind the curtains and she wanted to stay longer in the comfort of the bed next to her husband's warmth.

The alarm clock rang, shattering the peace in the instant it took for her to reach out and silence it. Danny stirred slightly and moaned and Rachel wanted to hold him again as she had in the night when he had cried in her arms. But though she waited for what seemed a long time, he did not wake and so finally, reluctantly, she slipped out of bed to go upstairs and begin the day's routine by waking the children.

In the kitchen her mother was making toast. 'Is Danny all right?'

The children appeared sleepily in the doorway.

'Go and eat your porridge,' Rachel told them. 'Before it gets cold.'

They turned and disappeared and she could hear them arguing but she was too tired and sad to intervene. 'He had nightmares.'

'Poor chap,' her mother said. 'It can't be easy for him.'

Rose passed over fresh toast from under the grill and Rachel spread a thin smear of jam across it. 'Can you try and keep Dad off his back?' she said. 'At least for a while?'

Rose gave her daughter a rueful smile. 'He was just trying to help.' She saw her daughter's expression. 'But I'll do my best,' she added quickly. 'I'll do what I can.'

Kate appeared, rumpled and dishevelled in her pyjamas but still beautiful even after the late shift at the hospital. She yawned and stretched.

'I heard Danny screaming in the night. Is he all right?' Kate took the half piece of toast Rachel gave her and pulled off a bite-sized piece. Then she licked the stickiness from her fingers.

'I'm not sure he's ever going to be all right,' Rachel said.

'Oh, he will,' Rose told them. 'It's early days yet. He'll come to terms with it eventually. You'll see.'

The two sisters exchanged glances and finished their toast.

'I've got to go,' Rachel said. 'Or I'm going to be late.'

'What about Danny?' Rose asked. 'Shouldn't we at least get him up?'

'Let him sleep. He wouldn't want us to fuss over him, and he said he can get himself out of bed and into the kitchen for a wash.'

'If you're sure?'

'I'm sure.'

She called to the children to say goodbye then hurried out through the back door and into the drizzle. Heavy cloud hung low in the sky, gun-metal grey and threatening more rain. Rachel shivered and pulled her coat closer round her. At the end of the driveway she turned down the hill that led to the Green, preferring to walk in the rain across the park than catch the bus, hating the smell of it and the way it lurched across the potholes. The trams had been better but they were long gone, one of the war's earlier casualties.

The Green was quiet in the wet, no children dawdling on their way to school, and the path that wound down the hill beside the allotments was spattered with mud and glistened with the rain. She stepped carefully, avoiding the puddles and the worst of the mud, and the long grass that grew there now lay beaten and flat after the storm. But it was still pretty with a jewel-green freshness, and the elm trees spattered her lightly as the leaves shifted with the breeze and dislodged their burdens of rain. She touched the bracelet under the cuff of her coat and thought of Danny.

He had woken twice in the night, drenched in his sweat, screaming, and she had held him as she used to do with the children when they were frightened by the air raids. His terror scared her, the cause of it unknown, and his helplessness in the face of it a side of him she had never seen. But he refused to talk about it, would not say what images, what memories haunted him, so she knew she had given him little comfort. Afterwards, he had slept again quickly and as she lay next to him, unable to sleep, she was filled with a longing to be close to him that she thought would burst her heart. Once, unable to resist, she shifted to lie her body up against him and stroked the dark hair back from his temple but he flinched and groaned with her touch so she withdrew her hand. For the rest of the night, she had lain sleepless and still.

The library was nestled near the bottom of the hill by the station, a red-brick Victorian building with a high ceiling and long windows that let in the light. She had loved it since her childhood and had never wanted to work anywhere else. Now, she hurried in through the side door, oblivious to its charms: she was late. She must have walked slower than usual, lost in her thoughts, and although Mrs Pitman said nothing the reproach was clear enough in her expression. The chief librarian was a small woman and shrunken-looking as though she had once been much taller, and she ran the library in an atmosphere of petty ill humour. She peered across the half-moon spectacles, thin face drawn into a frown as she waited for Rachel's apology.

'I'm sorry,' Rachel obliged. 'But my husband came home yesterday … He's in a wheelchair …'

The older woman's natural sourness apparently fought with the desire not to seem unpatriotic. 'Poor fellow,' she managed to say. 'Italy, wasn't it?'

'Yes. At Anzio.'

'A bad business, that.'

'But we took Monte Cassino at last yesterday. So that's good news.'

'Hmm. Well. You'd better get on.' She turned away.

In the office Rachel hung her coat and hat on the rack. They were dripping and she was surprised: she hadn't noticed the heaviness of the rain. Then Jane rushed in, shaking water from her hair with her fingers. Drops sprinkled over the desk and floor.

'Late again.' She was out of breath as she hung her coat next to Rachel's.

'I was late this morning too.'

'You've got a good excuse. I haven't.' She turned from the coat rack to look at Rachel, sweeping wet hair back from her face with one hand, pretty features flushed from hurrying. 'How is he?'

Rachel hesitated, unsure what to say, the habit of loyalty to her husband hard to break even with Jane. The truth would be a betrayal. 'He's all right,' she said. 'Considering.'

'He must be glad to be back though,' Jane said. 'To see you and the children. He probably just needs some time to adjust. After all, he's been through an awful lot.'

'I know. And you're right. Perhaps I'm just expecting too much.'

Jane glanced up at the clock on the wall above the door. 'Once more into the breach …'

Rachel laughed. 'Oh go on!' Then she followed her friend out to the desk at the front of the library and opened the doors. Mrs Pitman ignored them both.

DANNY WOKE with the sense of hopelessness and anger that haunted all his days. Trails of the nightmares played across his thoughts, and he remembered Rachel holding him, her own face wet with tears, trying to comfort the man she used to love, the man he left in Italy.

Anger flared in him as restless energy in his limbs, and pain in the space where his legs used to be. The rest of his life in a wheelchair. For what? To hold some stinking beachhead that should have been won long before he ever got there. The whole campaign had been rotten to the core, a list of bad decisions from the top: they should never have been there in the first place. Some fucking general's scheme for glory, no doubt.

And how many poor sods had died because of it? Well, maybe they were the lucky ones. It was over for them – no crippled life stretched out endlessly before them, no more days and nights of memories and dreams they could not escape.

He tensed the muscles of arms and clenched his fists,

feeling the strength there, aggression balled in them, confined, no outlet to release it. He wanted to run and punch and shout with all the vitality of his youth. Instead he slowly opened his fingers one by one and let the tension seep from his arms, and the energy, unexpended, turned inwards on him as bitterness.

The house was quiet: unnatural, he thought in a city so large. He relieved himself into the bottle by the bed, then slid across into the chair. Rachel had left him his dressing gown across the back of it and he shrugged it on, trying to ignore the way it fell loose across his lap, no legs to give it shape. Automatically he reached to the window and yanked back the curtain, peering out to the silent street outside. There was no one, no sign of life, just a solitary cat sleeping on the garden wall. He let the curtain fall and turned away to light the day's first cigarette. He drew back hard and the heat in his chest made him feel alive.

Beyond the door of the bedroom the front door to the house creaked open and slammed shut. Heels clicked down the driveway. Kate, he guessed, on her way to the infirmary for the afternoon shift. He followed her in his mind until the sound of her footsteps died away and the house settled again into a quietness that was unnerving.

A city should be busy, he thought, lively and full of people. He remembered the shop before the war, only a short walk away from this silent suburb but a different world, and one that was beyond him to get to now. There would be life there: the shop at the hub of a myriad of roads that led off the Gloucester Road, an ancient artery that stretched from the heart of the city through its northern suburbs, on and out of Bristol all the way to the city whose name it carried. Once, he and Rachel had taken a bus for the hell of it all the way there. It had taken most of the day and they had got back on the last bus late in the evening to face a roasting from George.

Later on, after they were married, they would sit after work in the window of the flat above the shop and watch the people down below. The constant hiss of the traffic, and the trains on the railway bridge clanking restless through the nights had been company, a reminder of the world they belonged to.

Now was quite alone in the hush, and he had no idea what he could do with himself to pass the hours until he had company again to distract him from his misery.

THE DAY PASSED SLOWLY. The library was quiet because of the weather, people mostly coming to sit and read the newspapers out of the rain, or to check the casualty lists on the board that hung just inside the door. There were new names each day, other women's husbands or sons or brothers, and Rachel knew she was lucky that her man had come home at all. A few of the regulars came in and asked after Danny. She told them he had got home safely and thanked them for asking. The hours until five o'clock dragged, and the women said goodbye to each other on the steps outside in the rain.

'It'll be all right,' Jane said. 'You just need to be patient.'

Rachel smiled. 'Yes, I know. And I'm sure you're right. Thank-you,' she said, but it was hard to put his coldness from her mind, and the rage in him that wished that he was dead.

'See you tomorrow.'

'Tomorrow.' Then as she turned to walk back up the hill she remembered Jane's boy, young and smart and keen in his RAF uniform, shot down early in the war, nothing left of him now. Danny was home and he was safe and that ought to be enough for her so she tried to set her mind against the doubts and walked home, across the Green, thinking of nothing.

Her headache was pounding by the time she got home, and it had seemed to be a longer walk than usual. Her mother was in the kitchen preparing dinner as she stepped through the door.

'Are you all right, dear?' her mother said. 'You look very tired.'

'I am tired.' Rachel slipped out of her coat, and hung it in the cupboard. 'Have the children been okay?'

'Fine. Haven't heard a peep from them – I don't think they've left Danny's side since they got home.'

Rachel smiled, fears lifting with the news. Maybe Jane had been right. Maybe it would just take time.

'Hi Mum,' Charlie said in the living room, without lifting his head from the broken wooden soldier that his dad was helping him to fix.

'Give your mother a kiss,' Danny told him.

Rachel went to the table and kissed each child in turn. Then she bent to her husband and kissed his cheek too. He did not flinch or turn away.

'How was your day?' she asked him.

'Quiet. I didn't really know what to do with myself.' He passed the toy and the glue to his son to stick it together as he had shown him. 'How was work?'

'Quiet too. I was late this morning and Mrs Pitman was in a bad mood all day.'

'She always is,' Charlie said. 'She's a right old sourpuss.'

'You fix your soldier,' Danny said.

'Yes Dad.'

'But did you manage all right?' Rachel asked. 'There wasn't anything you needed?' She had been thinking all day about him stuck there alone, unable to reach things, to do basic tasks, knowing how frustrated it would make him. He had managed to drag himself up the stairs to the bathroom the night before to wash but there was still so much he could not do.

'I managed,' he said. 'But I did think that if we could put a ramp up to the outside lav, I could use that instead of the commode. Be nicer for everyone, that.'

'What's a commode?' Jean looked up from her drawing of a soldier, her brown eyes, Danny's eyes, wide with curiosity.

'It's a kind of toilet,' Charlie told her, with all the authority of his eight years, 'that looks like a chair.'

'Why?'

'So you can have it in the living room, or the bedroom, and no one knows that it's actually a toilet.'

Jean considered this for a moment, colouring in the soldier's hat as she thought. Then she said, 'What's the point of that?'

'Dunno,' Charlie shrugged.

Danny looked up at his wife and smiled, and when she placed a hand on his shoulder he let it rest there, so that for a moment they were brought close again by their love for the children. A faint hope shimmered. His muscle was warm and solid in her palm how it used to be, and she wanted to stay there longer. Then her mother called out to her from the kitchen and the moment broke. She lifted her hand away with reluctance and went out to help with dinner.

On Sunday morning Danny refused to go to church with them.

'Why should I praise a God who could let this madness happen?'

'To thank him for letting you live? For us?' Rachel was pleading with him in the privacy of their room. 'To keep Dad happy?'

He shook his head.

'And because it's somewhere we can all go together,' she

went on. 'We can take it in turns to push the chair up the hill. Wouldn't you like to get out of the house at least?'

He took a deep breath, and she tried to ignore the desperation in his voice.

'Rache, listen,' he said. Rachel stopped pacing in front of the door and turned to face him. 'I'm not going. All right? All those pitying Christians, asking about what had happened to me. I'd rather go to war again than face those hypocrites.'

'All right. If that's what you want,' she sighed. 'I'll see you later then.'

'See you later. Have a nice time.'

She flashed a false smile at him and swung out through the door to the hall where her parents were waiting. Listening to every word, no doubt. The front door slammed shut and he heard the children running down the drive, Rachel's voice calling out to them to stay in sight, and then the house fell quiet as the voices faded into the distance.

PEACE SEEMED to reign in the comfortable suburb, large solid houses with their windows blinking, indifferent in the sun, and it was easy to forget about the war that was raging not so far away. The air was clear and fresh after the rain. Puddles in the pot holes reflected the sun and the glare on the wet pavement was blinding. Rachel's father walked ahead, his wife one step behind, trailing him anxiously, hoping to please. Rachel followed on, taking her time, and after their first burst of running the children lagged so that she had to turn and call them often to catch up. The solitude and the clean coolness of the day were pleasant, and she tried not to think of Danny at home.

At church they took their usual place a few rows from the front, dwarfed by the grandeur of the great gothic arches, the vicar high above them in the pulpit. She had grown up in this church through Sunday School and the girl guides: her earliest memories of Christmas were bound up with the carol service there, the primary school just next door. It was peaceful and familiar and the ancient rhythms of the liturgy soothed her, her spirit lifted by the hymns. But when she knelt to pray she realised that she no longer knew what to ask for. For so long she had prayed to God to bring her husband home, but the man He had finally sent to her was different from the man who went away. Danny had come home to her a stranger, and there seemed to be no place to begin to get to know him.

Patience, Jane had counselled, give him time. Maybe she was right, Rachel thought. Maybe inside Danny there still remained a kernel of himself untouched by the war that in time would grow and flourish and bring him back. But as she whispered this hope in her prayers she felt no answering sweep of faith, and she rose from her knees still uncomforted.

The family walked home in silence, the children running on ahead this time, George Kirby's mood still black enough to keep them all from talking until three RAF fighter planes roared low overhead, shattering the stillness of the morning. Charlie stopped running and pointed at them, turning to the adults and shouting.

'Spitfires! Grandpa look! Spitfires!'

George hesitated, reluctant to break the taciturnity of his mood until finally he relented and allowed himself a smile. 'Where d'you think they're going?' he called.

'To get the Germans!' Charlie shouted back.

Rose smiled at her daughter as Charlie jumped up and down, waving madly at the planes before they banked and moved away out of sight beyond the rooftops. Jean stared after them with her sad brown eyes as the Spitfires droned into the distance, and silence began to settle until Charlie took over the noise of their engines, swerving and swooping down the road, arms outstretched, imaginary Messerschmidts exploding all around him. The others followed him home without talking.

'Had a nice time at church, did you?' Danny asked George, as the older man skirted past the wheelchair in the living room to his chair in the corner.

George scowled and opened the newspaper before he noticed the jazz that was playing on the wireless. Kate appeared, and grimaced at her sister as their father leant over and yanked the button round to turn it off.

'Don't you like jazz, George?' Danny said, with a wink at his wife.

'Don't,' she mouthed.

'American rubbish.'

'I'd have thought a sophisticated fellow like yourself would have enjoyed a bit of jazz …'

The muscles in George's cheek began to twitch but he said nothing more, staring resolutely at *The Sunday Times* in front of him.

'I'm going outside,' Kate said, yawning. 'It's such a beautiful morning.'

'I'll come out with you,' Danny said. 'I could do with some fresh air.'

Rachel followed them out through the kitchen and stopped at the back door, watching the children as they played in the garden. Kate was struggling with the wheelchair on the small step up to the overgrown lawn and they were laughing as between them they tried to manoeuvre him through the grass. When they stopped Danny gave her the cigarette he had rolled and her hair fell forward across her face as she bent to him to light it. She flicked it back with a careless movement and as they laughed again Rachel wondered how long it would take their father to notice that his younger daughter smoked. She turned away, envious of their easy company together, and went back inside to help her mother with Sunday lunch.

AT THE TABLE the arguments started again.

'How was church?' Kate asked, her tone light and friendly in the heavy atmosphere.

'Fine,' Rachel said. 'The vicar talked about …'

'You should have come,' George interrupted. 'It's been a while.'

'I didn't get in till late last night,' Kate answered. 'I wasn't even up when you left.'

'We all work hard, you know.'

'Except me, of course,' Danny said. He flicked a sly look at Rachel and she turned her face away.

'Except you,' George agreed.

Rachel lowered her eyes, appetite gone, depressed by Danny's baiting of her father. Once, he would have bitten his tongue for her sake, tried at least to keep the peace, but his hatred had turned poisonous, George an easy target for his venom. She would have thought he had seen enough of fighting.

There was a silence until Rachel's father spoke again. 'Any more thoughts on that?'

'On what?'

'Getting out and doing something with yourself?'

'Not really. I've only been back a few days.'

'There must be something you can do,' George insisted, and Rachel felt a surge of the same hatred. She kept her eyes averted, and closed her lips.

Danny shrugged and kept on eating.

'I know it sounds harsh, but you need to be doing something with yourself. Get a bit of self-respect. It's not good for a man to be idle.'

'It's not good for a man to have no legs,' Danny whispered in the silence. 'But there's fuck all I can do about that either.'

'Danny!' Rose exclaimed. 'The children!'

Danny turned to her. 'Sorry Rose.'

'I've warned you about your mouth!' George's voice was raised.

'Leave him alone, Dad,' Kate said then, getting up from her half-finished meal, squeezing her narrow hips out from the table and heading towards the door. 'Please? For all our sakes?'

Her father said nothing, but the muscle in his cheek quivered again with the tension, and they finished their meal in silence.

Rachel combed her hair at the small dressing table in their room, getting ready for bed. In the mirror in the half-light of the bedside lamp she could see Danny in his chair behind her.

'What does he want from me?' he was saying. 'What does he bloody expect me to do?'

Rachel turned on the stool to face him, watched him drag himself from the wheelchair to the bed by the power of his arms. They were still strong and broad and in his vest she could see the flexion of the muscles of his shoulders. She longed to run her fingers across the dips and grooves of them, and remembered nights of his body over hers, the hardness of his muscles as she held his arms.

'He's ashamed of me,' Danny said, settling himself under the covers. He cradled his head in his hands and she had to look away – it seemed wrong somehow that his upper body should remain so fit, so beautiful. 'He was ashamed of me when I worked in the shop and he's ashamed of me now.'

'He wanted me to marry a doctor, or an engineer,' Rachel said. This was old ground, and comforting in its familiarity.

'Not a greengrocer. Well I can't even do that any more, so

now I'm worse than useless. That's it, isn't it. He thinks I'm a worthless piece of shit …'

'Keep your voice down,' Rachel whispered.

'I'm not lazy,' Danny went on, and he did not lower his voice. 'And I'm not a coward. I've done my bit. More than my bit. I've always worked hard. It's not my fault I'm a sodding cripple. What've I got to do to prove myself?'

Rachel sighed and said nothing. There were no answers. But she thought it strange that her father's opinion still hurt him so much, when there was so much else to grieve for.

'He's a miserable old bastard who designs planes for other men to risk their necks in.'

'That isn't fair.'

'Taking his side are you?'

'Of course not.'

'You sure about that?'

'I married you didn't I?'

'Yes, but I was different then …' He trailed off as the anger waned, and only the sorrow of what he had lost remained.

'After the war we can get our own place again,' Rachel said. 'Then things'll be better. You'll see.'

'How can we get our own place on what you earn?'

'I don't know,' Rachel said. 'But we will. We have to. We can't stay here for ever.'

Danny laughed, and it was as though another man had taken his place in the bed. A man she could be married to and be happy. 'That's my Rache,' he said. 'Never one to be beaten by the facts.'

'You've got to have dreams,' she shrugged. 'Or what's the point?'

His smile faded, and as he turned his head away from the lamp, his face grew dark in shadow. 'I don't know, Rache,' he whispered. 'I really don't know what the point is any more.'

There was a silence and outside the evening rain

hammered against the garden. They could hear it splattering on the path beneath the window, the gush in the corner where the guttering leaked.

'The shop's still empty, you know,' Rachel said. 'I went past it the other day. It's all boarded up but the sign is still there. Lock & Sons.' And every time she passed the place she felt a tremor of regret. All the memories of their marriage were held inside it, and leaving it still seemed to be a loss of faith. But there had been no other choice: memories did not pay the rent.

'It would have broken Dad's heart to see that,' Danny said. 'That shop was his life.'

'We could do it again, Danny. Have the shop I mean. After the war, when the shortages are over.'

'How?'

'I could give up the library.' Hope lit inside her, a possibility to make things better, take them back to how they used to be.

'You never would before.'

'There was no need before.'

Danny was silent, thoughtful, as Rachel finished brushing her hair. Then he said, 'You'd hate it.'

'I'd rather do that than be here.' Always in her parents' house she felt herself as watched and judged and criticised and she was harder on the children than she should have been, wary of her father's disapproval. It was a different world from the easy freedom they had enjoyed in the flat above the shop before the war, Danny's parents close and loving, a life that had once seemed to give her everything. And now that Danny was home perhaps they could start again. They would work the shop together and remake the life the war had broken.

She got up and moved round the end of the bed to her own side and when she got under the covers she lay facing him as they had always used to lie together in bed, talking over the day. But he did not turn his head towards her and his eyes were fixed on the ceiling above his head.

'Good night, Danny,' she whispered, and just touched the dome of his shoulder with her fingertips, the skin cool and smooth and hard across the muscle. With her touch he turned his head to her, as though surprised by her presence so close.

'Night Rache.' Then he turned away from her and in the quiet each of them drifted slowly into sleep, quite alone.

Chapter Four

The invasion of Normandy was on everybody's lips, the fall of Rome the day before forgotten in this new excitement. Italy seemed irrelevant with the opening of the new front and no one doubted that this was the beginning of the end. In the library no one talked of anything else. Books were forgotten and people came in with updates from their wireless sets at home. A sense of achievement hung in the air, a feeling that the tide had turned at last. The elation was infectious.

It was only walking home in the late afternoon that the exhilaration began to wane. In the aftermath of the excitement she was tired, and the walk seemed longer than usual and more arduous, the hills very steep. Usually she enjoyed the walk up Whiteladies Road at the end of the day, the Victorian shopfronts still grand even if mostly they were empty. But today she noticed only the remaining signs of bomb damage, buildings scarred or destroyed, craters pitting the road, reminders of the toll of the war so far, and even the promise of the Normandy landings could not bring back what was already lost.

Haphazard gusts of wind caught at her umbrella and by

the time she turned off the main road she had given up the struggle with it, preferring to let the cold rain fall against her hair and face. The same wild weather in Normandy someone had said, and in her mind was an image of a beach somewhere, the beach that Danny fought to hold, the brutal truth of what such landings really mean. She would be pinning up longer lists of casualties on the library board in the days to come. Such a waste of life, she thought, of hope, of youth. There had to be a better way.

Over dinner her father was expansive, his spirits high with the news of the landings, and Danny was quiet, thoughts turned inwards, Rachel guessed, on images of other beaches, other landings.

'This is it,' George was saying. 'History will remember this day. For the first time we're going to give Hitler something to worry about …'

Rachel and Kate exchanged glances.

'We beat him in North Africa, we've got him on the run in Italy, but they were sideshows compared to this.'

Rachel felt her husband tense beside her, the heat of restrained anger rising from his skin. He stopped eating, carefully placed his knife and fork one next to the other across his plate. 'Some sideshows,' he murmured.

George turned abruptly. 'What did you say?'

'I said, some sideshows.'

His father-in-law was silent for a moment, the ebullience of his mood deflating with the interruption. Then he said, 'What do you mean by that?'

Danny ran his fingers back and forth around the rims of the wheels. Rachel's eyes followed their movement, hands that had held a gun and taken life. She turned her face away from the thought of it.

'I mean,' he said softly, 'that without those sideshows the invasion could never have happened.'

'Well no,' Rachel's father admitted. 'But that isn't what I meant. I was just saying that the fall of Rome doesn't mean much any more now that we're in France.'

'It means a lot to the men who fought for it.'

'Of course it does. Battles always mean a lot to the men who fight in them. But in the greater scheme of things, winning France is what matters …'

All eyes went to Danny, who backed his chair away from the table and took himself out through the door to the garden without another word. Rachel was moved by his dignity, and hated her father for his tactlessness.

Smoke from Danny's cigarette trickled in through the open window and she wondered if she should go to him, or if he would rather be alone with his thoughts and his memories, if her presence would disturb him. Undecided, she sat in the silence until the moment had passed and it seemed too late to go to him any more. The others finished their meal without talking but Rachel had lost her appetite.

THE LANDINGS on D-Day were still on everyone's lips when an officer came to visit Danny at the house. Rachel opened the front door to him, and he seemed somehow out of place standing there on the drive in the early summer sun. In one hand he held a cane but he stood upright and he wore his uniform well. Taking off his hat when she appeared he ran a hand across hair that was auburn. A light sweat coated his forehead, pale skin flushed with the warmth, a few light freckles brushed across his cheekbones. His eyes held Rachel's without wavering and their intensity was uncomfortable. She dropped her gaze and mumbled a good afternoon.

'Good afternoon,' he replied. 'You must be Mrs Lock?'

'That's right.' She looked up at him, surprised that he knew her name.

He smiled and the sternness left his face. 'My name is Andrews. I served with your husband in Italy.'

Rachel nodded – the name was familiar from Danny's letters home, and the letter Andrews himself had written her when Danny was wounded.

'I was in the area, and I just called to see how he's getting on.'

'That's very kind of you. Please, come in.' She stepped back, embarrassed now to have kept him standing on the doorstep. Then she led him through to the living room where Danny was bent over the table, fixing a neighbour's watch.

'You've got a visitor, Danny,' she said. 'Lieutenant Andrews.'

For a moment Danny did not raise his head, apparently engrossed in the detail of the watch. Then he swung the wheelchair round to face them. Shouts from the children in the garden drifted in on a breeze, and George's voice, telling them to mind his plants with the ball.

'He's a captain,' Danny said. 'Not a lieutenant. Can't you see?'

Rachel flicked a glance to the officer. 'I'm so sorry,' she said. 'I just remembered you were a lieutenant from Danny's letters. I didn't think …' She could see now the captain's pips on his epaulettes then remembered the letter he had sent her, and cursed herself for a fool.

'That's quite all right,' he replied. 'You aren't in the army. There's no reason for you to notice the difference.' He smiled again, and Rachel felt a hot flush of resentment that her husband had made a fool of her in front of him.

'I'll make some tea,' she said.

'That would be lovely.'

The door to the kitchen swung to behind her and she could

hear only the low rumble of her husband's voice, the officer's murmur inaudible through the half-closed door as she made the tea. Through the open back door to the garden she could see her father stooped over the vegetable patch with a trowel, and the children flickered in and out of view behind the garage as they chased the ball across the patch of lawn. When she went back into the living room with the tea tray, Andrews was still standing as she had left him. The conversation stopped abruptly and left a residue of tension.

'Please sit down, Captain Andrews,' she said.

'Thank you.' He moved to the armchair by the unlit fire and in the bright sunlight that flooded the window, the room seemed shabby and tired with its faded wallpaper and old inherited armchairs. She wished she had suggested that they have tea in the garden but it seemed too late to suggest it now. She poured tea for them all.

'Are you back on leave?' she asked him.

'No. Unfortunately not,' he replied. 'I was wounded, only slightly, but I'm not deemed fit for active service any more so they sent me back here.' He lifted the cane from where he had leant it against the chair as if to confirm the story. 'And now I'm based at the Artillery Grounds, instructing officer cadets at the Training Unit there.'

'I'm sorry to hear that you were wounded.'

He gave a slight shrug. 'Thank you.'

There was a silence and all of them sipped at their tea. The football thudded on to the concrete just outside the window. Charlie scampered briefly into view as he ran to fetch it, and George's voice was raised in annoyance. Andrews fished in his pocket and pulled out a couple packs of Woodbines.

'I brought you these.' He passed them across.

'Ta.'

'You're very welcome.'

'Still don't smoke?'

'No.'

'Or drink?'

'The odd glass of wine now and then.'

Danny half smiled. Then he said, 'Any news of the boys?'

'Some. I'm afraid I heard that Harry Wilkes was killed a couple of weeks ago. I'm sorry. I know he was a friend of yours.'

The hardness fell from Danny's face. He drew back hard on his cigarette and held the smoke a long time in his lungs before he let it go.

'So Harry didn't make it after all,' he murmured. 'Funny, that. We all thought Harry had the luck of the devil. So many near misses. If anyone was going to make it, it was going to be Harry.' The two men locked eyes, an understanding between them that Rachel could not share. 'How did it happen?'

'I don't know.' The Captain shook his head. 'I didn't get any details. And I've had no news of anyone else.'

Danny nodded and observed the cigarette between his fingers. A silence fell in the room, though they could hear the shouts of the children, carried easily on the warm air. The sounds of summer, Rachel thought.

'It's a beautiful day,' Andrews said.

'Yes, isn't it. Summer here at last, hopefully.'

'Hopefully.'

Conversation faltered in the awkwardness and Rachel looked across to Danny for help but he stared into his tea and said nothing.

Andrews tried again. 'Do you work, Mrs Lock?'

'Yes,' she said. 'I'm a librarian, at the library on White-ladies Road.'

'Yes, I know it,' he smiled. 'I've been in there. It's not far from the Artillery Grounds.'

'You like reading?'

He nodded. 'History mainly. And some fiction. But I have

to confess I only went there once and that was to read the newspapers out of the rain.'

Rachel smiled. 'A lot of people do that.'

'I'm sure they do.' The Captain drained the last of his tea and Rachel took his cup and put it back on the tray.

'I should go,' he said. 'I only popped in to see how you were getting on, Danny. I don't want to keep you from your work.' He stood up and nodded towards the watch, spread carefully in pieces on a cloth across the table. 'You always did have a way with machinery.' He turned again to Rachel. 'Your husband was a useful man to have in the platoon. He could fix anything, pretty much. Very handy indeed.'

Rachel smiled, pleased by the praise of her husband, but she saw Danny's hesitation in taking the officer's proffered hand.

'I'm glad you're all right,' Andrews said. 'Hopefully I'll see you again.'

'P'raps.'

'It was nice to meet you, Mrs Lock.'

'I'll see you out.' She followed him into the hall and opened the door. Above the houses at the front the sky had darkened, a mass of slate-grey cloud moving in that warned of rain. Both of them lifted their eyes to scan the change.

'So much for summer,' Andrews said. Then, 'How is he?'

Rachel sighed, unsure how much to say. 'He's coping. More or less.'

'Give him time,' he said. 'He's been through a lot. More than you can know.'

'He won't tell me anything.'

'Some things are too hard to talk about.'

The Captain's eyes shifted back to the clouds in the distance and she thought that he too had been through a lot. Then she wondered if he woke like Danny weeping from his dreams at night, and if he had anyone to hold him.

'I'll call in again,' he said, 'If you don't mind.'

'No. Of course I don't mind. It would be nice to see you again. Thank you for coming. It was kind of you.'

'It was my pleasure.' He smiled and lifted his cap to his head then turned and walked away. She watched him go, the lopsided gait as he limped down the drive and out of sight. When he was gone she turned and went back inside. Danny looked up from the watch.

'He liked you,' he said.

'Don't be ridiculous.'

'I may be a cripple, but I'm not fucking blind.'

'Danny, don't,' Rachel said. 'Please don't. He came to see how you were.'

'Came to gloat, more like.'

Rachel paused with the tray held awkward and heavy in front of her. 'I don't understand.'

'And you liked him,' Danny said, ignoring her.

'Now you *are* being ridiculous,' she retorted, but a flush of guilt betrayed the lie. She stood for a moment longer, the tray growing heavier, and waited for him to reply but he reached out for the watch instead and began to work on it again. Concentration lined the heavy face as his fingers worked the delicate moving parts with surprising dexterity. A man who could fix anything, Andrews had said.

Then, tightening her grip on the tea tray, Rachel made her way out through the door to the kitchen and stood at the sink, but her mind was miles away from the washing up, resting instead on Andrews, wondering idly if she would see him again.

THE PUB WAS Kate's suggestion, a way to get them out from under George's irritability, a first trip for Danny out of the house. The girls took turns to push the wheelchair, struggling with it up the hill until Danny grew frustrated at their efforts and began to turn the wheels himself. It seemed to take all his strength of will to make it, the muscles of his arms and shoulders straining against the unaccustomed exercise, but there was a new sense of purpose about him, a memory of the Danny she had married.The children went off to explore the garden behind the pub, and it was hard to get the wheelchair over the small step to the door of the bar. Inside it was crowded, a busy Sunday lunchtime, filled with the smell of warmth and beer and tobacco. Mostly the people were civilians, men too old to be fighting, the odd youngster still too young. A few uniforms coloured the throng, the olive drab of the services and the dark blue of the ARP. People moved back to make way for the wheelchair when they saw it and voices dropped to a murmur of embarrassed sympathy.

There was no one there they knew: it was not a pub that Danny would have chosen, and the pity was clear in men's faces; pity and unease. The sense of strength that had seemed to come with the exercise left him in an instant. He spoke to no one, his eyes on the ground, and Rachel stood close to the chair, alert and protective as she watched her sister buy the drinks at the bar and flirt with the man who served her.

With the pint in his hand Danny drank greedily, a distraction from his rage, and Kate said quietly behind him, 'Maybe this wasn't the best time to come.'

Rachel nodded in agreement and moved round to the front of the chair to crouch down, her face a little lower than her husband's. 'Shall we just stay for the one?'

'No,' Danny answered, but he did not look at her. His gaze was hard, and focussed on some point ahead of him that Rachel could not see. 'I want another one after this.'

'Are you all right?' she said softly.

He turned his face towards her but his eyes still seemed

distant and impossible to read. 'I'm fine. And I want to stay for another one. All right?'

'All right,' Rachel said, standing up. 'If that's what you want.'

'It is.' He lifted his beer to slug down the last of it and finally met her eyes with a look in them that dared her to disagree. She took the empty glass from his hand and went to the bar and as she waited to be served a man spoke at her shoulder. She recognised him from the days in the shop.

'Hello love. Is that for Danny?'

'Yes.'

'I'll get it.'

'He wouldn't want you to.'

'Then don't tell him.' He moved in closer and Rachel saw the deep lines in his face, careworn eyes. 'I was in the last one, you know. Lost an arm at the Somme.' He slid the coins across the polished wood of the bar. 'From one old soldier to another.'

Rachel glanced back over her shoulder towards Danny but he was talking now to Kate, and laughing.

'Thank you,' she said. 'It's kind of you.'

The man nodded and moved away, disappearing away through the crowd towards the dartboard at the back. Rachel paid for the pint with the money he had given her and took it back to her husband.

'What did he want?' Danny asked, after the first mouthful of beer. 'Chatting you up was he?'

'He was just asking after you. He knew you from the shop.'

Danny grunted.

'He lost an arm at the Somme, he said. He seemed like a nice fellow. Sad though. Sad eyes.'

Danny followed his wife's gaze in the direction of the dartboard but the man was out of sight behind the crowd. He turned his attention back to his beer, and Kate and Rachel stood awkwardly, conversation between the two of them too difficult with Danny there. In amongst the good-natured hubbub of Sunday drinkers, Rachel felt very alone.

Danny finished the drink quickly, swigging it down, his first pints, Rachel realised, since he got back, and when the glass was empty she took it and moved a little way through the crowd to put it on a table. Then Kate took her place behind the chair and struggled to push it across the heavy carpet. He could probably have done it more easily himself, Rachel thought.

Outside, a fine drizzle had begun to fill the air. Kate went to get the children, wet and muddy and breathless from the garden, and together they wandered slowly back down the main road.

'Sorry, Danny,' Kate said. 'I didn't think it would be like that.'

'Ignorant bastards,' Danny spat.

Instinctively Rachel turned to check the children, but they were trailing some way behind, examining some rocks they had unearthed in the garden and their father's words were lost in the air.

'They were embarrassed,' Kate said. 'They didn't know how to act.'

'Like I said, ignorant bastards.'

Rachel said nothing, wary, Danny volatile now and likely to take offence at anything. They walked home the top way along the main road to avoid any upward slopes and as they passed the church, a few stragglers were still leaving after the later service.

'I'll push if you like,' she said to Kate.

'I'll do it myself,' Danny told her, and as Kate let go of the handles, he spun the wheels in his hands, propelling himself forward with ease on the downward slope. He moved a little way ahead, and Charlie and Jean raced after him. He did not turn as they called out but he slowed down and let them draw level.

The two sisters walked side by side in silence. Once they could have talked to each other all day and night, but since Rachel had moved downstairs they had barely spent any time together, and it was hard to know what to say. The new awkwardness surprised her – they had always been friendly enough before.

'Are you all right?' Kate said at last, as Danny turned the corner out of sight ahead of them, the children either side of him.

'I'm fine,' Rachel said. 'Why?'

'You seem … sort of … out of sorts …' She seemed reluctant to say it, as though she might offend.

'I'm fine,' Rachel repeated.

Kate slowed, labouring over the words she was trying to find. Then she stopped walking and turned to her sister. She said, 'You seem unhappy. Miserable, actually.'

'I'm not miserable.'

'Well, that's how you seem. I thought you'd be happy to have Danny back. It's all you wanted for so long and now he's here and you just seem really … down.'

Rachel sighed and began to walk on slowly, annoyed with her sister, searching for a way to explain that would end the conversation. She was not close enough to Kate to confide completely, a slight rivalry between them that had always kept the most precious secrets from being shared.

'I am glad he's back,' she said at length. 'But it isn't exactly how I imagined it would be. We aren't the same people any more and it's taking time to adjust. That's all.'

'I know that ,' Kate replied. 'But all the same …'

'All the same what?'

'All the same, I think it'd be easier for Danny if you tried to be a bit more cheerful.'

They reached the corner. Danny and the children were already nearly at the bottom of the hill and they could hear Jean's squeals of fear and delight as she sat on her father's lap, the chair spinning dangerously.

They walked on a few paces in silence before Kate said, 'I just want you both to be happy. That's all.' Then she broke into an easy run to catch up with the others and Rachel watched her go, saw her litheness and her energy, the smile on her face as she reached them laughing and breathless, and thought with envy that her sister might be right.

On weekday lunchtimes the pub was less crowded and as the weeks of summer passed, Danny found his way there more and more often. It was release for him to get out, somewhere to go away from the oppressive atmosphere of the house: even when he was alone there he hated it, his dependence written in the walls and the furniture.

He tried all the various routes to get there, testing his muscles against the hills, and the struggle and the soreness were a distraction and proof of being alive. He found it was best to take the short sharp hill near the house that levelled out to a more gentle slope along the main road. He could do it in twenty minutes on a good day, and he came home a different way, taking his time to go past the Green on the downward slope. Sometimes there would be children from the school playing football or cricket and he would stop by the gate to see if he could pick out his own children among them. Once he saw Jean but she was absorbed with her friends and did not notice him.

He found friends of a sort in the pub, men he could pass the time of day with, men who showed no interest in his past or the war in Italy, so that he could sit with them and enjoy a pint as though nothing had changed, and almost bring himself to forget about it too. *Drowning your sorrows*, he had heard people say, but they were never really drowned, more like submerged for a while, just out of sight beneath the surface, with their shadows still plain if you cared to take the time to look. So he kept his eyes averted for the time he was in the pub and found that afterwards, when the sorrows re-emerged, that they had lost a little of their power to haunt him.

Rachel knew that he went, that he was drinking too much, but she said nothing, just grateful for the peace it seemed to give him. He slept better on the days that he drank, nightmares dulled by the alcohol, though she worried when she began to smell the whisky on his breath in the evenings, his father's hip flask he had carried through the war refilled each time he went to the pub. But there was nothing she could do to stop him, too wary of him now to even mention it, afraid of stirring up the anger or that other emotion she could not name, a deeper darker hurt in him that scared her more for being unknown.

Try to be more cheerful, Kate had told her.

She turned on the wireless after dinner for *It's That Man Again*, comedy she had shared with Danny's parents and her children before they left the shop. Charlie still used the catch-phrases now and then and it always raised a smile: it had been too long since she had listened to it, accustomed now to the more serious fare that George preferred.

'Do you remember it?' she asked Danny over the theme tune, 'from before you went away?'

He nodded.

'It was your Dad's favourite. He used to laugh and laugh. Even after Vic went. It was about the only thing that ever cheered him up.'

Danny observed her, and as the madcap patter of the programme began, she wondered if he understood the effort she was making. Then all of them were laughing; even her father managed a smile or two, and Rachel looked around the room with pleasure.

Afterwards she suggested a cuppa and when Charlie replied with a sombre 'I don't mind if I do,' in perfect mimicry, they all laughed again and on her way out to the kitchen she caught Danny's eye. There was a smile still in it, and a flicker of something else: love perhaps? hope?

She hummed as she made the tea, a lightness in her she thought she had forgotten.

Chapter Five

Early in September, when the days were still bright and warmed from the memory of summer, Captain Andrews came in to the library. Standing to one side of the desk he waited patiently to speak to her while she waded through a pile of books to be renewed for an elderly borrower. She saw Mrs Pitman glance over once or twice, curious, but the Captain seemed oblivious, focusing so intently on Rachel that she grew self-conscious, and felt the first beginnings of a blush creep over her skin. Finally the renewals were finished, and he stepped forward to face her over the counter.

'Good morning, Mrs Lock.'

'Morning, Captain Andrews. What can I do for you?'

'I was wondering how I might become a member of the library.'

Rachel smiled. 'You waited all that time to ask me that? You were standing right next to the notice.'

He followed the direction of her nod with his eyes. 'Ah, yes,' he said. 'So I was.'

She waited and watched as his eyes skimmed down across the information. His features were fine, she noticed, high cheekbones and a narrow nose, and she found it hard to imagine him in the brutality of battle.

'So would you like to join?' she asked.

He finished reading and turned back to her. 'Yes. Very much.'

Reaching under the desk she handed him a form. 'Fill this in and I'll issue you with some tickets.'

'Thank you.'

Another borrower came to the desk and Andrews moved aside with his form. Rachel stamped the woman's books automatically, without noticing.

'Thank you,' the woman said.

Rachel looked up in surprise.

'For the books.'

'Oh yes,' Rachel recovered herself. 'You're welcome. I'm sorry. I was miles away.'

The woman smiled again and her eyes strayed for an instant towards Andrews. Rachel looked away, embarrassed.

'That's perfectly all right,' the woman said, and after she had gone Rachel stood feeling foolish and uncomfortable and very hot. She dabbed at her face with a handkerchief and tried to calm the raucousness of her emotions. Andrews stepped in front of her again and slid the form across the counter.

'Your name's Christopher,' she said.

'Kit,' he replied. 'No one ever calls me Christopher.'

'Kit,' she repeated, looking up at him. 'It suits you.'

He laughed and the sad intensity left his eyes so that he seemed much younger. Rachel dropped her gaze to the form, made shy by the new intimacy of his Christian name, and Mrs Pitman lifted her head towards them at the sound of his laughter. This time he noticed and moved in closer to the desk.

'Am I getting you in trouble?'

'Not yet.'

'I wouldn't want to get you in trouble.'

Rachel said nothing and busied herself with his tickets. When they were done she put them down and he reached out to slide them across the counter with his fingers. Long fingers, she noticed, slender hands. There was no ring.

'The history section is over there,' she said, pointing to the back of the library.

'You remembered.'

'And the fiction is near the front here.'

'Thank you.'

She watched him move away between the rows of books and heard the muffled thud of his cane on the wooden floor. Then she turned to help another borrower with an enquiry.

'Who was that?' Jane whispered a few minutes later, standing near so that Mrs Pitman would not hear.

Rachel started in surprise at her closeness. She had not noticed Jane come back from her tea break.

'An officer that served with Danny in Italy,' she said. 'He was his platoon commander.'

'What did he want?'

'To borrow books.'

Jane raised an eyebrow in disbelief and Rachel looked away, self-conscious, becoming afraid of the strength of feelings she was not supposed to have. There was a pause and both women looked across towards the back of the library. He was out of sight amongst the shelves.

'He seemed very nice.' Jane paused. 'Is he married?' A smile twitched at the corners of her lips.

'I don't know,' Rachel lied. 'I didn't ask him.'

Jane laughed and picked up a pile of books and walked away. Rachel saw the bounce in her step, her prettiness, and hoped that Andrews would not notice her. Then she left the desk for Mrs Pitman and went to the office for her tea break so that she would not have to see him again.

But later, when he was gone, she was sorry she had not been there to say goodbye to him.

On Fridays the library closed at lunchtime and Rachel finished early. Outside, it was a beautiful autumn day, the sun warm in a clear blue sky, a slight coolness in the air with the first beginnings of the new season. A few leaves had begun to drift down from the plane trees that lined the road: it was Rachel's favourite time of year. She stood for a moment on the steps of the library, drinking in the freshness. Relieved to have finished early, she walked up Whiteladies Road towards home without hurrying, oblivious of the blank and blinking windows of the empty shops and the uncleared rubble, trying only not to think of Andrews. But the image of the blue eyes was clear in her mind, and she smiled with the memory of the way he had looked at her. Danny had been right; there was no mistaking that he liked her. What on earth could he be thinking? she asked herself. He must know it was impossible. She straightened her shoulders and walked faster, strong with resolve to be colder to him next time, to avoid him altogether if she could. But even as she decided, a part of her was sorry and thought how nice he was.

By the time she got home, she was warm from the walk, and the cool of the house was quite welcome. In the kitchen Kate was sitting at the narrow table staring into space, miles away. She jumped at her sister's sudden presence.

'I'm sorry,' Rachel said. 'I didn't mean to startle you.'

'That's all right.'

Rachel turned to light the stove and began to make a sandwich for herself and tea for the both of them. Kate's eyes drifted back into far away space. Rachel observed her sister with wry amusement as she worked. 'Who is he?' she asked.

Kate snapped herself back to the kitchen. 'How did you know?'

'I've seen that look before.' Kate had never been single for long. Whenever she and Kate were out together, it was always Kate that people looked at, Kate that drew admiring looks, and she basked in the power of her magnetism. But her interest in each of her men flared hot and bright and briefly: she had been leaving a trail of hurt and bewilderment behind her ever since she turned fourteen. Rachel had never understood what gave her sister such allure, nor why she chose to use it so recklessly. She poured the tea and passed a cup to her sister who blew across the surface gently before she drank.

'His name's Paul.'

Rachel leant against the counter next to the stove. 'Is that all you're going to tell me?'

'Promise you won't tell Dad?' She looked up and Rachel nodded. 'He's American. A G.I.'

No wonder she didn't want their father to know, Rachel thought. She took a bite of her sandwich. It was yesterday's bread and dry in her mouth. There was no butter. 'I hope he's worth it,' she said.

'Oh he is,' she replied. 'He's wonderful. I've never met anyone like him.'

'I've heard that before.'

'No,' Kate insisted. 'Not like this. It's different this time. It really is. I think he's the one. I think I could spend the rest of my life with Paul.' She turned to Rachel with eyes that were bright and pretty with earnestness. 'I feel like I've already known him all my life.'

'Where's he from?'

Kate smiled, delighted to be able to talk about her man to someone. 'Texas. He's just got the loveliest accent.'

'And a nice uniform?' It was hard not to be cynical. The city was full of G.I.s and their reputations went before them.

Kate almost choked on her tea. 'Give me some credit,' she spluttered. 'I haven't just fallen for an accent and a uniform. They're just part of it. Part of him.' She sighed. 'You'll have to meet him. All the girls at the hospital thought he was gorgeous too when they saw him. They were ever so jealous.'

'I'd love to meet him,' Rachel said. 'How long is he here?'

Kate shrugged and grew serious. 'I don't know. It's like it was with Danny. They aren't told when and they aren't told where. It's hard, isn't it?'

Rachel nodded, remembering when Danny had finally embarked after all those months of training and waiting and wondering. And now he was back, in pieces, and she thought how little they had known back then.

'I'm very happy for you,' Rachel said. 'But just be careful, won't you?''

'Don't worry about me. I can take care of myself.'

Rachel smiled and said nothing. They were silent a while, finishing their tea. Then Kate spoke again.

'So how are things with Danny?'

Rachel hesitated, long years of habit still keeping her loyal. She said, 'About the same. He goes to the pub most lunchtimes now.' She shrugged. 'I suppose at least it gets him out of the house.'

'Gets him drunk, more like,' Kate said. 'You don't have to lie to me for him. I know what he's like.'

Rachel shrugged. 'Then you know how he is. So why ask?'

'I just wondered if things were better between the two of you.'

'We manage,' Rachel said.

There was a silence, the conversation over, and a slight sense of guilt for her curtness wheedled through her thoughts.

'I'm sorry,' she said. 'I don't mean to snap. It's just hard sometimes.'

Kate nodded, but her interest had faded with Rachel's reticence, her mind quickly moving back to Paul. She took her cup to the sink and rinsed it out.

'I'm going upstairs to get changed,' she said, when she had finished. 'I'm meeting Paul this afternoon.' She smiled with the thought of it and the tension with her sister was forgotten. 'See you later.'

Rachel watched her go before she turned to wash up her own cup. Then the back door swung open and Danny was there, struggling to manoeuvre the wheelchair through the narrow entrance. He was drunk.

'I've been at the pub,' he told her.

'You don't have to explain.'

'I'm just telling you where I was. Did I hear Kate?'

'She's gone upstairs. She's going out this afternoon. She's got a new man.'

He lifted a derisory eyebrow. 'Poor bastard.'

Rachel ignored the sarcasm, and put the kettle back on the stove to make him some tea.

In the living room, drinking their tea, they were awkward. It was hard to think of things to say to him any more, and she remembered the easy unending conversation they used to share, though what they had ever talked about she could not think. Nothing important probably. Nothing deep. That had not been their way, feelings known and understood without the need for words. She missed him. She missed him worse now than when he was away, because then at least there had been the hope of his return to keep her going. Now she knew the Danny she loved wasn't going to come back. The war had sent back a stranger who had no love for her. She tightened her lips against the desire to cry and wondered if she should tell him that Andrews came in to the library. Better not, she thought. Better not to mention it. Instead, she said, 'How was the pub?'

'Are you trying to be funny?'

'No. I just wondered. Did you see anyone you know?'

Danny half smiled with wry amusement, and looked up from the tea he held in his lap, observing his wife. She shifted in her chair, uncomfortable under his scrutiny, and turned her face away, gazing out of the window towards a garden still bathed in sun.

'I can't work you out,' he said.

'What do you mean?' She turned to him then, surprised by his words.

'Don't you care that I'm drunk?'

'Of course I care.'

'But you haven't said anything. Once, you would've given me hell.'

'That was then. When we were different people. What can I say now that would make a difference? You wouldn't care even if I did give you hell. You'd probably just tell me where to go.'

He took a cigarette from the packet of Woodbines and lit it, drawing back deeply, holding the smoke in his lungs for a moment of pleasure before he lifted his chin and released it into the air above him. He said nothing, and the silence hung heavy until Rachel got up and took the teacups out to the kitchen. Then she went out into the garden and breathed in the fresh air until the tears no longer threatened at the corners of her eyes.

THEY WERE all at home for dinner that night except Kate, and they sat uncomfortably crowded around the dining table, elbows bumping, everyone irritable. Charlie was subdued and wary, having fallen foul of his father's temper for talking back to his mother, and Jean, as ever, was following his lead. It pained Rachel to see her children so cowed, so afraid of their father.

'I saw Fred Lennox this morning,' Rose said. 'Their Henry's been killed, somewhere in France, he said. They got the telegram yesterday.'

Rachel remembered she had seen his name on the list at the library, but in her own sorrows she had quite forgotten it. 'How's Mrs Lennox?' she asked.

'Devastated, apparently. Quite gone to pieces.'

'Of course she is,' George said, lifting his fork to make the point. A piece of mashed potato fell from it back to the plate. Charlie turned to glance at his sister with a barely stifled giggle and Rachel pretended not to see. 'He was a fine lad, with fine future ahead of him. He was all ready to go to university before the war.'

'He was going to be an architect,' Rose said.

George lifted his eyes from the plate and looked at Danny. 'Good job that,' he said. 'Being an architect. People will always need houses to live in, whatever happens. You can support a family on that.'

'It's not much use to him now though is it?' Danny answered, without looking up.

Rachel flinched, waiting for the fight to follow.

'I'm just saying …' Her father lifted his hands before him in hurt defence as though it were Danny that had begun the aggression. '… that it's a good thing for a man to have a profession.'

'Even if he is dead.'

There was a pause and in the silence Rose found her daughter's eyes with hers, anxious and afraid. Rachel looked away, unable to give her mother the reassurance she wanted.

'Anyway,' Danny said, gazing round the table. 'I'm a working man myself now, so you can keep your comments to yourself.'

The others stared at him and he smiled in satisfaction.

'You've got a job?'

'Yes, George. I've got a job. It's only part time, mind. But it's a start.' He took another mouthful of food, enjoying himself, basking in his father-in-law's incredulity.

'Where?' Rachel asked. 'Where are you going to be working?'

Danny finished chewing his mouthful. 'At the pub.'

George scowled and turned his attention back to his meal. 'Doing what?'

'The books, ordering, paperwork. Not so different from the shop really. Jack's cellar man got called up a while back and he's been doing it on his own ever since. Reckons it's too much for one man. So I offered.' He shrugged as though his words were unimportant.

'That's wonderful,' Rachel said. She was astonished, and hurt that he had said nothing earlier when they were alone. But she smiled and kept her feelings hidden beneath a thin layer of composure. 'When do you start?'

'Next week,' he replied. 'So I'm a working man again, George. That should make you happy. What do you say?'

George regarded his son-in-law for a moment before he answered. Rachel waited, watching him, tension thick in the silence as he considered his reply.

'I'm very pleased for you Daniel,' he said at last. 'A man should have a job if he can.'

Rose glanced at Rachel, eyebrows lifted in baffled surprise, and Rachel half shrugged in response. Then Danny spun to face his wife. 'Happy Rachel?'

'I'm happy.'

'Even though it's the pub?'

'Even though it's the pub.'

But she had her misgivings and she was sure that he must know of them.

In the morning when she woke she lay still for a while, reluctant to leave the warmth of the bed for the morning cool. She was tired, a bad night with Danny's dreams, and thoughts that kept her from her own sleep in the peaceful hours between.

The way that he had looked at her at the table when he had asked if she was happy, the same look he used to challenge her father. It was as if he saw them both as enemies now, the whole family against him. She switched on the bedside lamp and turned her head to look at him across the pillow. He lay facing her, curled up on his side with his hands tucked in close to his chin, the same way Charlie often slept, and his face was tranquil in quiet deep sleep, no sign of the terror of last night nor the bitterness of his days. She wanted to reach out and smooth the dark hair back from his temple, so that he would wake and return the caress, and love her as she needed to be loved.

What happened to you over there, Danny? she murmured. *What happened that changed you so much?*

He breathed on, deeply, oblivious. Upstairs, she could hear the footfalls of her parents in the bedroom above and the irregular short steps of the children on the landing to the bathroom. The clock ticked round towards the hour and Rachel forced herself from the bed and got dressed, silent so as not to wake him.

The morning was grey outside on the way to work, but dry and fresh, and the walk through the Green and down the hill was pleasant. Empty shop windows blinked at her as she passed down Whiteladies Road, but their bareness went unnoticed now; it was years since they had held displays. Most of them had closed down anyway, nothing more left to sell. A bus roared past her up the hill, old engine straining, its passengers invisible behind the grimy windows. The conductor hung on the back step, arm wrapped round the pole. Rachel walked quickly, growing warm in the cool autumn morning, and by the time she reached the library she could feel the warmth of sweat beneath her arms and along her spine. She was the first to get there, before Mrs Pitman, and in the quiet she set about making the tea. Mrs Pitman arrived as the pot was brewing.

'Morning, Mrs Pitman. How are you?'

'I had a bad night.' Her face puckered into a frown. 'My father took a turn for the worse. I don't think it'll be long now, God bless him. It'll be a relief for us all when he goes.'

Rachel said, 'It must be very hard for you.' No one knew how old Mrs Pitman's father was, but his daughter had been looking after him for years, her own husband long since dead and buried.

'It is. It's been a terrible burden all this year. Terrible. I pray to God I never get like that because there'll be no one to look after me as I've looked after him. No one.'

Rachel did not quite know what to say. 'Your daughter's still in London?'

'Yes, yes. At the War Office. I'll telephone her today though I don't expect she'll be able to get away.'

Rachel poured the tea and gave a cup to Mrs Pitman. The old woman sipped it absently and showed no inclination to get started, so they stood next to the urn in the office and drank together in silence with the door open that led through to the library. No one came in to the reading room and the lending library did not open until half past.

'Well,' Rachel said finally, when the clock showed nine-thirty. 'I suppose we'd better get started.'

'Yes, indeed,' Mrs Pitman agreed. 'No use worrying about it all. Business as usual, then. Business as usual.'

RACHEL WAITED on the step outside the heavy wooden door, scanning for her sister amongst the people on the hill. A young child ran past, scuffing in the unswept autumn leaves, and his mother jogged breathlessly behind, calling out to him to wait. He kept on running and the woman looked up and shot Rachel an exasperated smile. Rachel smiled back, a moment of shared understanding, then turned her eyes up the hill again to look for her sister. Kate was still nowhere in sight, late as always, and Rachel's gaze wandered to the bombed-out church across the road, a pile of rubble now, still uncleared. Before the war they had opened and closed the library doors by the bell of its clock, and the chimes had marked the passing of the day. Now it seemed normal that all that was left was the low stone wall against the pavement, a pile of stones, and the small shabby hall at the back that served as the new place of worship. It was hard to remember exactly what the church had looked like.

People hurried past her against a wind that had turned chill in the last few days, winter breezing in early this year, and Rachel dug her hands deeper in her pockets, wishing that Kate would hurry. Eventually she emerged on her way down the hill, and Rachel moved off the step to meet her.

'Am I late?' Kate asked.

'Yes.'

'Sorry.' She shrugged as though it were nothing to do with her, and the two sisters walked off down the hill, chatting about their day. Absorbed in their conversation they took little notice of passers-by, most of them heads down, clutching their hats against the gusts of wind. Rachel had taken hers off, and they laughed as one young man lost his and had to scurry after it, chasing it among the legs of the crowd. Finally he caught it and when Rachel looked up again at the faces, she saw Captain Andrews a little way ahead, making his way towards them. For a moment she panicked and turned her head away to pretend she hadn't seen him, but he had already spotted her and it was too late. In three more paces he was in front of them.

'Mrs Lock.' He touched his cap.

'Captain Andrews.' She smiled but she was awkward in his presence, exposed again beneath the directness of his gaze. 'This is my sister, Kate Kirby,' she said, and hoped he would not see her blush.

'Miss Kirby.'

'You can call me Kate,' her sister laughed, and jealousy hardened in a knot in Rachel's stomach: her sister's natural ease with Andrews touched a chord of rivalry.

'So you're Captain Andrews,' Kate said, and Rachel looked away, ashamed of herself.

He laughed. 'Yes. I'm Captain Andrews.' Then he turned to Rachel, the smile still around his eyes, irresistible. 'Day off?'

'No, no. The library closes early on Fridays. We were just going for some lunch.' She wanted to get away from him, afraid that her feelings were plain for them both to see, cringing inside at the thought of it.

'I was doing the same. Would you care to join me?'

Rachel swallowed and glanced at her sister. No plausible excuse came to mind.

'That would be lovely,' Kate said in the pause, 'Thank you.'

'There's a nice place I know down on Cotham Hill. Shall we?'

He turned and led them through the crowd across the road and it was quieter off the main street where they could just walk with the three of them in a row along the pavement. Once or twice Andrews dropped behind to let someone go past and each time he did so the sleeve of his greatcoat brushed against her arm.

It was not far and though they took a table next to the window, the glass was steamed up so much that they could not see out to the road. Kate rubbed a small patch clear with her hand to peer out but it filled again with condensation almost straight away, and she gave up with a shrug. The restaurant was small but it was warm inside and pleasant, with white walls and tablecloths, and there was a hushed atmosphere amongst the diners that was surprising.

They ordered the soup and there was a silence until Kate said, 'So, Captain Andrews, have you got the day off?'

'No, not at all,' he replied. 'Actually, I'm AWOL.'

'Really?' Kate gasped.

He laughed and flicked a glance to Rachel. 'No, not really. I'm allowed a lunch break. And there's not much happening at the moment, so I can take my time.'

'A bit different from Italy, then,' Rachel said.

Andrews nodded and the smile left his eyes, and Rachel wished she had said something different.

Kate said, 'Danny used to talk about you sometimes in his letters.'

He tilted his head with interest.

'He used to say you weren't bad for an officer. That they were a lucky platoon to have you.'

'Did he?' Andrews murmured, thoughtful for a moment before he recollected himself and smiled at them both. A crooked smile, Rachel noticed, that touched the left side of his mouth before the right, so that often it was only half a smile.

'Any plans for the weekend?' he asked.

'Work,' they said in unison, and laughed.

He turned to Kate. 'What work do you do, Kate?'

'I'm a nurse.'

'That's a hard job.'

'It's all right,' she shrugged. 'At least I'm here, instead of over there, in France or Italy or somewhere. That would be much harder.'

'Yes,' he agreed. 'They do a very dangerous job.'

There was a silence and Rachel found she was wishing that Kate were not with them, that she could talk to him alone. With the three of them it was hard to think what to say.

'I wanted to go overseas when I first qualified,' Kate went on. 'But they said they needed me here. I was disappointed at the time but now I'm glad. After all the stories I've heard.'

She smiled at him and he returned the smile but afterwards his eyes touched Rachel's for an instant, and so she knew he had no interest in Kate, in spite of her prettiness. A small group of officer cadets passed behind them to the door and Andrews touched a hand to his temple in recognition of their salute. The door opened with a tinkle of the bell and a wave of cold air swept into the room. Rachel shivered.

'Where are you from originally?' Kate asked him.

'Marlborough.'

'I love Marlborough,' Rachel said. 'We had an aunt who lived near there when we were children and we used to go there for holidays sometimes. I remember finding a swan's nest on the river one year. I thought it was the most magical thing that had ever happened.'

He smiled. 'I like it too. I was very happy there. I used to teach at the college.'

'And you taught history,' Rachel said with a smile. 'Am I right?'

'Yes. Quite right.'

'Hence the interest. Will you go back to it after the war?'

'Probably. I did think about staying in the army but that isn't an option now.'

'Because of your leg?' Kate asked.

'Yes.'

'Does it give you a lot of trouble?'

He hesitated. 'A little,' he said. 'I can walk on it all right. But I can't run, so I'm not much use as a soldier any more.'

'I didn't think officers needed to run,' Kate said. 'I thought they got driven about in staff cars.'

Andrews laughed. 'I'd need to be a few ranks higher for that, I think.'

Kate shrugged, unabashed. 'So what did you do to it?'

'Shrapnel. Around the knee.'

'That must have hurt.'

'It did.'

There was another silence and the soup arrived. It was delicious and they ate eagerly, warming themselves from the inside.

'We've never been in here before,' Kate said between mouthfuls. 'I don't know why. But we'll definitely come in here again.'

They finished their meal and sat full and contented in silence for a time. Then the Captain called for the bill.

'Thank you,' Rachel said. 'That was lovely.'

'It was my pleasure,' he answered. 'But I really must be getting back now.'

He stood and helped them with their coats and as Rachel shrugged herself into hers, the backs of his fingers just brushed against her neck. She shivered and dropped her face away from him to cover the embarrassment. Outside, they walked together back to the corner where their routes parted.

'It was nice to meet you, Kate,' he said. And to Rachel, 'I've got some books to bring back. I think they're probably overdue, so I might see you again in the library.'

'I hope so. Thank you again.'

'My pleasure.' He nodded and touched his cap then turned and walked away. The sisters stood watching him make his way back to the Artillery Grounds but he did not turn and Rachel was glad. She would have been ashamed for him to know they had watched him for so long.

ANDREWS WALKED BACK SLOWLY, unaware of the wind or the traffic on the road. He was thinking only of Rachel, and the impossibility of what he felt, a need that threatened to unravel him.

He had stayed away from her after the first time, reneging on his promise to visit her husband again, afraid to see her in front of him, aware of his own transparency. He had hoped that in time her image would fade from his thoughts, that she would become a woman in his memory he might have loved in a different life. But no matter how hard he tried to train his thoughts away from her, her picture stayed in his mind, the details vivid and persistent; the angle of her head when he caught her in a moment of thought, the cadence of her voice when she spoke, the pale fine line of her wrist encircled by the bracelet he knew must have come from Syria. Jealousy shivered through him every time he thought of it – the precious metal against such fair skin. It should have been a present from him: other fingers had no right to clasp its beauty around her arm.

In front of him a gust of wind snatched a sheet of paper from the pavement and lifted it across his path, twirling it haphazardly on the road. It heaved and shivered across the tarmac, then caught in the wheel arch of a passing jeep. The vehicle roared on, oblivious. Andrews followed it with his eyes distractedly while the rest of him was dislocated by the thought of Rachel, the shield of self-sufficiency he had erected to protect himself in Italy completely shattered by their meeting. She had opened him again to the possibility of feeling, and left the nerve ends raw and vulnerable.

So the library had drawn him as a thirsty man to water and his reward had been the knowledge that Rachel felt the same. He remembered the blush that spread across her skin that day as he watched her work, the way she checked his finger for a ring. Afterwards she had hidden from him, nowhere to be seen when he went to the desk to take his leave, and that had told him everything.

Sleepless that night he had vowed not to see her again.

He lay awake for most of the night, tormented by the struggle between his heart and mind. She was the wife of one his men, he kept telling himself, a man he had commanded many times in desperate battle, a man it would be wrong to take from. It could not be. Whatever he felt, it could not be. He could not allow himself to be in love with Rachel.

Then today they met again by chance and all his resolve just failed him. Like butter in the sun it melted at the sight of her, a force he had no power to deny. However wrong it was, he could not help it: it was far too late to stop himself from falling.

He was at the gate before he knew it, and he had no memory of the journey there. He stopped, surprised, and automatically returned the sentry's salute. Then he paused to straighten himself, trying to turn his mind away from Rachel and towards the business of the afternoon. He only half succeeded.

'We saw your Captain Andrews today,' Kate told Danny in the living room at home.

Danny started in surprise and the half-full teacup fell from his hand. 'Fuck it!' he hissed.

There was a silence and both children stopped their game to stare at him.

'Charlie, go and get a cloth from the kitchen,' Rachel ordered. The boy got to his feet, stepped over his sister lying sprawled on the rug, and disappeared through the door. He returned a moment later cloth in hand. 'Thank you.'

She took it and knelt by the wheelchair to mop up the mess. Danny let her wipe his hand and wrist, the arm of the chair where the tea had spilt, without complaint.

'Are you all right?' she asked him gently. 'You didn't burn yourself?'

'I'm fine.'

'That's good.' She smiled at him but he turned his face away from her. Then she took the cloth out to the kitchen and stood at the sink to rinse it out. It was hard to stop herself from crying.

'So how was Andrews?' Danny asked her as she stepped back through the door.

'He seemed fine.'

'He bought us lunch,' Kate said. 'Which was nice of him.'

'Very nice.'

Kate exchanged a glance with her sister, taken aback by the sarcasm.

'And what did you talk about?'

'Nothing much,' Kate said quickly. 'Small talk. You know, the usual thing.'

'No. I don't know.'

Kate looked to her sister for help. Rachel said, 'He told us he was a teacher before the war. In Marlborough.'

'Was he?'

'You didn't know?'

'No. We never socialised. He's an officer.'

There was a silence and Danny dropped his eyes to the paper that was on his lap, the edges frail and still wet with tea.

'Shall I make you another cup of tea?' Rachel offered.

He shook his head and they sat in silence a while longer, the tension seeming to shrink in around them, and the only sound was the hushed nervous whispering of the children.

Chapter Six

'This is Paul,' Kate announced one Sunday in October, a last glorious autumn day before the winter hit to stay.

The American stepped into the living room behind her. He was tall and pale with a boyish face but beneath the uniform his frame was wiry and strong. Kate moved to be beside him, a protective hand on his arm though he did not seem to need it.

'Nice to meet you, sir.' He proffered a hand to the father of his girl and though George grasped it firmly he could not disguise the judgement on his face, nor his distaste.

'You too,' George nodded.

They stood for a moment, each sizing up the other. Danny observed them from his chair at the table, a half smile at the corners of his mouth: the other daughter now with a man who was unsuitable. He watched, interested to see how the young man would take the hostility.

George said, 'Kate didn't mention that you were … American.'

'She didn't?' Paul smiled and laid his hand across Kate's. 'Well, I am.'

'So I can see.'

'This is my sister Rachel,' Kate said quickly, 'and her husband Danny. And this is my mother, Mrs Kirby.'

He nodded to each of them as they were introduced and took the hand that Danny extended. He seems all right, Danny thought. And George obviously hated him, so that was in his favour.

'Please sit down,' Rose said. 'Would you like some tea?'

'Thank you.'

The American took a chair at the table across from Danny. The two men looked at each other for a moment in silence. Danny wondered what Kate had told him, how much history the young man knew. Then Paul said, 'Where did you get hit?'

'Anzio.'

'Anzio, huh? I heard it was really bad there. Like the Great War.' Then, 'What happened to you?'

Tension descended and everyone's attention turned to Danny. He hesitated, the memory half-buried now, kept under mostly by drink and willpower, a place he did not want to visit again. The American was waiting, his young face interested and eager, still naïve, no idea what he was going to, what he would have to see and do when he arrived. For a moment, Danny was almost sorry for him, aware of how brutally that innocence would soon be stripped away. If, that is, he survived beyond the first few days.

'It was a mine,' he said. It was the best he could manage, the first time he had spoken of it. Blood pumped through him in quick hard surges, and he reached to the table for a cigarette to calm himself, struggling to control the trembling of his fingers as he lit the match, enraged by his weakness. Hands that were always steady under fire shaking now at the mention of a memory. He sucked back hard on the cigarette and the heat of it was hard and comforting in his lungs. He coughed. Then, to cover up his feelings he said, 'It was probably one of your lot's.'

'An American mine?'

Danny nodded.

'That's too bad. I'm sorry.'

'Not half as sorry as I am.'

'No. I guess not.' Paul dropped his eyes to the forage cap in his hands, turning it lightly between his fingers.

There was a silence until Rose came through from the kitchen with the tea. She laid the tray on the table. 'How do you take your tea, Paul?'

'How it comes,' Paul answered, and Danny wondered if he would have liked to ask for two sugars, if he were just being polite. Poor sod, he thought, falling for a Kirby girl, trying hard to please.

Rose filled the cups in turn and dished out the cake that Kate had made that morning. She gave the children extra big pieces, a special treat. They bolted it down, then at a nod from their mother slipped out to the garden to play.

'So how are you finding England?' she asked. 'Do you like it here?'

'Very much, Mrs Kirby. It's so very different from home.'

'Where is home?' Rachel asked.

'Texas. A place called Bay City.' He grinned. 'You've probably never heard of it, right?'

Rachel smiled. 'Right.'

He laughed and took a careful sip of his tea.

'So what did you do before you joined up? George asked.

Judgemental bastard, Danny thought. Here it comes.

'I was a cab driver,' Paul replied. 'It was a great job. Out and about all day, meeting people. I loved it.' If he noticed George's sneer he made no sign. 'And what do you do, sir?'

Danny smiled, liking the American more for his self-respect, and the fact that he had no fear of them.

'I'm an engineer. At the BAC,' George's tone was clipped with irritation. 'I suppose you've heard of them?'

'Of course.'

'Well, it's lovely to meet you at last,' Rose said.

'You too, ma'am. I've heard a lot about you all.'

'I bet you have,' Danny murmured.

Rose smiled, trying hard, but her husband's silence cast a shadow over all of them, and made them ill-at-ease.

'You're a rifleman?' Danny asked then.

'He's a sniper,' Kate said. She touched Paul's arm with pride and he covered her fingers with his own.

'Not yet, he's not.'

Kate's breathing quickened. 'But he will be.'

'You haven't killed anyone yet?'

'I haven't met any Germans.'

Danny nodded, and Paul's gaze hung on the other man's face, waiting for him to go on. 'It's a hard thing to do the first time,' Danny said. There was a pause. Then, 'D'you remember the first time you killed an animal?'

'Uh-huh.'

'How did you feel?'

'I was eight years old,' Paul replied, eyes still locked with Danny's. 'It was just a bird, with a stone from a slingshot, but I cried for hours.'

'But it was easier after that? A bit easier each time?'

'Yes.'

'It's the same with people.'

Paul nodded, and Danny half smiled at him as he took another Woodbine from the packet. Then he half threw half slid the pack across the table towards the American. Paul took one out and the two men lit up. Kate reached across and took one too and her father looked up when he heard the second scrape of the match. There was a silence as Kate breathed smoke into the air above them.

'Put that out,' George said.

'Who, me?' Kate replied.

'You know who I'm talking to.'

'You let him smoke.' She gestured towards Danny with the hand that held the cigarette.

'He isn't my daughter,' George snapped back. 'And I'm not having a daughter of mine smoke in this house.'

Kate lifted the cigarette to her mouth and drew back, letting the smoke trickle out from her lips. She was reckless and defiant, made courageous by the presence of the man at her side.

'I'm warning you.' George rose from his chair so that he loomed over the small group at the table, but she was not cowed.

'Leave her alone,' Danny said. 'What difference does it make? In a few months time she'll be gone and living in America and doing exactly what she likes anyway.'

The older man turned to him, pointing, hand shaking with rage. 'You keep out of this. This is nothing to do with you.'

Danny shrugged, indifferent.

'Is that true?' Rose turned grief-stricken eyes to Kate. 'Are you going to go to America?'

'Yes. It is. Paul and I are going to get married,' Kate almost spat. 'And I can't wait to get out of here.'

Rachel stared at her in disbelief and shock.

'If you come back, that is,' Danny said to Paul. 'And in one piece. Come back like this and she won't marry you. You know that, don't you?'

Kate's gaze flicked to the floor and Danny saw the rapid rise and fall of her breathing as she fought to contain her fury. There was a silence, all eyes on the couple, waiting. When she looked up again at her family her eyes were dark and hard and the hatred in them encompassed everyone.

'Why the hell would I want to stay here?' she breathed. 'I hate you all.' She turned to Paul. 'Come on. Let's go. We aren't welcome here.'

Paul stood up and mumbled a goodbye and thank you to Rose, then followed his fiancée out of the house.

No one moved or spoke as the slam of the front door reverberated through the silence. After a while Rose got up from her place at the table and began to load the cups back on to the tray. Rachel watched her for a moment before she moved to help, and George sank down into his armchair. He reached across to turn on the wireless next to him and an American voice filled the room. George swore before he yanked the knob round to find the BBC again.

Chapter Seven

The drinking helped the nightmares. He had it under more control now, not the frenzied need for forgetfulness of when he first got back. The job helped. Gave him a purpose and something to do with the hours of his day instead of just thinking, and remembering.

SOMEWHERE IN ITALY there was a farmhouse – a golden stone building on the top of a hill. He had no memory of the name of the place but by then they had all come to seem the same to him, another farm, another hill, another river, remembered only for the men who never left them: the river that took O'Grady, the hill that killed Stan Hodge, the names on the map long forgotten, or never learned. Years ago, Rachel used to say she would like to go to Italy, see the art in Florence, the canals of Venice, St Peter's Square in Rome. They would look at pictures together sometimes, in magazines, and dream about a holiday.

But his Italy was a different place, a cultured graveyard.

The artwork meant nothing to him, nor the history, and it seemed obscene to him that people should care that a statue or a church had survived undamaged when a man had been blown to bits right next to it. Sometimes in the village churches where they were billeted at night, too wracked by nerves and shock to rest, he would touch the carved Madonnas with his grime-ridden hands and wonder what the lifeless eyes had seen, what other battles they had witnessed, what brutalities, all passing unrecorded except by that dead immortal gaze. He had seen the villagers bow their heads before such statues, or cross themselves in faith, lives risked at times to protect the sacred forms. He would have smashed them all, defaced each holy work of art in every church they saw, if it would have brought just one man back and restored a fallen life. How could anyone have faith in the midst of all of this?

They had been given orders to investigate the farm, to take it if they could, bring prisoners. It was a lot to ask of fifteen weary men, all that was left of the platoon, and no idea what risks the farm might hold.

They crouched now, huddled at the bottom of the hill, hidden from the house by the rising land and the hedgerow, scared again, terror in their bones. He had thought at first that battle would get easier, become less frightening each time, but now he knew the opposite was true. Every time was worse than what had gone before, every fight one more chance to die and his turn getting closer. It was a simple matter of statistics – the odds against surviving got longer every time.

He looked along the line of men. Not many left from the landing at Sicily, faces now beside him whose names he did not know. Replacements, whose eagerness to prove themselves before the old hands made them dangerous. It was better not to try to get to know them, though most of them would probably be gone before he ever got the chance: he preferred to stay close to the men he knew and trusted. He looked across at Sergeant Hayes, peering through the bushes, exchanging the binoculars with their officer, discussing tactics. The three of them had been together from the start: Hayes had been a private when they met way back in Syria, a different world, another life. They had played at war back then, trained and exercised, no clue about what really lay ahead. Now it seemed impossible that anything else existed but war and cold and pain and fear. Now he was a different person.

He swung his head the other way. Next to him lay Walker, helmet tilted forward across his face against the winter light, taking forty winks wherever he could find it. Danny was constantly amazed at the man's ability to sleep, here for instance, in this stinking freezing mud-filled ditch, while the others nerved themselves up for action. He smiled, and sank down lower on his haunches to light a cigarette: drawing back, the smoke was warm inside him. For a moment, he tried to conjure up a pleasant sense of warmth: the memory of a picnic on a summer's day, or a pint before the fire at the pub on a bitter winter's night. But the only heat he could remember was the heat of sweat and struggle, of exhausted stumbling with a heavy load. He took another drag on the cigarette and coughed and tried to stop himself from thinking. Hayes turned his head towards him.

'Get the men up. This is what we're doing …'

Danny prodded Walker, who woke up easily, and all the men's attention turned towards the crouching officer, whispering hoarsely in the quiet afternoon. From the distance came the sound of gunfire, the thunder of artillery, the snap of small arms closer by, but the sounds were so familiar they barely noticed: it was too far away to worry them, someone else's battle, the normal backdrop to their days.

Lieutenant Andrews was talking quickly, asking questions, making sure they understood. Danny dropped the fag end into the water at his feet, listening hard, tiredness giving way to the alertness of his nerves.

Maybe this time they would be lucky. Maybe this would be the only farm in Italy the Germans would not fight for, and they could walk right in and take it. But he thought the odds were probably against it. Jerry fought for everything, no inch was ever taken easily, every mile of ground in Allied hands bought and paid for handsomely with blood.

'On my command,' Andrews said.

Their movements seemed too loud in the silence as they crept towards the points for jump off. On the left flank, Danny's men crouched down behind the bushes, peering up ahead as next to them the Bren group got their weapon ready. To their right, Andrews waited with the others.

Danny turned his gaze towards the officer. He could feel the wet of sweat on his back and his armpits as he waited for the gesture that would send them out across the open ground. It was a steep hill, exposed, and he tried not to think about whose dying image that farmhouse would be.

The signal came and the men began to run, bodies bent low, rifles cradled and ready to fire. Halfway up the field the German gun began, spitting metal across the grass, two men down already. The left flank ran for cover but the others dropped, hidden now, lives dependent on the ground's unevenness, the small depressions that saved them from the hissing steel. Danny's group made cover, sinking down behind the ruins of a wall, and as the Bren gun opened fire behind them, the mortar shot its screen of smoke. They waited, breathing hard, straining for the seconds' silence the Germans needed to reload. He glanced across to where Andrews lay flattened beneath the spray of bullets. Above the din of gunfire he heard someone screaming out in pain.

Then Andrews' head was raised a fraction, mouth open in a shout.

'Fall back!'

The words were lost but Danny knew the shape they made. He looked back up the hill towards the farm and saw the self-propelled gun shake off its camouflaging branches and move forward into view. Fuck. He gestured to the others and in the moment when the Spandau's rip of fire fell silent, they turned and raced back down the hill, balance hard to keep in the downward leaps of panic.

The big gun lobbed its shell and missed, aim too long. The men thudded into the ditch, squatting down, hidden from the Spandau as it started up again. He was breathless, panting, wet with sweat, the freezing mud unnoticed in his relief to be alive. He turned and peered above the ditch's rim. Two men lay lifeless on the slope and one was stirring, screaming, trying to drag himself towards them but barely moving. Danny swore and looked away. Peter Lewis.

They got up again and slid and stumbled through the mud towards the deeper safety of the woods. The Spandau rattled leaves amongst the bushes as they ran and behind them the self-propelled gun found its line and shattered through the cover that just a while ago had seemed to offer safety. They reached the woods below the ridge and stopped in amongst the trees, breathing hard, and as the others rested with their backs against the tree trunks, the signaller tried to force the radio into life. The gunfire stopped and the sound of Lewis dying filled the silence. Danny lit a cigarette and smoked it fast with trembling fingers. The radio was dead.

'We've got to go back for him,' Danny said.

Andrews looked up from squatting by the radio. He shook his head. 'No.'

'We can't leave him there like that.'

'We can't go back either. It would be suicide.'

The others in the squad looked away, their sympathies divided.

'I promised I wouldn't leave him,' Danny breathed. 'I promised I'd see him through it.'

Lewis had been just a frightened boy at the beginning, latching on to older braver Danny. The two of them had hit it off, an unexpected friendship, and Lewis grew up quickly, proved himself courageous and dependable, with a wicked sense of humour. He was Danny's closest friend.

'I'm going back for him.'

For an instant Andrews wavered, flicked his eyes towards the dying man. Then he shook his head. 'No. I'm sorry. No one's going back. We'll send a party for him after dark.'

'He'll be dead by then.'

'I'm sorry.'

Danny bit his lip. He could taste the salt of sweat and the bitter earthy grit of spattered ingrained mud. He spat, and the sputum landed close to Andrews' boots.

'Is that an order?' He wiped a filthy hand across his mouth.

'Yes. That's an order. Now let's go.'

The others kept their eyes averted as they heaved their aching bodies from where they rested on the ground and followed Andrews back down towards their line. Reluctantly, Danny followed on behind.

THE SOUND of Lewis dying on that winter's day had stayed with him, recurring through his life at unexpected times, the memory tripped by the touch of a breeze in a certain direction, a chance remark or a sound that seemed to have no connection at all. In his dreams, that day came back to haunt him often, variations on a theme.

And the guilt for leaving Lewis festered like the worst of wounds: he had left his friend to die alone on the word of a man he would later come to hate.

Chapter Eight

'Why is Dad so cross all the time?' Charlie asked at bed time. 'He clipped me round the ear for nothing tonight. I hadn't done anything. Nothing at all.'

Rachel tucked the covers up round her son and shivered in the cold bedroom. In the next bed Jean lay watching with quiet dark eyes that were impossible to read. Beside her on the pillow, as always, was the doll her dad had given her, the embroidery wearing thin from constant use.

'You must have done something.'

'Well,' he said, glancing across at his sister. 'I might have scowled at Jean a bit. But it was just a scowl, that's all. Honest.'

'He doesn't mean to be angry with you.'

'But he hit me. It isn't fair.'

Rachel sighed. She was tired from work and the constant effort to keep the peace. Like walking on eggshells most of the time, having to be wary of his moods, always watching her words in case she said something that might set him off. And Charlie was too old, too clever now, to fob off with half-baked fibs. He could see what his father had become and he was old enough to remember how he used to be.

'D'you remember what Dad was like before he went away?' she asked him. 'How he used to play with you and run about?'

Charlie nodded. 'He used to take me to the Green every Sunday. We used to play football. He said he'd teach me cricket too when I got older but then he went away.'

'Charlie,' Rachel said gently. 'I know it's hard with your dad at the moment. That he's a bit unpredictable. But you know I'm sure he wishes he could play with you like he used to. And that's the problem. That's why he's so sad and angry. Because he can't do any of the things he used to do. And he never will be able to.'

'Because of his legs?'

'Yes.'

Charlie thought about this for a moment, running his hands across the quilt back and forth. Then he sat up again, another question forming on his lips. 'Is that why he drinks?'

'Who told you he drinks?' She was staggered, almost winded by the blow of her son's understanding. He was growing up faster than she knew.

'Other boys at school,' Charlie said. 'They say he's drunk every lunchtime. That's why he works in a pub. Because he's a drunk.'

No wonder there are wars, she thought: the gift of cruelty is innate. 'What boys?'

'All of them, Mum. They all say it.'

'And what do you do when they say it?'

'I tell them they're liars. And sometimes we fight about it.'

'Oh Charlie. Have you been in trouble at school for fighting?'

'No,' he replied. 'Well, only a bit.'

Rachel smiled, and stroked the hair back from his temple. 'Try not to fight over it. It's better that you don't fight.'

'I'll try.'

'That's a good boy.'

'I just want it all how it used to be, Mum …'

'Me too, darling. Me too. Shall I read you something?'

'Yes please.' Charlie reached out and chose a book from the pile on the table by the bed, then held it closed on his lap for a moment, thumbs running gently across its cover. Jean still lay silent and thoughtful, eyes wide open, taking all of it in.

Rachel gently prised the book from under Charlie's hands. She knew there was more he wanted to say but she was too tired to draw it out of him now. She said, 'You just have to patient with him, Charlie. Give him lots of time and love and hopefully he'll come round. That's all you can do. That's all any of us can do.'

He said nothing and she opened the book and began to read:

'*Roger, aged seven, and no longer the youngest of the family, ran in wide zigzags, to and fro, across the steep field that sloped up from the lake to Holly Howe…*'

Jean began to doze quickly as she read, weariness overcoming her interest. But Charlie hung on every word and every time she thought that she should stop, he begged her to go on. He was battling with his tiredness, staving off sleep just to have more of her company; so much of her was taken up now with work and Danny. She should read to them more often, make more time to be with them: they were growing up so fast and she felt as though she hardly knew them.

It was late when finally she closed the book, and she watched her son drifting slowly into sleep, eyelids growing heavy in the hard-fought fall from wakefulness. She smiled. They were so peaceful in their sleep, angelic, and she sat and watched them for a while, growing colder in the darkness.

'You were a long time,' her mother said, when at last she went down.

'Charlie wanted me to read.'

Rose smiled and nodded and went back to the ironing.

'Here,' Rachel said. 'Let me do that. You've been on your feet all day.'

'Thanks love. I appreciate it.' Rose gathered up the clothes she had already done and took them upstairs to the airing cupboard. Rachel took her place at the board. The fragrance of the fresh laundry was pleasant and soothing and as she worked she did not allow herself to think of anything.

IN THE BEDROOM, late when the rest of the house had gone to bed, Danny watched his wife undress. She turned half away, self-conscious in front of him, as she had always been. A modest girl, he thought, sweet and kind and innocent. A good wife. He had never doubted she would be faithful. When other men in the company were fretting about their women alone for so long and England full of Yanks, he had never worried for a moment, sure of Rachel's loyalty. But now he was home again and they were strangers. His fault that, he knew, but there was nothing he could do to change it, too much inside him from the years away.

'Turn round,' he said softly. 'Let me look at you.'

She froze, reluctant and embarrassed.

'I can still look at you, can't I?' he said. 'Even if I can't touch.'

She turned slowly, dropping the arm that shielded her breasts. She stood straight, soft breasts still round as he remembered them, nipples hard with the cold air. She hadn't changed, he thought, still the same soft lines and pale skin.

'You can touch,' she said.

'There's no point,' he replied. 'Can't bloody do anything, can I?'

'We can still love each other.'

He closed his eyes, unable to face it, the thought of

touching her when down there would not work. It was too shameful. Better not to start it. Not to even try.

'Put your nightdress on and get into bed,' he told her.

She stood a while longer in the cold, hoping he guessed, to tempt him, but all he could see was her awkwardness in front of him, her embarrassment, and he realised he didn't want her anyway. Maybe a different girl, one of the whores he had seen in Italy, girls who knew how to tempt a man; maybe a girl like that could have coaxed him into loving her a little. But not Rachel. That had never been their way, and she didn't have it in her to seduce him. He settled himself beneath the covers and lay on his back, head propped on his hands while he waited for her to get into bed.

'I still love you,' she said, lying close, gazing up at him, the same trusting girl he had married. He tried to remember when he had stopped loving her.

'I don't want your pity,' he said.

'It isn't pity,' she replied. 'I'm your wife and I love you and I want for us to be happy again.'

'You think we can be happy? Really?'

'We could at least try.'

He let out a half laugh of derision. 'How?'

'This is our life now. We have to make the best of it.'

He turned his head on his hands to look at her, still young and pretty and hopeful, her soul unscarred by war, sights and sounds no man should ever know.

'This isn't a life,' he said. 'This is living hell.'

She slid back from him, unable to meet his eyes, and for a moment he was sorry that she was caught up in the wash of him sinking, but reaching out to her now could only pull her under too.

'Do you hate me very much?' she asked.

'I don't hate you.'

'Are you sure?'

'I don't hate you Rache,' he said again.

But there was nothing she could do to help him any more, and he wished that she would give up trying. He heard the stifled sniff, the start of tears he knew she would not let him see.

'Good night, Danny,' she whispered.

'Good night Rachel,' he said. Then he reached out and turned off the lamp and lay with his back to her, but he could still hear the muffled sobs until he fell asleep.

THAT NIGHT RACHEL dreamt she was with Andrews. There was no war and they lived in a cottage by the sea but they were not happy because there was something she had lost and though she knew it was something terribly important, she could not remember what it was. So she searched and searched along the cliffs above the sea, and scrambled down the face of them and searched among the rocks that were strewn across the beach. Then she waded out into the water but she could not find what it was so she waded deeper and deeper and the water was cold and she could not keep her footing as the sand shifted with the tide beneath her feet. Then on the wind she heard her name and turned to see who was calling and there was Andrews on the cliff, waving to her, but he was far far away and he could not help her so she turned back to keep looking in the cold cold water, stumbling and flailing but still going deeper until it was over her head, but she did not find what it was she had lost.

She woke confused and afraid, her mind still grasping for the thing she had lost. Beside her Danny slept heavily, exhausted from the terrors of his night, peaceful now and serene in sleep. Then she remembered what he had said to her before they slept, and her own dream slipped from her thoughts. She slid out of the bed away from him, unwilling to face the truth of his words. Somewhere inside him the old Danny must still exist, she told herself. Somewhere deep down, beneath the nightmares and the anger, his heart was still the same. But now, for the first time, she could not make herself believe it. He left more than his legs in Italy, she thought. He had left the whole person that he used to be.

In the kitchen Kate was leaning on the counter and crying. 'Paul's shipping out today,' she sobbed. 'He phoned me at the hospital last night.' The rest of her words were choked in her tears. 'He's … gone …'

Rachel stood and said nothing; what words of comfort could she give?

'And you don't even care,' Kate accused, wiping at her face with the heel of her palm. Even in tears she was pretty, Rachel thought.

'Of course I care,' she soothed. 'But there's nothing I can say, is there?'

'You don't know what it's like, how much it hurts.'

'I do,' Rachel said gently, placing a comforting hand on her sister's shoulder. 'I know exactly. But it gets easier with time. You'll see.'

Kate shook her head as if unwilling to believe it, then swung herself away and out of the kitchen. Rachel heard her take the stairs two at a time, the slam of the bedroom door. She stood for a moment to collect her thoughts, her sister's self-absorption sometimes hard to bear. The tea did nothing to revive her spirits.

During the night it had snowed but by morning there was only rain and the sky was dark and heavy above her. As she stepped outside a gust of wind spattered her with rain and almost wrenched the door from her hand. It was too wild to walk to work she decided, so she trudged instead to the bus stop, her umbrella useless in the wind. She was drenched before she even got there, her wool coat heavy and cold, and as the memory of her dream wound itself through the understanding that Danny would never come back to her, she felt herself sinking into hopelessness. This was going to be her life now, loveless and miserable, and the days stretched out endless before her.

The bus arrived, swaying and loud and overcrowded. She pressed herself into a space by the door and the wind whipped the rain in her face as the vehicle took off. Then it lurched way across a pothole and the passengers who were standing stumbled and cursed. Rachel wrapped her arm more tightly around the pole and hung on.

'Road's a disgrace!' said the woman next to Rachel.

'Government's got more important things to spend its money on,' a man's voice replied.

The woman said nothing in reply but went on grumbling to herself close to Rachel's ear until they reached the stop for the library. Rachel jumped off with relief, glad to be away from the press and the noise. On the pavement as she waited to cross the road an army officer hurried past and her heart jumped in the moment before she realised that it was not Andrews.

By the time she got to work her woollen stockings were sodden from the spray on the road and she towelled herself dry in the office while she waited for the urn to boil for tea. Then Jane put her head round the door. She was smirking.

'Your officer friend is at the desk,' she said.

'Really?' The image of her dream slid into focus in the forefront of her mind, clear and vivid. 'He asked if you were here.'

Automatically, Rachel touched a hand to her hair, in rats' tails because of the rain, but there was nothing she could do to make it better.

'Thank you,' she said. 'Tell him I'll be right out.'

Jane disappeared and Rachel took a deep breath before she

opened the door and went across to the desk. 'Captain Andrews.'

'Mrs Lock.'

'What can I do for you?'

He smiled and dropped his eyes and for the first time she saw him look uncomfortable. The shyness made him younger, almost boyish, and without noticing, she took a step back, away from him.

'I was hoping,' he said, lifting his face again, 'that you might agree to have lunch with me today.'

She hesitated, searching for the strength to refuse.

'Please?'

Rachel lowered her eyes to the counter and rubbed at the worn wood with her fingers. 'I can't,' she whispered. 'I'm sorry.'

'It's only lunch.'

'I know,' Rachel said, though she was aware that it meant far more than that, to both of them. 'All the same, I can't. It isn't right.'

He swallowed and nodded, and a new line of tension touched his jaw as he tried to hide the disappointment. Rachel kept her eyes averted so she would not change her mind and it was more difficult to do than she could ever have imagined.

'I understand,' he said.

'Please go,' she asked him. 'Please don't come here again.'

'I have to get my books from somewhere,' he replied. 'You wouldn't deny me my books would you?'

She smiled, in spite of herself. 'No. Of course not. You can come and get your books.'

'Thank you.'

There was a pause and she wished he would go before she weakened and changed her mind.

Finally, he said, 'I'd better go. And you'd better get to work. I wouldn't want you getting in trouble on my account.' He touched his cap, then he turned and was gone. Rachel blinked against the tears and dragged her feet back to the office.

'What did he want?' Jane asked, handing Rachel tea.

'Nothing.'

'Oh, come on,' she pleaded. 'He must have wanted something. Tell me something interesting. I could do with a bit of gossip.'

Rachel wiped her eyes and tried to smile. 'He asked me to lunch.'

'I hope you said yes.'

'I said no.'

'Why? It's only lunch.'

'I'm married. To one of his men.'

'Oh, live a little.'

Rachel shook her head. They drank their tea and the clock ticked round to half past.

'Well,' Jane said at last, moving to the door. 'If you don't want him, can I have him? He is rather lovely, don't you think?'

'Yes. He is lovely. And no, you can't have him.'

'Greedy,' Jane laughed, and let the door swing shut behind her. Beyond it the library began to fill.

RACHEL WAS MISERABLE ALL MORNING.

'Oh for God's sake,' Jane said at eleven. 'Why don't you just ring him and tell him you've changed your mind?'

'I can't,' she replied. 'It isn't that simple. Besides, I don't know the number.'

'He's at the Artillery Grounds, isn't he? The number can't be that hard to find.'

Rachel was silent and at twelve she hurried out into the rain, desperate for fresh air and movement. Just outside the door she almost ran into a man who was sheltering from the weather in the porch. It took her less than a heartbeat to realise it was him. Startled and confused, she backed away down the steps so that she was standing in the rain. It fell coldly against her face and hair: she had left her hat inside.

'Mrs Lock.'

She nodded in response but did not look at him, knowing she could not refuse that smile a second time.

'I was hoping you might have changed your mind,' he said.

'Well, I haven't.' She turned and half ran along the pavement down the hill away from him. She had no umbrella and he followed her with his, trying to hold it over both of them. From the corner of her eye she could see him as he limped along beside her, struggling to keep up as she wove her way between the people that were passing them. The street was busy in spite of the rain, workers out for their lunch break.

'Please, Rachel?'

The use of her first name stopped her and as they stood in the middle of the pavement in the rain she could feel the water seeping inside her shoes. An American army truck roared by on its way up the hill, covering them with spray and passers-by walked round them, irritated.

'Don't you take no for answer?' she demanded.

'Apparently not.'

She laughed then, in spite of herself, all her will to resist him gone with the sight of the smile in his eyes. They walked on together and she let him guide her to the same restaurant as before. They were silent until they were settled at a table by the window.

'Thank you,' he said.

'For what?'

'For coming.'

The waiter appeared.

'Would you like the soup?' Andrews asked.

Rachel nodded and he ordered two bowls of soup. The waiter turned and went away.

'I'm married,' she said then, leaning forward so that he would hear her lowered voice. 'To one of your men. We can't do this.'

'He's not actually one of my men any more.'

'Don't split hairs.'

He lowered his gaze and began to finger the cutlery. She had not seen him rattled before, and she shared his discomfort. She should have stayed firm and said no. 'I'm sorry,' she said.

'You don't have to be sorry,' he replied. 'It's I who should be apologising. I shouldn't put pressure on you like this. It's wrong of me. Please forgive me. I really didn't mean for this to happen. Do you forgive me?'

'Yes,' she whispered. Of course, she thought. Of course I forgive you.

They sat in silence then, uncomfortable with each other, neither of them knowing how to go on. The soup arrived and dispersed a little of the awkwardness, giving them something to do. Rachel said, 'Actually, part of me is glad that you came back. But only part of me.'

He smiled. 'Well, all of me is glad I did.'

They ate some of their soup, a little more at ease with each other. Then, because it seemed ridiculous to sit with him in silence, Rachel said, 'Tell me more about yourself.'

'What would you like to know?' He was smiling, and though his company was easier now and less awkward, guilt gave the pleasure a bitter edge.

'I don't know. What makes Captain Andrews tick?'

'Call me Kit.'

'Kit.' She sounded the name on her lips and thought again how well it suited him.

'I'm Rachel.'

'I know,' he replied, and she recalled that he had used her

name earlier on the road outside. 'I remembered it because my mother's name is Rachel.'

'Really?' Absurdly, she was flattered. 'And your parents live in…?'

'Marlborough.' He paused. 'Would you like to know about my parents?'

'It's a start.'

He smiled. 'All right. My father's the vicar of a small church just outside Marlborough.'

'He must be very disappointed in you.'

Andrews looked baffled.

'Chasing after married women.'

He laughed. 'Ah, but he doesn't know. You see, I've never done it before.'

Rachel smiled. 'So, you grew up in Marlborough?'

'Yes. Then I went to Oxford and read English and History. Then I returned to Marlborough to teach until I joined up. That was in 1941.'

'You volunteered?'

'I did.'

Rachel nodded and broke more bread off the roll to dip in the last of the soup. There was a silence for a while but it was comfortable and in spite of everything she was glad to be there.

'How's Danny?' Andrews asked then.

All the pleasure of being with Andrews dissolved in a surge of guilt. An urge to confide fought with her natural loyalty, and for a moment she was confused.

'It isn't easy,' she managed to say.

Andrews watched her, trying to read between the lines. 'I'm sure it isn't,' he replied. 'Are things getting any better?'

'Not really. He's got a part time job …'

'That's wonderful.'

'… but it's at the pub so it's a bit of a mixed blessing really.'

'He's drinking a lot?'

She nodded.

Andrews said, 'He was a good soldier, Rachel. The best in the platoon, utterly dependable. But he saw a lot of his friends get killed, and he took it hard.'

Rachel was silent, emotions torn and battered between the two men. She had no idea what she felt any more.

'Are you all right?' he asked her.

'Not really,' she whispered. Then, catching sight of her watch she said, 'I've got to go.'

'Of course.' He called the waiter over and paid for the meal, then helped her on with her coat. She felt weak and close to tears, and when they got outside into the rain he offered his arm to her and she took it, huddling close to him under the umbrella, gripping on to him tightly for support. He walked with her to the library steps and when they stopped she slid her arm out from his, hurriedly, afraid, suddenly aware of how close to him she had been.

Andrews turned to face her. 'Can I see you again, Rachel?' he said.

She closed her eyes against the confusion but it made no difference. She could still sense him there, so near, and for a moment she thought she might be going to faint. She opened her eyes as he took her arm to steady her and all she was aware of was the pressure of his hand against her elbow and the blueness of his eyes.

'Rachel?'

'Yes,' she whispered. 'Yes.'

He smiled with relief and brushed the backs of his fingers against her cheek. She moved her head against them, drawing strength from his touch.

'I'll come when I can,' he said. 'It isn't always easy to get away.'

'I understand.'

'But I'll see you very soon. I promise.'

She nodded and watched him turn and walk away, the straightness of his back and the limp, his form growing smaller as he went away from her. She stood until he disappeared, blinking against the rain, and her heart beat fast with the danger of what she had done.

At home Kate was still in tears about Paul, alone in her bedroom, inconsolable.

'Come on, Kate,' Rachel coaxed. 'You're going to make yourself ill.'

'I can't help it,' she sobbed. 'I can't, I can't.'

Rachel sat on the edge of the bed and Kate drew her knees in closer to her chest, leaning her back against the headboard. Her eyes were red and puffy from so much crying. She looked awful.

'You can't go on like this,' Rachel said.

Her sister lifted her face and stared, then dragged the heel of her palm across her tears. 'What do you know?'

Rachel said nothing.

'You don't understand. You don't know what it's like.'

'Yes, I do,' Rachel replied, hurt and resenting the implication. 'I do understand. It was the same when Danny went.'

Kate shook her head. 'It's not the same.'

Rachel shifted back a little, hardening. 'What do you mean?'

'It's not the same thing at all.' Kate rested one cheek against her knees but her eyes stayed on Rachel.

'Why isn't it?'

'You and Danny …' she began. 'You and Danny … you didn't hurt like this.' She lifted her face then, eyes full of defiance, a challenge for her sister to disagree.

'How dare you,' Rachel whispered. 'How dare you assume you know how much I hurt? You've got no idea.'

'I don't think you even cried.'

'Not in front of you perhaps.'

'But you didn't even miss a beat. It was like nothing had changed.'

'I had the children to think of. I didn't have the luxury of time for self-pity.'

Kate's face puckered in disagreement and disbelief and for the first time in her life Rachel thought her sister was ugly. 'The children were nothing to do with it. You just didn't love Danny like I love Paul. You never have. You don't know how. So don't tell me you understand what I'm going through because you don't.'

Rachel got up from the bed and moved away. At the door she turned back. Her sister was still huddled on the bed, wrapped in her own self-pity and anger. She hesitated, half-tempted to make a fight of it, to voice her contempt for Kate's histrionics over a man she would most likely have forgotten in a month. But she was too weary to care, and too sad on her own account to bother. She said, 'You don't know me at all.'

'Just go away and leave me alone.' Kate did not bother looking up.

Rachel left her and plodded down the stairs, gripping the rail to steady herself.

'How is she?' Rose looked up from her sewing as her daughter sat at the table to watch her husband lay out a pack of cards in a game of patience. Charlie stood at his side, watching too.

'Impossible,' she said.

'What did you say to her?' Danny asked.

She shrugged. 'What can you say?'

'I hope you didn't tell her he'll be fine, because there's a good chance he won't be.'

He looked over the cards, fingering the ones in his hand for a moment before he began to play. He took his time, letting Charlie point out to him what cards he could use.

'No,' she answered. 'I didn't tell her that.'

'That's good. Because no one comes back fine. No one. It's in your head it gets you, even if your body's in one piece.'

She said nothing, but she thought of Andrews and wondered what nightmares troubled him.

Danny put the ace of diamonds up and Charlie shifted the two to go on top of it. His father nodded in approval. 'You want to finish it off?'

'Can I?'

'Go on.' He moved the chair back a bit to let the boy slide in front of him and lean against the seat but the game was over quickly, and Charlie moved away, preferring the more certain safety of the rug. He found his pencil case and some paper and, lying down on his stomach, began to draw.

Danny took out a cigarette. His hands were trembling as he tried to light the match and he swore when it did not catch until the third attempt. Once it lit he drew back hard and flicked the broken match into the ashtray. Smoke curled into the air above him, calming him, and George coughed automatically from his chair in the corner. Danny turned to Rachel.

'Game of rummy?'

'If you like.'

He shuffled the cards, hands quick and agile now, steadied by the cigarette, then dealt. They played and Rachel lost every hand.

'What's wrong with you?' he asked after a while.

'Just tired, I think.'

'Worrying about your sister, more like.'

She smiled. 'Maybe,' she said, but her thoughts had not been on Kate.

'She'll be all right. She'll get over it.'

Rachel nodded and laid down her first winning hand.

'There you go.' He smiled. 'You know, she's a lot tougher than you give her credit for,' he said, collecting the cards to deal another hand. 'She can care take of herself. She's harder than you know.'

He dealt, the cards neatly skimming the surface of the table, but he left them face down for a minute when he finished so that he could light another cigarette. Rachel watched him, the deep breath of satisfaction, the cough that always followed.

'What do you mean?' she asked.

They picked up their cards and began to play. He raised his eyes and looked at her across the top of his cards as though he were appraising her for something. 'Just, she's not a baby any more, and she'll get over him. You don't need to worry about her. That's all. It's your go.'

She turned her attention back to the game and quickly lost the next hand.

Chapter Nine

When does infidelity begin, Rachel wondered as she crossed the park at lunch time on her way for the afternoon shift at work. Does it start with a word? A look? A touch? When does it become too late to remain a faithful wife? A week ago Kit touched his fingers to her face and as she rubbed her cheek against them, a promise had been made. Now she wanted him with every cell within her, and the giving of her body seemed as nothing against the treachery of her mind and her emotions: in every sense that mattered the betrayal was already done.

Kate had been right – she never loved Danny like this.

AT WORK she was called to the office straight away so that Mrs Pitman could haul her over the coals for conducting her social life within the precincts of the library. It seemed that the Captain had called that morning and asked for her, and Mrs Pitman had taken exception. The old woman was furious, glaring at Rachel above her glasses with rheumy eyes, but

Rachel did not care. She made her apologies in a dream and wandered back out to the desk with a smile on her face. Captain Andrews had come and that was all that mattered.

'What was all that about?' Jane whispered between borrowers.

'She's taken a dislike to Captain Andrews. I'm banned from talking to him.'

Jane rolled her eyes. 'She should be working for the Nazis.'

'Was she awful to him?'

'Icy.'

Rachel smiled. Then they heard the office door swing to and they moved away from each other and worked on without talking.

THE DAY WAS BUSY, and she had little time to think of Kit, but when they closed up at last at nine o'clock, the disappointment of missing him twisted through her. She stood on the step outside in the cold with Jane to say goodbye then stayed a moment to watch her friend hurry off through the darkness before she moved off the step to walk up the other way.

'Rachel.' His voice was almost a whisper close behind her and she turned abruptly, startled. He caught her arms in his hands and held her in front of him. 'Rachel.'

'You made me jump.'

'I'm sorry. I didn't mean to startle you. I just didn't want to get you into any more trouble.'

He smiled, his face lit by the soft lamp that glowed above the library door and they stood for a moment of indecision before he let her arms go and stepped back. Embarrassed by the sudden intimacy, he looked away, self-conscious. 'Forgive me.'

She nodded.

He smiled again, still shy. 'I was hoping you'd let me walk you home,' he said.

'That would be lovely,' she replied. 'If it isn't too far for you.'

'Walking's fine. Really.'

'If you're sure.'

He offered her his arm in response and she took it and they strolled up the hill. Once or twice she remembered that the night was almost freezing but for most of the way she was oblivious of everything but his presence by her side and the soft murmur of his voice.

'You can't come to the library again,' she said.

'I know.'

'Was she very rude to you?'

'Not exactly. But I got the message.'

'Yes,' Rachel smiled. 'She's very good at that.'

'Was she very angry?'

'She accused me of moral turpitude and besmirching the library's good name.'

Andrews laughed. 'And we've only had lunch together.'

An atmosphere of tension settled then and they walked in silence, made serious by the knowledge that lunch was only the beginning and that Mrs Pitman's assumptions were wrong only in their timing. They entered Redland Green and walked past the chapel and the tennis club, both deserted now. Near the bowling club they found a bench and sat down. Though the blackout had long been declared over, the lamps in the park had not yet been replaced and the darkness surrounded them, heavy with secrets. They were completely alone, the night too bleak for walkers, and Rachel shivered. There was a small space between them on the bench and they did not touch.

'I used to play here as a child,' she said. 'It was just grass then and a swing and a seesaw over there.' She gestured with her hand to show him where but he did not follow it with his eyes. 'The tennis club was here even then, but they've been growing hay here since the war began and now there's not much space for the children to play.'

'Do you want to stop this, Rachel?' he said. 'Before it's too late?'

She swivelled on the bench to face him but they were in shadow and she could not see his expression. She felt as though she were sliding towards him on ice so thin it might break at any moment, and she knew all that awaited her was the cold grip of the water underneath. But she could not stop the slide, and she knew, too, that the water would be as cold whenever she fell. She could not be without him.

'I think it already is too late,' she whispered.

He nodded and shifted forward towards her. 'You're sure?'

'Yes.'

'I'm glad,' he said. Then he reached a gloved hand to her face, lifted it to his and kissed her.

Afterwards she sat back away from him and cried as he stretched his arm along the back of the bench and twisted loose strands of her hair in his fingers.

'Don't cry,' he said. 'Please don't cry.'

'I'm sorry,' she replied. 'It's just … I've never thought of myself as an unfaithful wife. All the time that Danny was away I never even looked at another man, never even considered it, though lots of other women did. Lots of women I know didn't wait.'

She looked up at him, his face leaning close in the gloom.

'I loved Danny,' she went on. 'I really did. I suppose I still do in a way. But he's changed so much and I just don't know …' She trailed off. There was no need to say more and she did not want bore him with it all.

He said nothing but slid his arm round her shoulder, moved closer in to her and kissed her again. Then she rested her head against him, the greatcoat rough against her cheek.

They sat for a while, the time unmeasured, and his closeness filled all of her senses, all of her thoughts.

'We'd better get you home,' he said eventually.

'Yes.' She was freezing but she wanted to stay there all night with him holding her. She could have frozen to death there and been happy. Anything but the loneliness of the water beneath the ice. Andrews stood and helped her up and she found that her legs had grown stiff from the cold.

'Does the cold affect your leg?' she asked him.

'Yes.'

He put his arm round her and pulled her tight in against his body and they walked the rest of the way in silence. Near the house they stopped in the shadows between the intermittent street lamps, only half of them working.

'I'm on late again tomorrow,' she said.

'Then I'll walk you home again.'

They kissed again but briefly because they were close to home and she was afraid.

'Tomorrow, then.'

'Tomorrow.'

He turned and walked back the way they had come and she watched his back disappear into the darkness, the tap of his cane on the pavement growing fainter. When she could no longer see him she straightened her hat and hurried through the gloom to the house.

As always, she went round to the back door. Inside, her father and husband were arguing. She could hear her father's raised voice through the window as she passed and as she made her way through the kitchen dread seeped coldly through her, its chill deeper than the bitter night outside. She hesitated, breathing slowly, searching for the courage to face them. Then she thought of Kit's mouth against hers, the roughness of his cheek against her forehead as he held her, and opened the door that led from the kitchen to the living room.

'Leave him alone,' her mother was saying. 'It isn't worth it.'

'He's drunk and I'll not have a drunkard living in my house!'

'So fucking throw me out and have done with it then!'

They fell into silence when she appeared in the doorway and all of them turned towards her. Danny's eyes were glazed and vicious and she looked away so that he might not read the guilt there.

'Your husband is drunk,' George said. Then he waved a hand in dismissal and brushed past her on his way out to the kitchen. The door slammed shut behind him and Rachel hoped it would not wake the children.

'They've been fighting,' her mother told her.

'I heard.' She looked at Danny and watched all the fight go out of him. He sat slumped in his chair, a wreck of the man he used to be, staring blankly into space before him.

'I'll leave you to it,' Rose murmured from the doorway. 'Good night.'

'Night Mum,' she answered. Her mother's footsteps on the stairs sounded tired, and they heard her cross the landing to the bathroom. 'I'll make some tea,' she said.

Danny said nothing, still staring.

She went back out to the kitchen where her father stood at the sink, leaning hard against it on his hands. His breathing was hoarse, his face still flushed with anger. When he heard her behind him he turned.

'How long has he been drinking like this?' he said softly.

'A while.' She was surprised he had not noticed before now. 'I thought you knew.'

He shook his head and shifted to one side of the sink so that Rachel could fill the kettle from the tap.

'How long is a while?'

'It's been gradual. It didn't just start overnight.'

He sighed. 'I don't suppose working at the pub helps much, either.'

'No.' She lit the stove and stood close to the flame for warmth.

'You never should have married him.'

'Ssshhh…' she hissed. But a part of her a wondered now if perhaps he was right: had he known all those years ago what Danny would become? Then she dismissed the thought straight away, ashamed of it. Danny had been changed by the war and no one could have foreseen that.

'It has to stop.'

'He needs it,' Rachel said. It was second nature to defend Danny against her father. 'He needs it to cope.'

'Other men cope without it.'

'Other men are not in his situation.' Anger rose so swiftly that she had to clench her fists and jaw to contain it.

'There are other men a lot worse off than he is. He's got you, the children, a job … He needs to pull himself together. He needs to take care of his family. It's what a man does.' He sounded exasperated.

Rachel swallowed, breathing hard, searching for the words to make him understand.

'He's a cripple, Dad,' she whispered. 'He can't walk, he's totally dependent on me, on you. He has the most terrible nightmares. God only knows what he's been through and the drink at least stops him from dreaming. How would you feel in his situation? Wouldn't you feel like drinking?'

'It doesn't solve anything,' George replied.

'Maybe not,' she shrugged, 'but it eases his pain. Surely you can understand that?'

Her father tilted his head, as if he were trying, after all, to make sense of it. When he spoke again his voice was lower, and she heard the hurt and weariness beneath the words. 'He's always had you under his spell. Even now you defend him. I've never understood what you see in him, why you can't see him for what he is. He turned you against me years ago, and I've never really known what it was I did wrong. I only ever wanted to protect you.'

She nodded, too close to tears to speak.

'But I failed,' he went on. 'And here we are.'

'I'm sorry, Dad,' she managed to whisper. 'For all of it.'

He touched her arm with his fingers in a rare half moment of affection. Then he said, 'I'm going to bed so I'll leave him to you. I wish you luck.'

She said nothing but when he had gone she held her face in her hands and fought back the tears until the kettle boiled. Then she made the tea and took it through to the bedroom where Danny was waiting for her. He took the cup and cradled the warmth in his palms against the chill of the room. Rachel shivered.

'How did it start?' she asked.

He shrugged. 'I was drunk.'

She sat close to him on the bed and watched while he fumbled to roll a cigarette, the tea balanced precariously on the arm of the chair. When the cigarette was made and he had lit it he lifted his eyes to her and through the redness of the alcohol they were sad and full of shame, the eyes of a man who has been broken by life. Her own betrayal of him disgusted her.

'I can't help it,' he whispered. 'I need it.'

'I know.'

'It dulls the nightmares, you know. It stops me thinking, remembering. Otherwise it's always there, Rache. The memory of it. It's like I can't switch it off unless I have a couple of drinks.'

'I know,' she repeated.

They sat in silence, each drinking their tea, the bitter night settling round them, and she thought of Kit limping back to his billet without her.

'We should go to bed,' she said.

He nodded and stubbed out the cigarette and she took the cups back out to the kitchen. When she got back to the bedroom he was already in bed, but she knew from his breathing that he was not yet asleep.

'Are you all right?' she whispered.

He was silent.

'Good night.' Then she lay for a long time until finally she slept and mercifully dreamt of nothing.

THE NEXT NIGHT Andrews waited for her on the opposite side of the road, leaning against the low stone wall that bordered the bomb site of the church. There were few people about, a frigid November night that threatened more rain, and the sparse street lamps with their broken bulbs did little to dispel the cold and the dark. He wrapped his arms tighter around himself against the chill, and waited.

Just after nine the door opened and automatically he rose from the wall, eyes picking out the detail of her through the darkness. She was not alone, and he hesitated by the edge of the pavement, watching her exchange goodbyes with the other young woman who worked there. Then the other girl hurried off down the hill, hands deep in her pockets, and Rachel stood on the step, stamping her feet against the cold. In a few strides he was with her.

'Rachel,' he said.

He had waited for this moment all day, living it over and over in his mind all through the hours since they said goodbye. He held her against him but she did not lift her face, and he let his lips rest against her hair. After a moment she moved back from him, linked her arm through his, and they began their slow meander home.

'It's good to see you,' he told her.

'You too,' she replied, but her smile seemed anxious and quick, and she would not meet his eyes.

'What's wrong?' he asked, heartbeat quickening with apprehension. 'What's the matter?'

'Nothing,' she replied. 'Nothing's wrong.'

'Don't lie to me,' he said softly. 'Please don't lie to me.'

They stopped walking and Andrews turned her to face him. They stood in silence for a moment on the empty pavement. A young couple on bicycles hurtled down the street behind them, weaving through the potholes, laughing. He waited till the sound of them had faded into the night, then lifted a hand to her face to raise it so that he could see her in the shadowy light. She could barely bring herself to look at him.

'Tell me what's wrong,' he urged. He traced the line of her cheek with his fingertips, felt the softness of her even through the leather of his glove.

She dropped her eyes, unable to face him, searching the pavement at their feet for an answer.

'Rachel?' He was desperate to know, terrified she would reject him after all.

'It's Danny,' she whispered. 'I feel like such a traitor.'

He was silent, afraid that with the wrong words now he could lose her. He watched her, her gaze still flicking restlessly across the ground, hoping to find a clue in her, the right thing to say.

'How is he?' he said in the end.

She lifted her eyes to him at that, and he breathed again. 'You saw him,' she said. 'You saw what he's become. He's a broken man …' She trailed off and, with her hands in her pockets, began walking slowly on again. He moved beside her but they did not touch.

'You have a right to be happy, Rachel,' he said.

'Why?' She turned to him and there was anger in her eyes. 'Why do I have any more right to happiness than he does?'

Andrews stopped and turned to her. 'Because you have a chance. Danny had his chance to be happy with you, to start again. And he didn't take it. Why should you have to suffer for that?'

Rachel said nothing, still walking slowly on. He held her arm to stop her.

'What kind of life can you have with him?' he asked.

She jerked her arm away from his hold then turned to face him. They were close enough that she had to lift her head to look at him.

'Are you going to make me happy?' she said. There was a challenge in her eyes, as though he were offering the impossible.

'Yes,' he replied. 'I am.'

'Can we be happy, you and I?' she asked. 'The way things are?'

'Yes,' he said again. 'I believe we can. Or I wouldn't be here.'

He could not now imagine living without her; already she was the meaning in his life, his only source of joy, and the battlefields of Italy were forgotten in her presence.

Rachel sighed, her resistance beaten by his sureness and her own desire.

'Aren't you happy now?' he said. 'Here with me now, just being together? Doesn't that make you happy?'

'Yes,' she admitted. 'But it hurts too.'

'I understand,' he said, and bent to kiss her, cradling her head in his hand, and he was surprised by the passion in her kiss

– he had expected more reluctance. Afterwards he put his arm around her waist and as they walked with their bodies close together he wished that they could go somewhere else and be warm and private without the bulk of all their winter clothes between them. There was nothing to say, no need for words, and the silence rested unbroken until they had almost reached the top of the hill. Then a group of servicemen tumbled from a pub and were brought up short by the sight of an officer. He loosened his hold on Rachel and slowed his stride to return their hasty salutes.

'Do you like being an officer?'

'Yes,' he said. 'And I'm good at it, in spite of what your husband thinks …' He stopped, furious with himself, remembering that Rachel did not yet know what Danny thought, that she had not yet heard that story.

'What do you mean? What does he think?'

'Nothing,' he said quickly.

'Tell me.'

'It's nothing, really … It's just that men and officers don't always see things quite the same way …'

Rachel smiled. 'I can't imagine Danny liked taking orders much.'

'No. He didn't. But even so, he was a good soldier. He was brave and dependable and you can't ask more than that.' He fell silent, and even Rachel by his side was not enough to coax his memory away from Italy.

'What's wrong?' she asked.

'Nothing.'

'Don't lie.' She squeezed his arm so that he turned to her briefly with a smile before he became serious again, the memories fresh and painful. 'What were you thinking about?'

'I was thinking that I should still be over there,' he said. 'With the men where I belong.'

'But what you're doing here is important.'

He shook his head. 'Not really.'

'You're teaching other men to be officers. Surely that's important?'

He said nothing and they walked on a few strides without talking. Then Rachel said, 'Do you really wish you were still there? I thought it was awful.'

'It is awful,' he replied, then wished he had said nothing. He didn't want to talk about the war with her, with anyone: it was better left unvisited, unsaid.

But she was silent then, and asked him no more questions as they walked on with their arms around each other and their bodies close together so that even through the thickness of their coats he was aware of her hip as it moved against his thigh. At the Green they found the same bench again, and this time they sat close together, thighs touching. A lone dog walker hurried past, hands deep in pockets, and the dog bounded ahead and paid them no attention. The air smelled of damp wool and wet earth and the cold felt as if it were in his bones. When the dark had swallowed the walker, Andrews took off his gloves and turned towards her. She melted into him, lifting her face to let him kiss her, and his hand fumbled inside her coat to cup her breast. With the warmth of her next to him and her lips against his, everything else ceased to exist. Finally, they moved apart, and he held her so that the weight of his cheek was against her hair.

'You aren't going to cry today?' he asked.

She sat up to look at him, ready to be angry, but then she saw the smile in his eyes, and laughed instead. 'No. I'm not going to cry.'

'Good. Then I can kiss you again with a clear conscience?'

'You can.'

He kissed her harder then, hungry for her, and in his need for her, his hand slid down from her breast to find her thigh beneath the heavy wool skirt, fingers caressing the cold bare skin and smooth dip of her groin, the rough hair and soft warm flesh beyond the line of underwear. With his touch there she took in a sharp breath and he remembered himself, where they were, and drew away from her abruptly.

'I'm sorry,' he whispered, looking down, ashamed to have lost control so utterly. 'I'm sorry.'

'It's all right,' she said.

He turned to her, burning with anxiety and desire. 'I'm sorry,' he said again. 'It's been such a long time.'

'Don't worry. It's all right. It's been a long time for me too.'

He gave her a rueful smile as she reached out to touch his face and he took her fingers in his hand and put them to his lips.

'I think I'm falling in love with you Rachel,' he said, surprising himself. It was not his way to express his feelings so easily.

'Do you?' Rachel replied, and the smile and delight in her eyes made him glad that he had told her.

'Does that make you happy?'

'Yes,' she said. 'It makes me the happiest woman alive.'

He kissed her again, slowly, gently this time, and neither of them noticed it growing late, nor the freezing drizzle that settled on their hair and coats. But afterwards, as they walked arm-in-arm through the night towards her house, sadness crept back over them both.

THE DAY WAS bright and clear on her next day off and there was no one home when she left so there was no need for lies. Ashamed of the shabbiness of her hat in the brightness of the sun she went without, and the winter air burned cold against her temples as she walked. It was hard to restrain herself from running like a child across the Green to meet him. On the other side of it she took the back way, avoiding Whiteladies

Road so she would not pass the library. The ways of the streets were well-known to her, the endless convoluted routes learned in childhood, this part of the city so familiar, a part of her. Just past the railway bridge on Hampton Road she cut through to the back of Cotham Hill, past the house of an old school friend – a dark Victorian building set back off the road – and recalled hours of girlish conversation in the cosy basement kitchen. It was years since they had seen each other, lives growing separate, and for a moment she was touched with curiosity, slowing her steps to think that she should call and find her friend again – once they had been as close as girls can be. Then she remembered Kit was waiting and the friend was instantly forgotten as she hurried on.

The Artillery Grounds were almost at the bottom of Whiteladies Road. A high wall topped with barbed wire and large wrought-iron gates announced its separation from the fine Georgian houses that surrounded it. A lone sentry stood guard in front of them. Behind the wide parade ground an old artillery gun from the Great War protected the door to the building. It had always been there, home to the local militia in the pre-war years but its presence was louder now that so much of the city was given up to the war.

Andrews was waiting outside the gate; she could see him there scanning the road for her even though she was early, and she quickened her pace, impatient to be with him. He saw her coming and lifted his arm to wave and she smiled and waved back and in a moment she was next to him. They stood together, not touching, and the pretence was painful to maintain. Then he took her arm and guided her away from the gate. She put her arm through his, and he smiled as they slowed down to a stroll.

'I wasn't sure if you'd come,' he said.

She looked up at him in surprise. 'Why ever not?'

He hesitated.

'Why not, Kit?'

'It doesn't matter.' He shook his head and turned to her. 'You came. That's all that matters.'

'Of course I came,' she replied. 'Wild horses couldn't have kept me away.'

His smile widened and she moved her body in closer to his and held his arm more tightly.

'Where are we going?' she asked.

'There's a hotel up here. It's quiet and we can have some lunch.'

'What time have you got to be back?'

'I told my C.O. that I was meeting a girl and he told me to take my time. This place was his suggestion.'

Rachel laughed at being called a girl and Kit leant in and kissed her hair.

'You're my girl,' he whispered.

They turned off the main road and soon they were in back streets that Rachel did not know. She had heard there was a swimming baths somewhere near but she had never been. As a girl she had swum at a baths nearer school – but it had been a long time since then and now she no longer even had a bathing suit. She should find time to take the children sometimes, she thought. It would be good for them.

They walked on in silence along a road of Victorian terraced houses that had once been fine but now were shabby with neglect, the rendering peeling, the paintwork dirty and discoloured. On the corner they stopped outside the doors of the hotel and Andrews turned to face her, his face close to hers.

'What do you want to do?' he said.

'What do you mean?'

He paused, eyes flicking nervously across the pavement at their feet as she waited. Then he lifted his gaze to Rachel's face.

'We could get a room,' he said softly. 'If you'd like.'

Rachel looked away, flustered. She was not expecting such a question so soon, and it caught her off guard. She could say nothing in the beat that he waited for her answer.

'Forget it,' he said quickly. She could feel the tension of his embarrassment, and the fear he had asked too much. 'We'll have lunch. I'm sorry, I shouldn't have suggested it.'

He took her elbow and guided her inside the hotel, into the dining room, before she could gather her thoughts again, and her own breath was short and quick with excitement. Inside, it was warm and pleasant, a good fire in the grate, and the air was filled with the aroma of food. Several of the tables were empty and they chose one near the fireplace and Kit helped her with her coat. Then, sitting across the table from him, she felt foolish for her slowness. He was tense, his anxiety plain in the way he would not meet her eyes.

A waiter came and they ordered fish and chips and when he had gone there was still tension between them.

She should have said yes, she thought. She should have been quicker.

'I'm sorry,' he said again. 'I shouldn't have asked.'

'I love you,' she whispered, the words rising unbidden, unplanned.

He lifted his eyes to meet hers, surprised. They were very blue that day and bright with sudden pleasure. 'Do you?'

'Yes.'

'Enough to be unfaithful to Danny?'

'I'm already unfaithful in all the ways that really matter.'

'Yes, I know, but …'

'Yes,' she said, because she knew it was hard for him to say the words he needed. 'Enough to be unfaithful in that way too.'

A half-smile lit his eyes and he reached across to touch her hand, turning the wedding ring gently round on her finger. His fingertips were cold against her skin and she shivered and withdrew her hand. He sat back then but he was sure of her again and the awkwardness had passed.

'How was your morning?' he asked.

'I spent most of it in queues,' she replied. 'At the butcher, at the baker …'

'… and the candlestick maker.'

She laughed. 'More or less. But I shouldn't complain. My mother does most of the shopping. Her hours are shorter than mine because of the children …'

'I thought about you all morning,' he interrupted.

'I'm sorry about the room. Next time. Next time I've got a day off. I promise.'

He nodded and fingered the peak of his cap on the table. She watched him, wondering what thoughts were in his mind. 'Kit?'

His eyes flicked up to hers and he smiled as though surprised to see her there. Then he observed the hat once again, rubbing at an invisible stain with his thumb.

'I was thinking about you and Danny,' he said, 'and how strange war is that he brought us together.' He raised his eyes and they were too intense for her to hold, so she picked up a knife from the table and traced the lines in the tablecloth with its blade. 'How did you meet him?' he asked. 'Tell me the story.'

She looked up and the light in his eyes had faded a little and she was more comfortable in their glow.

'It isn't very exciting,' she said. 'His parents had a greengrocer's shop that I used to pass on my way home from school every day. He worked there as soon as he was old enough and he loved it. He loved working with his dad. They were like peas from the same pod; a cheekiness about them that drew me in. Danny used to call out if he saw me passing, and throw me an apple or an orange.' She smiled with the memory, a happier more innocent time. Then her thoughts shifted back to the present and she grew serious and impatient with the telling. She shrugged. 'It just went on from there, really. But we had problems because my father didn't approve. He wanted me to marry an engineer or a doctor …'

'… or a teacher?'

'Yes,' she smiled. 'Or a teacher. He would have approved of you. You've got the right accent. The right background. And that's how he judges what people are worth.'

'He's not alone.'

'I know that. But Danny was a good man until … Italy … his legs …' She broke off, unable to find the words she needed to explain the confusion of all that had happened.

'I understand,' Andrews said. 'I knew him before Italy too. I know the kind of man he was.'

'Yes. Yes of course you did.'

'So you got married …?' he prompted.

'Yes. Eventually. Against my father's wishes. We lived above the shop and I studied to be a librarian. The children were born and everything was fine until the war, until Danny and his brother joined up and the shop hit hard times because of the shortages. Then Danny's dad died, and Vera gave up the shop, and I had to move back in with my parents …'

'It's a sad story.'

'I suppose it is. Though so many people have lost so much more. I have to remember that, and that I'm lucky to still have my family and my children and a house to live in.'

The food arrived and when the waiter had gone Andrews did not begin to eat but sat regarding her, thoughtful.

'What is it?' she asked.

'I was just wondering what the ending will be.'

Rachel shrugged. 'Who knows? I try not to think too much about it, to be more like you and seize the day.'

'Is that how you see me?'

'Isn't that how you are? Shouldn't the war have taught that to all of us?'

'Perhaps.' He smiled. 'Shall we eat?"

She nodded and they ate their lunch and afterwards they drank fresh coffee which was a rare treat. Then Kit's eyes wandered to the clock on the chimney. It was almost two o'clock.

'You'd better get back,' Rachel said. 'You don't want to take advantage.'

'Not this time, anyway.'

She laughed and looked away, made self-conscious by the expectation in his eyes. Then they left the table and walked out through the lobby into the cold afternoon. Clouds had drawn across the bright blue sky and without the sun to warm it, the breeze had turned bitter. Andrews scanned above them and buttoned his coat.

'Looks like rain,' he said.

Rachel nodded and took his arm and they strolled back the way they had come. But they stopped out of sight of the Artillery Grounds to say goodbye.

'When can I see you again?'

'I finish at one on Friday,' she said. 'Can you meet me then?'

'Yes. I should be able to. I've got some books to bring back.'

She smiled and he touched her cheek for just an instant because it was daylight and the street was busy. Then they turned and walked side by side without touching back to the gate.

Chapter Ten

On Friday Rachel waited on the steps when the library closed, huddled into her coat, collar turned up against the winter air, watching down the hill towards the Artillery Grounds. She waited for an hour, her feet growing painful with the cold, but Andrews did not come. So she wandered to the restaurant they had gone to before, but without him the soup was not as nice. She wished she had gone somewhere else.

Kate was in the living room, still only half awake after sleeping off the night shift. Rachel made them tea and they sat in the armchairs either side of the fire that barely glowed with faint warmth. She cradled the tea cup between her palms as she drank and the heat of it took the chill from her bones, but it was weak and tasteless, the week's ration running low. Kate sat across from her in a pair of old pyjamas and a dressing gown, feet pulled up beneath her, watching her sister with a strange hostile glare, as though the two of them were enemies. She was beginning to lose the soft roundness of her youth,

Rachel thought, a new hardness behind the pretty features. There had been no mention of Paul for a while, and she wondered if had been forgotten now, if another man had already taken his place. It half-crossed her mind to ask, but then she realised she did not really want to know. They drank their tea in silence, and Kate's gaze remained unwavering. Rachel shifted uncomfortably.

'What's wrong?' she said.

Kate leant forward in the chair. 'You're seeing Andrews, aren't you?' she hissed.

Rachel lowered the tea cup away from her lips, concentrating on holding it steady, panic rising with the uncertainty of what her sister knew. She shook her head.

'You were seen,' Kate snarled. 'One of the neighbours saw you. On a captain's arm near the Artillery Grounds. She told Mum.'

'So why did Mum tell you?' She was shaking with guilt and anger.

'Because she's worried about you, she said. And she asked me what I thought she should do.'

Rachel drained her tea and reached down to put the cup on the rug at her feet with slow deliberate movements, stalling, trying to calm herself. 'And what did you tell her?'

'I said I'd talk to you.'

Rachel said nothing.

'Tell me it isn't true. Tell me Mrs Ellis made a mistake.'

Rachel sat back and looked at her sister, pretty and tousled all bundled up in the armchair and did not know what to say.

'It isn't true, is it?'

'We had lunch,' she said in the end, because it was impossible to lie completely: they had been seen and it was better to meet the truth half way.

Kate sprang forward to the edge of her chair with an alacrity that startled Rachel, eyes dark with fury.

'How could you?' she said. 'How could you do that to Danny?'

'It was lunch.'

'You were on his arm.'

Rachel pulled her cardigan tighter around her against the cold and wished there were more coal for the fire. She was sick of weak tea and being cold, and she had no energy to fight against her sister's accusations.

'What's it to you, anyway?' she said. 'It's none of your business.'

'What if Danny found out?' Kate ignored the question.

'There's nothing for him to find out.' She was surprised how easily the lie came to her lips, and how much it mattered to keep the truth safe.

'It would destroy him.'

Rachel was silent. Guilt wrapped itself around her, and she could think of nothing else to say.

'Are you seeing him again?' Kate demanded.

'No,' she replied, and thought how she should have been with him that afternoon, how they should have been touching skin against skin in a room at the Old Road Hotel. If she closed her eyes she could still conjure the caress of his fingers against her face, the other hand searching beneath her clothes that night on the park bench in the freezing rain.

'Rachel?' Her sister's voice brought her back from the memory. 'You won't see him again? Promise?'

'Yes.'

'Properly.'

'I promise I won't see him again,' she said, but underneath her cardigan her fingers were crossed in the old ritual from childhood.

'So I can tell Mum that Mrs Ellis got it wrong? That she doesn't need to worry about it?'

'If you want.'

They sat then in silence as the room darkened with the fading light of the afternoon until the children came home from school, tired and hungry and bickering.

DANNY LAY in silence in the bed next to Rachel and she was restless too, and wakeful.

'Are you all right?' she asked him.

'I can't get comfortable,' he replied. The phantom legs were there tonight, aching and heavy, impossible to rest.

'Are you in pain?'

'Yes.'

'Do you want me to get you something?

'No. There's no point.' There were no drugs that could take the pain away, nothing to do but grit his teeth and bear it.

She turned on her side towards him, but he kept his gaze upwards to the ceiling to avoid the pity in her eyes. It was more than he could bear, that, the pity and the sense of duty that kept her trying to be nice. But her pity didn't help him, nor her kindness, and any love there used to be had died out long ago. The bracelet that he gave her was on the dressing table now, untouched, no longer clasped about her wrist each day as it had been at the beginning, a last symbol of her hopes abandoned. How could he blame her? There was no hope for them. There never had been.

'What were you arguing with Dad about tonight?' she asked him. 'I heard you from the kitchen.'

'Can't remember.'

'You must be able to.'

He turned his head towards her then, surprised that she still cared enough to ask. Or maybe she was just trying to show an interest, trying to distract him to keep his mind from the pain. He wondered how they had ever been happy together as man and wife – he couldn't imagine it now.

'Politics, I think,' he said.

'Tell me.'

'About Greece. All those communist partisans we killed.'

'He agreed with it?'

'He said, *C'est la guerre*,' Danny spat, disgusted. 'Those people fought with us for all that time and that's what we do to them. And he thinks it's all right.'

'I wish we could leave here,' Rachel said.

'What for?'

'To be on our own, without Dad on your back all the time.'

'It'd make no difference,' Danny said. 'I'd still be a useless waste of space.'

'You aren't a waste of space.'

'You're the only one who thinks so.'

'Is that what you think?'

'It's what I know. You don't see the way people look at me. Even my own kids despise me.'

Rachel sighed. 'That's because you're always angry with them,' she said. 'It's got nothing to do with your legs.' She stopped abruptly and shifted slightly away from him across the bed, afraid she had said too much, scared of rousing his temper. He saw the fear she had of him and self-loathing erupted through him, bitter like vomit.

'You hate me,' he said.

'No I don't.'

'You wish I hadn't come back. You all wish it. You were all happier before I came back. You think I don't know the tension I cause? You think I like living like this? Knowing my whole family wishes I was dead?'

'Please don't think that,' Rachel said. 'None of us wishes you were dead.'

'Well, I fucking do,' he whispered. 'I should've died in Italy with everyone else.'

He heaved himself partially onto his side to face away from her, and barely stopped himself from crying out with the pain in his legs. Staring into the darkness, he thought of Italy, and how the promise of home had once kept him going.

'I wish you could be happy again,' Rachel murmured to his back. 'I really do.'

He said nothing. He could not imagine happiness any more – it was a place that was far far away from him, an unreachable shore, and in his darkness he no longer even knew which way to turn to swim towards it. It was all he could do to keep his head above the water, the weight of his memories and his thoughts always tugging at his feet and threatening to drag him under. They lay together in silence for a long time, and only in the small hours did he finally start to drift off, weariness overcoming the pain at last.

WEEKENDS WERE ALWAYS FRAUGHT, nowhere for George and Danny to escape each other's company. Rachel worked most Saturdays and she was grateful to be out and away from it. Even in the morning before she left there were arguments, the children made fractious by the atmosphere, Danny's hand raised at Charlie as the boy made for escape through the kitchen door.

'When I get hold of you ...'

'You've got to catch me first,' Charlie taunted, and raced out for the garden.

Jean glanced up at her mother with nervous eyes and with a tilt of her head, Rachel sent her after her brother. The girl slunk away, her narrow body sliding easily through the half-open door, her face averted. Rachel wished she could take them both away to grow up somewhere less full of hate, and the image of the cottage in her dream touched a corner of her mind. She shrugged it away, wearied by a night of thoughts of Andrews.

Outside, on her way to work, she spoke to the children in the garden.

'Be good for Grandma. And don't,' she turned to Charlie, 'give your dad any backchat.'

'I hate him,' Charlie said.

'That's no way to speak about your father.'

He fought with the words on his lips for a moment but he could not stop them from coming. 'He's mean and he's miserable,' he blurted. 'And he's horrible to Grandpa and I wish he'd never come home. I wish he was dead.'

He stood in front of his mother, fists clenched, staring down at the path at his feet. Rachel touched his shoulder and guided him further into the garden away from the window so that they could not be heard from inside the house.

'Don't say that, Charlie,' she whispered. 'He's been through a lot. He doesn't mean to be angry with you all the time. It's just that he's angry at the world for what's happened to him. He's really very sad.'

'I don't care,' Charlie said. 'I hate him.'

He kicked at the frozen earth with his toe and Rachel wondered what memories he would keep of his childhood, how much of the hatred would stay with him.

'He's your dad,' she said. 'And I know you don't think so, but he loves you. Both of you.'

Charlie bit his lip against the words that wanted to come.

'So don't provoke him. Please?'

He looked up and gave her a reluctant smile.

'Just stay out of his way.'

'I'll try,' he agreed.

'Good boy. I'll see you at tea time.' She bent to kiss the top of his head and stooped to hug Jean. Charlie turned away and when he thought his mother was no longer watching he shoved his sister in the back. She turned and struck back with a flailing arm that made no contact then ran from him squealing to hide behind the apple tree. Rachel left them to it and set out on her way to work.

Chapter Eleven

Andrews had fretted when he failed to meet her, caught up in his work, unable to leave, and reluctant to phone the library for fear of getting her in trouble. He had seen her finally, briefly, when she finished work on Saturday, but she would not let him walk her home, telling him only they had been seen.

Now he waited for her out of the rain in the hotel lobby on a sofa that was worn and greasy with age. A *Telegraph* left from the weekend was strewn on the table in front of him. Restless and impatient, he tore his eyes from the window and picked it up, grazing the headlines without interest. A Woolworths in London had been hit by a rocket, a hundred and sixty dead, and Patton had finally taken the city of Metz. Nothing he had not already heard on the wireless. Bored with it, he dropped the paper back to the table and checked his watch. The minutes to five were passing slowly.

A minute past the hour Rachel hurried in from the cold, cheeks glowing, hair windswept and wayward beneath the shabby hat. Drops of rain clung to the sodden strands and she touched her fingers to them, sending a spray across her shoulders. He got up straight away and went to her then steered her by the elbow towards the desk.

'We've got a room booked for Mr and Mrs Andrews.'

The elderly clerk peered over his half moon glasses at the names on the register.

'Ah yes. Room 10.' He reached up behind him to a board for the key and slid it across the counter towards them.

'We'll be leaving early,' Andrews said. 'So I'd like to pay now.'

'Yes sir. Any luggage?'

'I've got a man picking it up from the station later.'

The clerk nodded. 'Very good sir.'

They walked up a flight of narrow stairs to a corridor dimly lit by a single unshaded bulb, and they had to peer at the numbers on the door before they found their room. It was small with old furnishings, but it was clean and neat, and the narrow window looked out on to the street below. In the road, two men in uniform were arguing, and though they could hear the raised voices, they could not make out their words.

Andrews took off his coat and hat and put them neatly in the wardrobe before he took Rachel's too and hung them next to his. She stood by the window looking out at the soldiers below as he sat on the bed and observed her; the line of her cheek in profile, the worn suit that hugged her waist and hips, drops of rain still in her hair. She seemed to him then the most beautiful thing he had ever seen.

Her eyes were lowered, watching the men in the road, and he thought that if he could not have her he would go insane. Hurt and rage and frustration mingled with desire. How could she be married to another man? A man who did not love her? He had seen the very first time they met how lonely she was in the company of her husband, how starved of the love she craved. Danny deserved to lose her, he told himself, and his sense of guilt was assuaged.

She stood now with her hands in front of her, twisting at her wedding band as though she could destroy it by sheer force of will. But she was miserable, her shoulder turned away from him, doubt in the seriousness of her expression. Perhaps he had brought her here too soon; perhaps he was asking too much.

'Are you all right?' he said.

She turned her head to him from the window with a smile that did not hide her unease and nodded. 'I think so.'

'Come here,' he said. 'Sit next to me.'

She moved across the narrow space and sat next to him, but there was distance between them, her reluctance a gulf he did not know how to cross.

'Rachel?' he said softly.

She turned towards him then and raised her eyes to his face. She looked as though she might be going to cry. He should have taken her out for dinner instead, he thought, waited until she was ready.

'I feel ashamed,' she whispered, and dropped her gaze to her hands in her lap, still twisting at the ring.

He touched a hand to her hair, smoothing it back from her temple so that he could see her in profile, her face lowered away from him in shame and confusion.

'Of being with me?'

'Yes,' she said. 'Of being here with you instead of at home with my family. Of lying and cheating. Of saying I'm working when it's my day off. I'm married, Kit. With children. I don't think I can do this.'

He withdrew his hand from her hair, then stood up and went to the window. It was not what he had hoped for and imagined, lying alone in the freezing attic room where he was billeted, thoughts of Rachel all that kept him warm at night. Doubt began to filter through his blood. Bringing her here had been a mistake: it seemed she loved him less than he supposed.

'They're still arguing down there,' he said. 'I wonder what it's about.'

There was a silence.

'I'm sorry,' Rachel said after a while. 'I'm sorry for spoiling it all and making it difficult.'

He turned from the window and leant against the windowsill, watching her. 'What do you want to do?' he asked. 'We could go out for dinner if you like. Or the pictures. We haven't got to stay here. I just thought that the privacy would be nice.'

'It is,' she replied, looking up, the first beginnings of a smile nudging away the sadness. 'It really is.'

She got up from the bed and went to stand by him at the window, watching the soldiers argue over some imagined insult, each threatening the other with violence, but neither willing to start the fight. She was close to him now, her shoulder brushing against his arm and he moved behind her, his hands on her shoulders. She leant back into him, and he touched his lips to her neck. Gently, he lowered the blouse from her shoulder, put his mouth against the cool smooth skin there. She shivered, and all his doubts were stilled: he had not been mistaken. His hands slid across her body, loosening buttons, inside the blouse, beneath her skirt. In the street below, the soldiers went their separate ways with curses and raised fists and the street became quiet again.

'Come to bed,' he murmured, and as he led her away from the window she kicked off her shoes and lay across the covers, watching him undress. Then he lay down beside her, his lips and hands beneath her clothes, urgent, forcing the skirt up over her hips, moving himself on top of her, inside her.

'Don't get me pregnant,' she whispered.

'I won't,' he promised.

Then all danger was forgotten as they moved together on the bed and nothing else existed for him but the pleasure of her closeness and the wish that the moment could go on for ever.

Afterwards they climbed between the covers against the icy sheets and held each other until they were warmed by the heat of their bodies and the worn cotton was no longer cold against their toes.

'I've missed you,' she said. 'I miss you every minute of every day. When you didn't come last week, I thought that I'd go mad.'

He smiled and leant up on one elbow, stroking her shoulder. 'Are you happy?' he asked. 'At this moment, are you happy?'

'I'm the happiest I've ever been in my life.'

'You don't care any more that we aren't really allowed to do this?'

She laughed. 'Not at all. Well, maybe just a bit. A very tiny bit.'

He laughed too, love and relief flowing through him in waves. 'I'm very glad.'

They lay in silence for a while, exploring each other's bodies with their hands and their lips, still immersed in the pleasure of each other till they made love again, slowly this time, learning how to please. And when they were finished there was a new intimacy between them, an understanding that went deeper than pure physical knowledge. They lay on their backs, looking up at the cracked cornicing and tatty lampshade.

'Danny doesn't deserve you,' Andrews said, rolling on his side to face her.

'Don't let's talk about Danny,' she whispered. 'Please? Not here, not now.' She looked up at him and touched a hand to his face and he was glad again that he had taken the trouble to shave before he came out to meet her. His cheek was smooth against her palm and he lifted his eyes to her and smiled. 'I'm sorry.'

'You didn't know him before,' she said. 'Before he got blown up and changed.'

'Yes, I did,' he replied. 'And probably better than you think.'

Then he rolled away from her and out of bed, closing the subject, wishing he had not brought up Danny's name. 'Shall we get some dinner?' he asked.

'No.' She snuggled deeper under the covers, reluctant to leave the warmth of the bed.

'Well, I'm hungry,' he said, laughing as he pulled off the covers and dragged her to her feet.

They dressed hurriedly in the cold and as they stood by the door ready to go, she asked him to kiss her again and he leant her against the door with the weight of his body and wished he could have melted into her and been a part of her always.

THEY ATE at another restaurant not far from the library. It was quiet and the few customers there seemed to be officers. Some of them were American, and their voices carried loudly over the hushed conversations. Andrews nodded to one or two men that he knew but they did not disturb them.

They were quiet with each other now, already saddened by the knowledge of soon parting, and when they had finished their food they left quickly, heading out into the night. The rain had stopped and left a fine sheen of cold damp air that made them shiver. They stood on the pavement and their breath came in clouds of mist before them.

'Is it all right if I walk you home?' Kit said. She had said nothing more about having been seen and he was reluctant to ask her, to give her more reasons not to be with him.

'Yes,' she smiled. 'It's late and it's dark. No one will see us tonight.' She took his arm and they strolled up the hill, their bodies close, strides matching, talking desultorily about this and that. Neither of them mentioned what they had done, what they would do in the future.

At the Green they stopped and sat down on their usual bench. She rested her head on his shoulder and he drew her in close to him, her nearness rationed and precious.

'I wish things were different,' she said.

'That there was no Danny?'

'No. Not exactly.'

'If there was no Danny we wouldn't have met.'

'I didn't mean that really. I just meant I wish we could be together.'

Andrews looked down at her, nestled safely in his arm, and touched his fingers to her hair.

'We are together, Rachel,' he said softly. 'We're as together as a man and woman can be.'

She nodded but he heard her sniff and felt the slight heave of her shoulders as she tried not to cry.

'I think we ought to sit on a different bench next time,' he said. 'This one seems to make you cry.'

She looked up at him with a half-smile, trying hard.

'That's better,' he said.

'I'm sorry.'

'It's all right. I know it's harder for you than for me.'

She smiled again, wider this time, and rubbed the last of the tears away. Reluctantly, Andrews checked his watch.

'We'd better get you home. It's getting late.'

'I'll say the bus was late.'

'Again?'

'They're very unreliable.'

He laughed and took her hand as they got up from the bench. Then they linked arms again and walked on along the path.

Chapter Twelve

Sunday morning. The wheelchair bumped against the door as he opened it and Danny heard the conversation in the kitchen stop. His wife and her sister were leaning against the counters, sipping tea. So different, the two of them, hard to believe they were sisters. Kate, already in her make up, pretty and slight and neat, energy simmering under the surface, and Rachel, softer and more gentle, a sweetness in her face that even his bitterness had not yet destroyed.

'Tea?' she said.

He nodded. 'Where is everyone?'

'Dad's in the garden with the kids, and I think Mum's upstairs.' She stirred the contents of the teapot and poured him a cup. He took it with a nod of thanks. Whatever else, he couldn't complain she didn't try to look after him.

'I'm going upstairs,' Kate said. 'Before Dad comes in and tries to make me go to church.'

'See you later, then,' Rachel took her sister's cup and moved across to the sink to wash it out. To Danny she said, 'Did you sleep all right?'

'Not bad.'

'No dreams?'

'No,' he lied. He had never told her that no night passed without dreams. Not always the big nightmares that woke him screaming, terrified, but dreams of death just the same, trails of their images haunting his waking thoughts so that he was never entirely free of it. But there was no need for Rachel to know, no way she would understand in any case.

'That's good,' she smiled.

There was a pause as he lifted the cup to his lips and he remembered he had left his cigarettes in the bedroom. He put the tea on the counter and backed the chair up towards the door.

'My fags,' he said, when she lifted her eyes in question.

'I'll get them,' she said quickly. 'It's easier for me. All those doors …'

'Ta.' He moved away from the door, wheels turning easily on the linoleum, and let her squeeze past. Then the others came in from the garden, the children sent upstairs to wash faces and hands and get ready for church.

'I don't suppose you'll be joining us,' George said.

'I don't suppose you'd really want me to, would you?' Danny answered.

'It would be nice to go as a family.'

Danny nodded and took the cigarettes from Rachel and lit up slowly, coughing as soon as the smoke hit his lungs.

'You ought to give that up,' George said.

'There's lots of things I ought to do,' Danny replied, and with the second drag his chest was quieter, quickly accustomed to the heat and smoke.

George said nothing and edged past the chair to the door. Rachel followed him, good girl going to church with her parents, and within a few minutes he was alone. Then Kate appeared and helped herself to a cigarette from the pack.

'D'you do that just to annoy your dad?'

She laughed. 'I do it because I enjoy it. Same as you.'

'I don't do it because I enjoy it. Not any more. I do it to stop my hands from shaking.' He lifted a hand and both of them watched it, observing the slight tremble that would escape the notice of a casual observer.

'D'you drink for the same reason?' she asked.

'I drink to drown my sorrows,' he replied.

'Of course.' She leant back against the counter, hands resting lightly on its edge either side of her waist, shifting often to bring the cigarette to her lips. She was jittery with nervous energy.

'Heard from Paul?' Danny said.

'He was in France, somewhere, last I heard. But that was a while ago.'

'You still going to marry him?'

She smiled. 'Maybe.'

'That didn't last long. Found someone else, have you?'

'Not yet.'

'You're a hard bitch, Kate,' Danny said. 'I always did like that about you.'

She laughed. Then, 'Well, you aren't going to like me for what I'm going to tell you now.'

His watched her more carefully, serious now. 'What?'

'Remember when Captain Andrews came here?'

'Of course I remember.'

'And you said you thought he had an eye for Rachel?'

'Yes.'

'Well,' she sighed. 'I'm afraid to tell you that I think it might be mutual.'

Danny moved the chair nearer to the table to stub his cigarette into the ashtray. The stink of stale tobacco was strong in his nostrils but he did not turn his head away from it, wanting to keep his eyes away from Kate, aware of the mockery in her tone, the enjoyment in the news. It was hard to believe that Rachel would do it, but even in his disgust he could see the attraction that Andrews might hold for her. An officer and a gentleman. A man who could give her love. He looked up at Kate, standing above him and hated her.

'Why're you telling me?'

She shrugged. 'I thought you ought to know.'

'Are you sure about it?'

'No, I'm not,' she replied. 'And I'm not sure how far it's got either. But they have definitely had lunch together and she was seen on his arm on Whiteladies Road.'

'Bastard,' Danny spat. 'That fucking bastard. I ought to kill him.'

Kate edged along the counter away from him and with her movement he lifted his head. It pleased him that his anger made her nervous, that he had knocked out some of her cockiness. She was far too sure of herself, that one. Always had been.

'What are you going to do?' she asked.

'What can I fucking do?'

'You could confront her about it.'

He gave a bitter laugh. 'And what good would that do?'

'She'd stop,' Kate said. 'If she thought you knew she'd stop. She's got a conscience, Danny. The guilt must be eating her away already. If you asked her to stop it, she would.'

Danny took another cigarette from the packet, tamped it hard against the box, considering. She was right, of course. He could stop it with a word. But why bother? In the end what did it matter? If she was happy… He remembered Andrews' face on the day that he came to the house, his interest in Rachel easy to see, a new life in his eyes though he had tried his best to hide it. And Rachel smiling, flattered by the promise she saw in him, a different side of her. A Rachel who was happy. He closed his eyes.

'I wish you hadn't bloody told me.'

Hatred for the officer began to simmer, memories of other fights with him licking at his thoughts. He shook his head, trying to clear the images away. He was breathing hard, pictures in his mind he could not bear to watch: snapshots of his wife with Andrews interwove themselves with memories, the lovers wrapped around each other against a background of the war, the blast of shells and screaming men, friends of his, men who died because of Andrews. The noise reverberated louder, taking him back into fear and danger. The same sights and sounds and smells as in his nightmares. The same sense of terror. He shook his head again as though the movement could dislodge the thoughts, but it made no difference. It was all still there, clear as reality.

Somewhere in the distance Kate's voice was calling him. *Danny … Danny … are you all right …?* But she was too far away to answer. He felt his body start to shake. Kate's hand on his arm recalled him with a start, and roughly he pushed her away. She stumbled back from him, frightened, but he did not care. He needed fresh air, room to breathe, and he propelled himself toward the door with one hard shove, slamming the chair against it in his need to escape.

The cold air against his face, in his lungs, brought him back to himself, quieted the racket in his head. Fumbling, he lit himself a cigarette, and dragged the back of a hand across his face to dry the tears. His hands were shaking worse than ever. Kate appeared beside him, arms wrapped around herself against the cold. She squatted down beside the chair so she could look up into his face. There was no trace now of the mockery of before, her features drawn tight with worry.

'Are you all right? What happened?'

'I'm all right,' he said harshly, drawing back deeply on the cigarette. He coughed, hard, and she drew back a little from the violence of the spasm. 'I'm all right,' he rasped.

She stood up, staring down at him, uncertain as he raised

his eyes to her and said, hoarsely, barely more than a whisper. 'Don't you fucking tell Rachel about this, all right?'

'All right,' she replied, nodding. 'All right.'

'Promise?'

'I promise.'

'Good. Now get inside and leave me alone.'

She hesitated, unwilling to leave him, afraid of what he might do.

'Fucking go!' he hissed at her, and she turned and left him on his own with his nightmares in the cold December morning.

MRS PITMAN WAS NOT at work the next day. Her father had finally died in the night and she had telephoned Jane with the news.

'Poor old dear,' Jane said. 'What will she have to complain about now?'

'You're wicked,' Rachel replied.

'I know,' Jane grinned. 'I know. Tea?'

'Yes please.'

Rachel sat at the desk in the office, watching her friend make the tea, and thought how attractive she was, pretty and slight and mischievous. Maybe one day she would get over Roger and find someone else to make her happy. She was far too lovely to spend her life alone.

'What are you looking at?' Jane asked with a smile, and Rachel became aware that she must have been staring.

'I was thinking that you're very pretty,' she said.

Jane laughed. 'Thank you. Roger used to say that I looked like an elf.' She turned away to fill the pot from the urn, then left it to brew as she went to sit back at the desk with her friend.

'So what's happening with you and your Captain Andrews then?' she said.

Rachel hesitated, the hot flush burning up her face and neck, her pulse racing with the mention of his name. In the pause Jane lifted a quizzical eyebrow.

'Nothing,' Rachel managed to say. 'Nothing's happening.'

'Are you sure? You've gone awfully red.'

Rachel hesitated again, unsure what to say. She wanted to tell her, to tell someone, but she was afraid to, her own disloyalty hard to admit.

'You can trust me,' Jane said. 'I won't tell anyone. And I won't judge you. I promise.'

'All right.' She took a deep breath. 'I'm seeing him.'

'Seeing him?'

'Yes.'

'Seeing *all* of him?'

'Yes.'

'Ooooh.' Jane got up to pour the tea and there was a silence until she sat down again at the desk with the cups.

'We should open up,' Rachel said.

Her friend glanced at the clock. 'There's another five minutes yet so you can tell me all about him.'

'There's nothing really to tell.'

'Oh, come on.'

Rachel did not know what to say. 'We love each other,' she said, in the end.

Jane nodded and took a sip of her tea. 'It must be difficult, what with your family and everything. However do you manage?'

'I lie.'

'You are a dark horse.'

Rachel laughed, unsure if it was meant as a compliment.

'Well, if you ever need me to cover for you, I don't mind. Just make sure you tell me first.'

'Thank you,' Rachel said. 'I may.'

They finished their tea, got up from the table and moved

towards the door. Jane opened it, then paused and turned back. 'Is he as lovely as he seems?'

'Yes,' Rachel smiled. 'He is.'

'That's good. I wouldn't want you getting involved with a bounder.'

'Thank you.'

The two women smiled then went out into the library and unlocked the doors to begin work for the day.

It was a week before she saw him again. He was leaning on the wall of the ruined church across the road and in the dark she crossed to him easily, little traffic by that time of the evening. He stood up as she reached him and lifted a hand to caress her face. Then he kissed her and all the doubts of his absence were forgotten.

'I was beginning to think you weren't going to come,' she said.

'That I'd had my wicked way with you and that was the end of it?'

'Not exactly.' She laughed, embarrassed, and he smiled and squeezed her hand.

'I'm sorry,' he said. 'I've been busy – we do exercises at night sometimes and I can't always get away.'

'I know.'

'Am I forgiven?'

'Of course.'

They walked on a few strides in silence, their fingers intertwined in the pocket of his greatcoat.

'How have you been?' he asked.

'I've been busy too.'

He was silent. Then, 'And how's Danny?'

She hesitated, unwilling to tell him the truth, afraid that he would fret and worry.

'The same,' she said, but it was a lie. Danny had got worse again in the last few days, violent nightmares every night, the same as when he first came back. And he could hardly bring himself to talk to her, no longer a cold indifference, but a more active hostility that was harder to take. She glanced up at Kit as they walked, and he turned and smiled his half-smile, so it seemed he had not noticed the lie.

They walked in silence then, comfortable with each other, and at the Green they sat on the first bench they came to. Rachel turned up her collar and shivered, shoulders hunched.

'Come here,' he said, and put his arm round her, drawing her into him. 'You're cold.'

She curled up against him, sliding her hand inside his coat to be closer to him, to feel the warmth of his flesh and the beat of his heart. 'I love you,' she said.

'I'm glad,' he whispered into her hair. 'Because every time I see you I half expect you to say you won't see me again, that the guilt is too much for you to bear.'

'I don't ever want to stop seeing you,' she said. 'I want to be with you always.'

She sat up to look at him in the semi-darkness, and straight away he kissed her, long and hard and passionate, and when he took his lips from hers both of them were breathless.

'Do you mean that?' he asked.

'Yes.'

'Then when can I see you again? When can we spend some time together?'

'Saturday.' she replied. 'At the hotel. I could take the day off sick.'

'Saturday.' He stood up and held out his hand to help her up. 'Come on. Let's get you home.'

They walked on hand in hand and stopped at the corner of her road, in the shadow between the street lamps. In the darkness neither of them spoke because it was too hard to say goodbye. Then Kit lifted her hand to his lips.

'Till Saturday,' he whispered.

'Saturday.'

She turned from him and hurried away and though she knew he stood watching her walk through the dark until she reached the driveway, she did not look back.

Only the bedside lamp was lit in the bedroom and in the soft light Danny sat next to the window, looking out, a book open on his lap though it was too dark there to read. For an instant Rachel panicked and wondered if he had seen her with Andrews. He couldn't have, she told herself, they had parted well out of sight of the house, but the unease of guilt remained. He turned towards her briefly when he heard the door but he stayed silent, closing the book and reaching across to place it on the table next to the bed.

'What're you reading?' she asked.

'A book someone gave me in hospital. Before they shipped me out.'

'What is it?'

He glanced across at the cover as if to remind himself. 'It's called *The Odyssey*. Here.' He picked it up and tossed it so that it landed on the bed close to where she was standing. She lifted it and examined the cover before she leafed through the pages. It was an old edition, Pope's translation, printed on pre-war paper, and it exuded the mustiness of old books so familiar to her from the library. It seemed to be rare and precious and she held it with reverence. On the inside cover there was an inscription.

Danny, it read, *I hope this helps to pass the time. All best wishes for the future, Kit Andrews.*

She closed it quickly, fire streaming through her at the sight of his name, aware of her husband watching her, judging her reaction.

'Are you enjoying it?' she asked him, keeping her tone even, and she was surprised by the calmness of her voice. But she wondered if he would hear the tremor underneath, or notice the trembling of her hands as she held the book between them.

'It's all right.'

She smiled and gently tossed the book back to him as if it meant nothing to her, then went across to the dressing table in the corner. From there she could see him in the mirror behind her, still watching her. She wondered what he could know to test her like this, what he had heard.

'Why are you sitting here in the cold?' she asked.

'I didn't like the company in the living room.'

'Has he been having a go again?'

'He doesn't have to say anything. It's there in his face every time he looks at me.'

She said nothing but took the pins out of her hair and shook it free before she began to brush it, trying to calm herself with the rhythm of the long even strokes.

'You were late again,' Danny said.

'I was late leaving,' she replied. 'With Mrs Pitman away its been a madhouse. I missed the bus so I walked.'

'I don't like you walking home. It isn't safe.'

'I told you. I missed the bus. And anyway, I hate it. Half the time it doesn't come and when it does it's crowded and smelly and full of drunks …' She stopped, aware that she was gabbling in her nervousness, saying more than she needed, making it worse.

'Drunks like me, you mean?'

'Not like you.'

'Like what?'

'Offensive lecherous drunks.'

He laughed and sat watching her as she got ready for bed and she was embarrassed to undress in front of him, uncertain of what he suspected, and conscious of the taste of Kit on her lips, her senses still filled with the scent of him.

'Don't turn away,' Danny said. 'You don't have to be coy with me.'

Rachel moved to her side of the bed and took her nightdress from its place under the pillow.

'Wait. Don't put it on yet.'

'The curtains,' Rachel said. 'People can see in.'

He swung the chair back to face the window, staring out at the half-lit street beyond. Briefly, above the roofs of the houses opposite, the new moon shone through a break in the cloud, a sliver like in story books, but it was gone again in an instant. Danny reached up as high as he could and yanked the curtains closed, then turned himself again to face her.

'Get undressed.'

She swallowed, hesitating a moment before she quickly slipped off her skirt and jersey to stand by the bed in her slip.

'And the rest.'

She stared at the floor as she slid out of the slip and unhooked her brassiere with trembling fingers, afraid of this new interest in her. In the thought of Danny's mouth against hers she could smell the alcohol on his breath and the roughness of his lips. He would not now be a gentle lover. She suppressed a shudder and hoped that all he wanted was to look.

'Don't worry, Rache,' he said, as if he had read her mind. 'I'm not going to do anything to you.'

She said nothing, standing shivering at the side of the bed, her nipples hard with the cold, waiting and wondering why she was allowing him to do this. Guilt, she thought. Guilt and pity, a potent combination. From the living room they heard the faint chime of the clock striking eleven.

'Seen Andrews again, have you?'

She shook her head. 'No.'

'Comes into the library does he?'

'Occasionally.'

'He liked you.'

'Don't be ridiculous.'

'And you liked him, eh?'

'Can I put my nightdress on now? I'm freezing.'

'You didn't like him?'

She ignored the question and picked up her nightdress, slipped it over her head. It was old and worn and there was nothing even remotely sexual about it.

'You didn't like him?' Danny repeated.

'He seemed all right,' she said, but she had got into bed and under the safety of the covers she was less afraid of him than before. 'Why do you ask?'

He shrugged and swivelled the chair away. 'No reason.'

She lay on her side and watched him as he hauled himself out of the chair and into bed and settled himself beneath the quilt, leaning out when he was comfortable to turn off the lamp.

'Good night, Danny,' she said.

He said nothing and within minutes he was asleep. But Rachel lay awake a long time wondering what he knew and what had given her away to him.

Chapter Thirteen

She caught the bus to the hotel, too risky to walk near the library, and though she was early Kit was already there and waiting. He stood up as soon as he saw her, his eyes intense and full of hunger.

'Rachel.' He gave her a small smile in greeting and she knew that upstairs he would not be so reserved. 'Have you eaten?'

'No.'

'Are you hungry?'

'Not really.'

'Good. I was hoping you'd say that.'

Rachel laughed, and they went up the narrow stairs into the corridor. The light bulb had blown and it took them a while to find their room, a different one this time, slightly bigger with a hand basin in the corner, looking out over a different street, another row of shabby terraced houses.

'I'll light the fire,' he said.

He squatted awkwardly before it, protecting his damaged knee, and the sixpence clattered loudly in the meter. In the dim light of the room the gas flame caught, lighting up blue and iridescent as she stood with him by the fire. Blue flames turned to orange and heat began to fill the room. Kit turned to her with a smile, his hair very red in the heater's light, his eyes very blue, and she smiled too. Then he took her hand and led her across the room to the bed.

The love they made was urgent and fast, his mouth hard against hers, his hands groping under her clothes to find the flesh beneath, yanking the buttons open in his impatience. There was no time for thought as he entered her, one hand clamped across her mouth to stifle her cries, and still it did not fill her need for him. It was over very quickly and they held each other still half-clothed on top of the bed covers. Rachel began to cry.

'Don't cry,' he said. 'Please don't.'

But she could not help herself and this time he did not try to tease her out of it.

'I'm sorry,' she whispered, when the sobs had subsided and she could trust herself to speak.

'It's all right,' he replied, brushing the tears from her face with his fingertips. 'It'll be all right.'

Rachel smiled and lifted her hand to his face to caress him, but he took it in his fingers and held it to his lips.

'I love you, Rachel,' he whispered. 'I really do.'

She smiled but no words would come, caught in the backwash of her guilt, and the moment passed. Kit sat up, straightening his clothes, and she knew that she had hurt him with her silence.

'Would you like some lunch now?' he asked.

'Could we have it sent up?'

'We can go down.'

'Wouldn't it be nicer to be alone up here?'

The hesitation was for barely an instant but she saw the struggle in the working of his jaw. Then he said, 'Yes. It would, of course it would. I'll go down and see what I can arrange.'

He gave her a half-smile, the hurt still in his eyes, and was gone.

She lay a moment where he left her, bare skin growing cold until she raised herself with effort, straightened out her clothes. Raking hasty fingers through her hair at the mirror by the sink, she could see the redness of the eyes in her reflection, and tried to look away. But they followed her, accusing, and so she forced herself to meet them.

Why did he choose you? she asked the image. Why not someone prettier, someone less sad? She tried to give herself a smile, but it turned out wry and disappointing, and she wondered what he saw in her. Whatever he had told her she could never see that face as beautiful, never think it anything but plain.

Perhaps she should have let Jane have him, with her chirpy prettiness and humour, a woman who could make him happy. Depressed, she turned away from the sink and knelt by the fire to wait for him.

He brought cheese sandwiches and they sat on the floor near the fire to eat because there was no table, and he was good humoured again. When they had eaten he lay with his head in her lap and she stroked his hair, short and neat beneath her fingers. For a long time they were silent and though she wondered what he was thinking she did not like to ask. Finally, he looked up at her and smiled, then twisted round to sit up facing her.

'Danny showed me the book you gave him the other day,' she said.

'*The Odyssey*. I gave it to him when he was in the hospital on the beachhead. I thought it might cheer him up a bit. I didn't really have anything else to give. Does he like it?'

'I'm not sure. He isn't much of a reader.'

'No. I suppose not.'

'It was very kind of you to give it to him though. It's a

lovely book.' She wondered how long and far he had carried it before he gave it away, what it had meant to him.

'It was nothing.' He smiled and reached a hand, palm outward, towards the fire, warming his fingers before it. Rachel watched him, the handsome face still in concentration, pale skin lit orange by the heater's glow. He must have felt her gaze because he turned to her again after a time and smiled.

'You're very thoughtful today, Rachel,' he said.

She looked down at her bare feet and stretched her toes.

'Is anything wrong?'

He moved closer to her, bending to search her lowered face, but she averted her eyes from him, afraid to answer the question. 'Tell me.'

She took a deep breath and raised her head to look at him. 'I think Danny knows,' she said.

'About us? How? How could he know?'

'I don't know,' she shrugged. 'But he asked if I'd seen you again, if I liked you. And he showed me the book that you gave him. He was watching me, trying to see how I'd react.'

Kit turned his eyes away and stared into the gas flames as if they might hold the answers.

'You know, he saw that you liked me the first time you came to the house …'

'Did he?' Kit turned to her again. 'That was very perceptive of him. But how could he know about us now?' he persisted. 'Could someone have told him?'

'No one knows except Jane.'

'Are you sure?'

'Well … I suppose there's Kate.'

'She knows?'

'She suspects. She asked me about it a while ago, after we were seen together and I told her there was nothing in it. I don't know if she believed me or not. But she wouldn't tell him even if she did know. She's my sister.'

He said nothing, still watching her in the warm light of the fire, close enough for her to be aware of his breath. She knew what he was thinking, that it was Kate who had betrayed them.

'She wouldn't have told him. I'm sure of it,' Rachel said.

'Perhaps,' he replied. Then he dropped his eyes to the patch of threadbare rug between them and a tension descended that Rachel did not understand. In the silence the hiss of the fire was the only sound.

'What shall we do?' she asked him, when the silence had become uncomfortable.

'What can we do?'

'I'm not giving you up,' she said. 'Whatever he thinks about it I'm not giving you up.'

'Good,' he replied, and stretched out again on the floor in front of her, his back to the heat, leaning on an elbow. Rachel reached forward to touch a hand to his face and he turned his head to kiss her palm.

'I'm sorry,' she said. 'It can't be easy loving me.'

'It isn't easy loving anyone.'

She laughed. 'No. I suppose not. I never thought of it like that.' Then, because she wanted to turn their thoughts from Danny, she said, 'Have there been many?'

'Many what?'

'Many women that you've loved?'

'No. Not many.'

'Tell me about them.'

He smiled. 'Why do women always want to know about past loves? Why is that?'

'Don't evade the question.'

He laughed for a moment, and they were close again and easy with each other, and Rachel thought how much she loved him. Then he grew serious as he thought about what to tell her.

'There's only really been one girl that I've loved,' he said finally. 'I mean really loved.' His eyes flicked to Rachel's, and for a moment she was sorry she had asked.

'You don't have to tell me if you'd rather not.'

'It's all right. It was a long time ago now, in a different life. Her name was Ursula.'

'What happened?'

'She married someone else and I joined the army.'

'That's it?'

'Yes.'

She laughed, exasperated.

'All right,' he said then. 'I'll tell you the story.'

He looked down again at the rug and with the fingers of one hand he tugged gently at the loose threads of wool.

'She was rich and well-connected and she came from London to spend the summer with some friends in Marlborough.'

'What did she look like?' Rachel asked.

'Blond, fine features, tall.'

She knew he wasn't telling her all of it. 'Pretty?' she asked.

'Stunning.'

'Go on. What happened?'

'I met her at a party.'

She had arrived on the arm of a friend of his but she talked only to him all evening. By the end of the night he was besotted, and he had lost his friend for good.

'After the party I took her home.'

'Did you now?'

He looked up quickly, unsure of her tone, then smiled when he saw she was laughing.

'What happened then?'

'We spent some time together. I suppose I should have realised she wasn't serious but I didn't. Looking back, I think I wasn't even the only man she had on a string. Then at the end of the summer she went back to London and forbade me to write to her or see her again. When I disobeyed and wrote anyway she sent back the letters unopened.'

'What an awful woman.'

He laughed. 'Yes. She was. I think I knew that at the time really – but I just got carried away. Then one day I saw her engagement notice in *The Times* and so I gave up all hope and joined up.'

'And here you are.'

'And here I am.'

Rachel lay down close to him, shielded from the heat of the fire by his body, so that suddenly she was cold even though the room had warmed. She lifted a hand to stroke his face and he closed his eyes and rubbed his head against the pressure of the caress.

'Do you still love her?' she asked.

'Not in the slightest.'

'I love you,' she said.

'I know,' he answered, opening his eyes. Then he rolled her onto her back and kissed her.

THEY TALKED through the afternoon and made love again, lazily on the rug on the heat of the fire. Then they slept for a while and woke in a panic because they did not know the time and it was dark outside. But it was still early so they dressed and left the warmth of the room, shivering outside on the pavement as the cold of the evening hit their faces.

'Where to?'

'This way,' he said, and led them away from the hotel until they found a small restaurant in Clifton Village that he had heard about. It was tucked away and well-hidden and though she had passed it often, she had never noticed it before. They had to wait for a table so they sat just inside the door, holding hands and talking in low voices, and each time the door opened a blast of chilled air blew over them. She was excited to be there with him, happier than she could ever remember.

Kit ordered wine that must have been black market. Rachel was afraid of getting tight, of getting caught at home, but being with Kit made her bold so she drank it anyway. Then after dinner they walked out again into the winter night and held hands as they made their way back through half-lit streets to the hotel. There they sat close together in front of the fire because the room had grown cold again in their absence with the coming on of the night. Kit brushed the loose hair back from Rachel's temple and her neck so that it fell behind her shoulders. The touch of his fingers made her shiver.

'Does Danny do this for you?' he asked.

She shook her head. 'He won't even touch me.'

'What about before? What was he like with you before?'

Rachel tried to think, to remember if he had once caressed her in the way that Kit was doing now, but she could not recall a time that they had ever been so close, so affectionate.

'He never touched me like you do,' she said. 'It just wasn't his way.'

'More fool him.'

'But we were happy,' Rachel said, 'In our own way we were happy.'

'Only because you knew no better.'

She swung round to face him. 'That's unfair,' she said.

Kit dropped his hand from her hair and averted his eyes from her anger. 'I'm sorry,' he murmured. 'I don't mean to upset you …' But he would never understand why Danny had not appreciated her more, why he still didn't.

'I know,' she whispered.

Silence fell, and they could hear the low hiss of the gas fire, its heat strong against their faces and their limbs. But they did not move away from it, the only brightness in the room. Rachel looked at her watch.

'It's almost nine,' she said. 'I should go soon.'

'I'll walk you home.'

'I can get the bus. It's a long way there and back.'

'Nonsense. Besides, I want to stay with you longer.'

'I wish we could stay here.'

'So do I.'

They sat for another moment of reluctance before they both got to their feet. Kit stooped to turn off the heater then turned to help Rachel with her coat.

'Shall we go?'

'I suppose we'd better.'

He opened the door for her and they went out into the gloom of the corridor, down the stairs. In the lobby Kit gave the room key back to the clerk and paid for the room. Rachel watched him from the doorway until he turned from the desk to follow her. Then they both stepped out into the bitter night.

At home there was shouting. She could hear her father's voice through the window as she passed it and her first instinct was to turn and run back down the drive to catch up with Kit. He would not have gone far yet, she thought. She could still easily go to him. For the length of a deeply-drawn breath she thought about it then steeled herself to go inside. Her mother was in the kitchen.

'What's going on?' she asked.

Rose shook her head and Rachel saw the tension in her face and the weariness of it all.

'I'm sorry,' she said. 'I wish we could go somewhere else and leave you and Dad in peace.'

Her mother smiled and put a hand on her daughter's arm. 'I know. But it isn't your fault, dear.'

A door slammed.

'I'm really sorry.'

'You go to him.'

Rachel went through to the living room where Danny sat slumped in his chair close to the fireplace, features set sullen and hard, his cheeks florid from alcohol and the heat of the fire. He was staring into the grate but not at the flames: he was looking beyond them to something she could not see.

'What was all that about?' she said.

He did not turn.

'Danny?'

'Nothing.'

'It must have been about something.'

'It's not important.' Then swinging round in the wheelchair to face her, 'You're late. Again.'

She glanced at the clock. It was past ten already. They must have wandered home more slowly than she realised.

'It was busy. I was late leaving.'

He glared, and the afterglow of her hours with Kit twisted into the fear of getting caught.

'I'm going to bed,' he said.

'I'll be there soon,' she replied. 'I'm just going to have a cup of tea and a sit down. Would you like a cup?'

'No ta.'

She stood back to let him through and he swore as the chair bumped against the door frame. When he had gone she went back to the kitchen where her mother was doing a last bit of cleaning up, getting things ready for the morning. She made tea for them both.

'Your father's almost at breaking point.' Rose said. 'I don't know how much more I can stand.'

Rachel stared into her cup, blowing absently across the

surface of the tea. Her mother had always been the peacemaker, rarely complaining on her own account but trying instead to soften the blows from either side. She could still remember the endless conversations between them before she married Danny, her mother patiently explaining her father's disapproval over and over again, hoping for some understanding, for reconciliation. Her attempts were not always appreciated, or even noticed, but Rachel knew without her gentle influence the family would have broken down years ago.

'It's hardest on the children,' Rose said.

She nodded. There was nothing she could say.

'You don't see them as much as I do,' her mother went on. 'Charlie's getting quite withdrawn. He avoids being with his father now. He'll play up in his room in the cold rather than be downstairs with him. I'm getting quite worried. He used to be such an outgoing child.'

Rachel sighed and the warmth of the memory of being with Kit grew cold, the cold chill of guilt taking over. She looked at her mother, thin and pale, worn down by life, and wondered if she still loved her husband. Had she ever thought of leaving? Or loved another man? Rachel had never considered it before.

'You must talk to him, Rachel, tell him how it's affecting the children.'

'He already knows.'

'Then why doesn't he stop?'

'He doesn't do it on purpose,' Rachel said quickly, irritated, hearing her father in her mother's words, defending Danny even now. 'He can't help it. He's the unhappiest of all of us.'

'And he takes it out on us and the children. I'm sorry, Rachel. I know you feel you have to stick up for him but he's been home for six months now: it's time he got over it and let us all get on with our lives.'

'He can't help it, Mum,' Rachel repeated.

'I honestly don't know how much more I can take. And your father's getting to the end of his tether.'

'But Dad's just as much to blame. He deliberately provokes him. Surely you can see that?'

Rose shook her head, as she turned away to take her cup back to the sink. Her sympathies lay wholly with her husband: any pity for her son-in-law had long since been eroded by Danny's bitterness and rancour.

Rachel said nothing but she understood her mother's frustration. Then she thought that if Danny were different and more like he used to be, she would have no excuse for loving Kit. She drained the last of the tea and took the cup to her mother who rinsed it out and left it upturned on the draining board. Both women stood for a moment in front of the sink, side by side.

'I'm sorry, Mum. I don't know what else we can do.'

Her mother turned with an anxious, half-formed smile and a shrug, and Rachel felt the guilt like a weight inside her. 'Good night, Rachel.'

'Good night, Mum.'

In the bedroom Danny was in bed, sitting up, waiting for her. 'Your mum had a go too, did she?'

'Not really. She's just tired of the bickering. We all are.'

'And it's all my fault, I suppose.'

'No,' she replied. She was tired and did not want to have this conversation. She wanted to lie in the dark and silence of the night and imagine that she was with Kit. She sat at the dressing table and began to brush her hair.

'So what did she say?' Danny persisted.

'Nothing much.'

'She must have said something.'

Rachel turned on the stool to face him. 'Actually, she wanted me to talk to you about Charlie. She thinks all the fighting is making him withdrawn.'

Danny dropped his eyes to his hands on the bedspread and the muscle in his cheek began to work. Rachel spun back to face the dressing table and watched him lift his head slowly to find her gaze in the mirror.

'Is that true?' he asked.

'He used to be such a happy boy. When you were away we used to talk all the time about how you would have liked this or that, or how you'd be proud of him for something he'd done. And now I think he's afraid of you.'

'Afraid?'

'Yes.' She stood up and began to undress but he did not seem to notice.

'Why's he afraid of me?' He looked up at her, eyes shot with hurt bewilderment. 'I don't beat him or anything.'

'No. You don't,' she agreed. 'But you're angry all the time, and he's too young to understand that it isn't his fault. He thinks all that anger is with him. All he wants to do is please you and make you proud of him. You're his dad.'

'And Jean?'

'I don't know about Jean. She's a strange one, that child. She watches everything and takes it all in but I've got no idea what she makes of it all. She'll never say.'

He was quiet as Rachel got into bed beside him, and they lay in a moment of silence before he reached out and turned off the lamp. Then he spoke into the darkness.

'Even my children fucking hate me.'

'Nobody hates you,' she whispered. 'We'd all love you if only you'd let us.'

He turned away from her to face the window and when he was settled she shifted too, getting comfortable, arranging the covers so that both of them were warm. When she was still, he spoke again.

'You don't love me,' he said. 'You used to. But you don't any more.'

She was silent.

'See? You don't even deny it.'

'I don't know what I feel any more,' she said.

'Pity,' he told her. 'Pity and obligation and that's about all.'

She propped herself up on one elbow to see him better but he did not move and it was hard to talk to his back in the dark.

'I wanted to love you, Danny,' she said. 'When you first came home it was all that I wanted. To have you back and be near you, to love and hold you and have you hold me. It was all that I dreamt about all those years you were away.'

'So?'

'You wouldn't let me. You were so angry and bitter that I couldn't get near you.'

'So it's my fault?'

'No. I didn't say that.'

'But that's what you meant. You wanted to love me but I made it impossible with my anger and my bitterness. That's what you said.'

'I don't blame you for being angry and bitter,' she whispered. 'How can I, after all that you've been through.'

'And you don't know the half of it.'

'No.'

'But you wouldn't have loved me anyway, even if I'd come back smiling.'

'What do you mean?'

'Look at me,' he hissed. 'What do you see? You remember when I used to have legs? When I used to have a dick that worked? How can I be any kind of husband to you now anyway?'

'It didn't matter.'

'Well it bloody well should've.' He was silent then, and she tried to remember when the love had gone completely, if she had fallen for Kit before or after it was over. She laid her head back down on the pillow and as she turned away from her husband her shoulder brushed against his back beneath the sheet. He flinched with her touch, and hurriedly she shifted further over so that they would not touch again.

After, she decided. Kit had come when the marriage was already over and there was nothing left of it to save.

'Good night,' she whispered.

Danny grunted in response. Sleep took a long time to come.

She woke to Danny screaming beside her and instinctively reached out a hand to calm him, but he shoved it away and sat up.

'Don't touch me!' he hissed at her. 'Don't you fucking touch me!'

Rachel drew back from him, afraid of his hatred, unsure if he was still in the nightmare.

'It's a dream,' she said from a distance. 'You were having a dream.'

She turned on the lamp and watched him, his head in his hands, hair soaked with sweat. Then he turned to her and his eyes were glazed with emotions she did not know.

'Don't look at me like that,' he whispered. 'I don't want your pity.'

'I'm sorry.'

'I want my life back,' he said. 'I want my fucking life back.'

Reaching out for his cigarettes, his hands were shaking and it was a moment before the tobacco caught in the flame of the match and glowed red as he drew back on it hard. He coughed when the smoke hit his lungs but when the spasm had passed he was calmer and his hands shook with less violence. There was a silence and upstairs they heard Rachel's father get out of bed and walk along the landing to the bathroom. It was four a.m.

'No one should have to see what I've seen,' Danny said. He took another pull on the cigarette and coughed again. 'No one. They may be dreams now, but they were real enough then.'

'Would it help to talk about it?' she offered in a whisper, though she was terrified he might accept, uncertain she could cope.

He turned and observed her for a moment, considering, then turned away and kept on smoking.

'You don't give up, do you?' he said. 'Even now you still think you can help.'

'You're my husband.'

'I was your husband.'

'For better or worse, remember?'

He laughed then, a touch of the old Danny. 'Well, it doesn't get much worse than this, eh?' He finished the cigarette with three short pulls on the stub, then crushed it into the ashtray with his thumb. 'I'm not going to tell you about Italy, Rache,' he said. 'It would break your heart.' His voice cracked and when he turned again to reach for another cigarette, his jaw was clenched to stop the tears from coming. 'It would break your heart,' he whispered. 'Now go back to sleep.'

'Are you all right now?'

He shrugged. 'You go back to sleep.'

She leant over to turn off the lamp and when her eyes became accustomed again to the darkness she could make out Danny's outline against the window. He was still sitting up, still coughing.

'Lie down,' she said. 'You'll get cold.'

'I'm fine,' he replied.

She turned on her side with her back towards him and heard the snap behind her as he struck a match to light another cigarette. She did not sleep again that night.

Chapter Fourteen

The stuffiness of the room made it hard to concentrate on the lecture he was giving. The cadets were bored and listless in the warmth, their training almost done, and in the exuberance of their youth they were desperate to get to war before they missed it, full of dreams of being heroes, he supposed, of finding death or glory.

Andrews glanced round the room at the fresh, unknowing faces, eager boys, barely older than the schoolboys that he used to teach. It was a crime to send such innocence into battle. Once, the men he knew in Italy had been as young; clean cut and naïve, minds and bodies still undamaged by the war. But that was not how he remembered them: the faces in his memory were of lined and haggard men, their eyes made sad by too much suffering, and old before their time. A lot of them had died. And others, men like Danny, alive but utterly destroyed.

He stopped talking, suddenly aware that it was pointless to go on: he had taught these boys, these men, the best of all he knew and the rest was up to them. They looked up in the silence, surprised, and stared at him.

'Any questions?' he said.

'No sir.'

'Then that'll be all.'

'Yes sir.'

There was no need to tell them twice. The room erupted in the clatter of them getting to their feet, and he turned away to rub the chalk marks off the board. Within a minute the room was empty and he could not recall the details of their faces, each of them unmarked in his mind, their futures too uncertain to allow himself to care.

Tidying up his papers, he placed them neatly in the leather briefcase before he turned his mind away from all of that and thought instead of Rachel.

In the downstairs mess, Andrews sat and read *The Times,* scanning the reports on the fighting in the Ardennes. He felt for the men in the middle of it: he knew what it was like to cower in bitter cold under German shells, with orders to hold the line.

He was alone. The others were still busy or had left but he had no desire to go back to his billet, a cold room in an unwelcoming house, the two old spinsters who owned it resentful of a stranger's presence. He preferred to while the time away here in warm familiarity, counting down the hours till it was late enough to pick up Rachel.

Ronnie Peters came in and called for the orderly to make some tea.

'Hello Andrews. And how's your girl?' he asked.

Kit looked up from the paper, but the other man's back was turned. 'My girl?'

'Yes. Your girl. You have got a girl, haven't you? I mean, everyone's talking about it. Works at the library, doesn't she?'

Andrews smiled and shook his head: they were like a bunch of old women how they gossiped.

The other man turned at the silence, and regarded him with interest. 'You haven't got a girl?'

'Yes. I've got a girl.' It was easier to tell the truth. 'And yes, she works at the library.'

'Good-oh. Lucky you. My girl's gone off with a Yank.'

'I'm sorry to hear that.'

'Yes. Rotten luck. She was rather splendid. I was thinking of asking her to marry me.' Ronnie sat on one of the other sofas that lined the walls and when the orderly returned with the tea, the two men drank in companiable silence as the minutes ticked slowly round towards the evening.

AT EIGHT-FIFTEEN HE was at the library desk, waiting patiently as Rachel worked, her lover unnoticed as she chatted and smiled, absorbed. She was beautiful, he thought, with her full lips and soft pretty eyes, and he smiled to himself with the memory of the taste of her. Without the war he would have spoiled her, bought her books and flowers and chocolates, taken her to see a show in London, but such luxury now was impossible and though he knew she loved him just as well without it, it still felt to him like meanness on his part.

The borrower moved away, brushing past him, and Rachel turned to talk to the girl that she worked with. Both of them laughed at some joke that they shared, and he knew from their gaiety that Mrs Pitman was not there. Then the other girl noticed him and nudged at Rachel, who swung round to face him with delighted surprise.

'How long have you been there?' she exclaimed. He saw the blush sweep up her neck and flood her cheeks with colour.

'A while.'

'Why didn't you say something?'

'I was watching you work, seeing what you're like when you don't know I'm here.'

'And what am I like?'

'Beautiful.'

'Oh, go on.'

'No,' he said quickly, 'I mean it. I could have stood here for hours, just watching you.'

She smiled, pleased, and reached across to take his books. Then the other girl was at her side.

'Introduce us,' the girl whispered.

Kit laughed and held out his hand to introduce himself and he saw the change in light in Rachel's eyes as she saw the two of them together. So he winked at her and she giggled, coy and girlish and delightful.

'Go,' Jane said then. 'Go home. I can close up.'

Rachel glanced up at the clock on the wall. 'It's not even half past eight,' she said. 'It's too busy.'

'I can manage,' the girl insisted. 'They'll just have to wait.'

Rachel cast her eyes across the library, considering.

'Trust her,' Kit said. 'She can manage.'

'Go on,' Jane repeated.

Lifting her hands in surrender, Rachel said, 'I'll just go and get my coat.'

'Thank you, Jane,' Kit said when she had gone.

'My pleasure,' Jane replied. 'Got to do what we can to keep the troops happy …'

He laughed and then Rachel was back with her coat on and together they stepped out into the night.

Outside it was freezing and Kit put his arm round her shoulders as she shivered, holding her against the warmth of his body. She nestled against him and as they stood on the pavement an overfull bus lurched past them on its way up the hill. A group of young soldiers, G.I.s, swung precariously in the doorway at the back, laughing raucously, and in the clear air their voices carried back down the hill.

'This way,' Kit said, and they walked down and off the main road past the station to a pub in a back street. There were mostly officers inside and Kit nodded briefly to a small group of men as he walked with her to the bar. He had hoped there would be no one there he knew: most of the instructors usually drank at the officers' mess.

He ordered brandy for them both because of the cold and they sat at a table in the corner.

'Cheers.'

'Cheers.'

The brandy was warm going down but sitting with Rachel in the smoky comfort of the pub the bitter night beyond the door was already forgotten.

'Jane seems like a nice girl,' he said.

'Yes. And she's a good friend. Her chap was killed a couple of years ago. He was a fighter pilot and they were going to be married. She was desperately upset, still is I think, but she puts on a brave face most of the time.'

He thought of the young men in his class earlier that day and said nothing.

'Perhaps we could find her someone,' Rachel said. 'There must be some nice fellows where you are?'

'Some,' he smiled. 'But most of them are idiots.'

'That's a shame.'

They took sips of their brandy.

'Perhaps *you* should go out with Jane,' Rachel said. 'Then

you wouldn't have to sneak about and you'd have a chance of making something of it.'

'You wouldn't mind?' he said, joking to cover the hurt of what she said: he still had hopes of making something of it with her.

'Of course I'd mind,' she laughed.

'No. I don't think so,' he said. 'She isn't my type.'

'And I am?'

'Oh yes.'

'I find it hard to believe that I'm anybody's type. Least of all a good looking officer like you.'

'Don't put yourself down, Rachel. You're beautiful. You have beautiful eyes and beautiful lips and your skin is soft and smooth and perfect …'

'You think I'm beautiful?' She was incredulous, and he hated Danny more for letting her believe anything different.

'Absolutely.' He was serious now, searching her face with his eyes, desperate to convince her. 'You're the most beautiful woman I've ever met.'

'Really?'

'Absolutely.'

'Thank you,' she whispered. 'No one's ever told me that I'm beautiful before.'

'I wish it had been me in that greengrocer's shop,' he said. 'I wish it had been me you used to visit after school.'

'I was a very plain child.'

'I doubt it.'

'You're very sweet to me,' she replied.

Kit smiled and they took more sips of their brandy. A young subaltern appeared at the table. He was red-faced and very drunk. 'Hello Andrews.'

'Spencer,' Kit nodded.

'Aren't you going to introduce us?'

'No.'

'Mind if I sit down?'

'Yes.'

The lieutenant hesitated, Kit's hostility filtering through the fuzz of his drunkenness.

'Leave us alone, Spencer,' Kit said. 'And go back to the bar.'

'Well, there's no need to be rude old thing,' Spencer answered. 'I just came to say hello to your girl.' He smiled at Rachel who gave him a small smile in return.

'Now you've said hello you can go back to the bar.'

'I'm going. I'm going.' He turned uncertainly and wove his way back to his party. They watched him go and saw the other men in the group glance over as he related what had happened. Kit ignored them and wished he had taken her somewhere else. They would be talking about her now, evaluating her worth, and the thought of such men judging her lit a dull and pointless anger. He shifted his stool to turn his back to the group and gave Rachel a rueful smile.

She laughed. 'One of the idiots?'

'Yes. I'm sorry.'

'It's all right. He seemed harmless enough. I'm sure he's quite pleasant when he's sober.'

'Yes. Actually, he is.'

They finished their drinks and it was time for them to leave. The night air was hard in their lungs as they stepped through the door, and above them the narrow strip of sky between the buildings was clear black velvet, studded with stars and a half moon, sharp-edged and luminous. They stared up, holding hands.

'It's a beautiful night,' Rachel said.

'Unless you're a flier.'

She gripped his arm then tightly with both hands.

'I hate this war,' she murmured. 'I hate the way all the

beauty has gone out of the world. We can't even enjoy a clear night any more because there are men out there who are dying because of it. I'm so glad you got wounded, that you can't fight any more,' she said. 'I'm glad you're here where it's safe. I couldn't bear it if you were in danger. It was bad enough with Danny. But with you I couldn't bear it. I just couldn't.'

Gently, he put an arm around her shoulders: there were no words he could say to comfort her.

'Let's go,' he said softly.

She loosened her grip and let him guide her up the hill on their slow wander home.

IN THE FOUR hours between a split shift at the library, Rachel lay with Andrews on the floor before the fire in the hotel room, her back and buttocks scorching red with the heat, her head resting on his chest in the lazy wake of making love.

'Is there anything about me you'd like to change?' she asked him, lifting her face to look at him. 'Anything at all?'

He smiled. 'Why do you ask?'

'I want to be perfect for you,' she told him. 'I'd change anything about myself if I thought you'd love me more because of it.'

'There's nothing,' he replied, rubbing his fingers across the heat of her shoulder. 'You're perfect as you are.'

He stared up at the ceiling, deep in thought until he wheeled round on to his side, propped up on an elbow, his face close to hers. 'Actually,' he said. 'There is one thing.'

She tilted her head to see him better. There was a smile in his eyes and at the corners of his mouth.

'What's that?'

'Your name.'

'What's wrong with my name?'

'I think Rachel Andrews would suit you better.'

She laughed but when she looked at him again the humour had gone from his eyes and his face had grown stern with seriousness.

'I mean it,' he said. 'I want you to marry me. I want you to be my wife.'

She swallowed, unprepared for this, and she could not look at him. 'I'm already married,' she said.

'You could get a divorce.'

Rachel pushed herself to her feet, needing to put distance between them, but the sudden movement in the heat made her dizzy and she stumbled and almost fell before she recovered herself and went across to the basin. She poured a glass of water and observed her reflection in the mirror. It was obvious to anyone what she had been doing – tousled hair and flushed cheeks, lips deep pink and swollen. She smiled at the reflection, remembering how she got that way.

'Rachel?'

She turned to him, sitting now before the heater, and thought he looked very beautiful, the whiteness of his skin in the orange glow, the auburn hair, and the sadness in his eyes from a life lived too near to death.

'Marry me,' he said again.

She refilled the glass of water and gave it to him as she sat down again by the heater, shivering from the moments away from its heat. She said nothing, thoughts and emotions too confused to answer him. He reached a hand to her face and lifted her chin so that she could not avoid his gaze any longer. His eyes were fierce with emotion.

'I don't know,' she whispered. 'I didn't expect …' Marriage to Kit had not seemed possible before, a life with Danny fated. She had just assumed that Kit believed the same and this offering of a dream threatened to dismantle her.

'Think about it,' he whispered, moving closer, close enough that his lips brushed hers as he spoke. 'Just think about it.'

'I will,' she murmured.

Then he moved a fraction more and his lips were on hers, hard and demanding before he lay her down across the rug and made love to her again.

Chapter Fifteen

The weekend passed slowly. Andrews thought of Rachel often, imagining her with her family, with Danny, and the images were hard for him to watch. So he thought instead about their life together, the cottage they would have near Marlborough, her children becoming country kids as he had been, then children of their own. Long peaceful evenings with the children all in bed and no more hurried stolen meetings.

Now he waited across the road from the library, leaning against the low stone wall of the church. It was raining and bitterly cold and, digging his hands deeper in the pockets of his coat, he shivered. Rain dripped cold on the back of his neck beneath the upturned collar. Someone had stolen his umbrella.

Rachel was late coming out and the old lady was with her so he waited where he was. But she saw him straight away and as soon as Mrs Pitman trudged off down the hill, Rachel ran across the road to meet him and threw her arms around him.

'I didn't know if you'd come in this weather,' she breathed, her lips against his cheek. 'It's a filthy night.'

'It's only weather,' he replied. Rain splashed up from the pavement and soaked his trousers. Rachel's legs were white and bare: it was a long time since stockings could be bought. He wondered why she chose not to wear slacks but he was glad of it: the awareness of her skin beneath the skirt aroused him.

'But I'm glad you did come,' she said.

'I thought you would be.'

She smiled and linked her arm through his and they walked without talking for a while, senses filled with the sound of the rain and the smell of it in the wool of their coats. When they turned off the main road it was more sheltered and the rain seemed less heavy.

'So how was work?' he asked.

'It was work.'

'And the lovely Mrs Pitman?'

Rachel laughed. 'She'll never change. And you?'

'It was work. Some good students, some not so good. I try not think about where they're going.'

She nodded and he wondered what she was thinking, if she had turned the thought of marriage over in her mind in the days since he had seen her, if the possibility occupied her every waking thought as it did for him. She turned to him.

'I was wondering, Kit …'

He smiled at her. 'Yes?'

'What will you do after the war?'

'I'll probably go back to Marlborough – they said they'd keep my job for me at the college.'

She was silent, but the grip of her fingers tightened on his arm.

'Come with me,' he said.

They slowed to a stop and turned to face each other on the narrow pavement. Behind him on the road a truck rattled past. He gripped the muscles of her arms in both hands and lowered his face to look into hers. The street was dark, the long-dead bulbs of the street lamps still not replaced, but even in the shadow he could see that she would not look at him.

'Marry me, Rachel,' he urged in a low voice.

She covered her face with her hands. 'I don't know,' she murmured. 'I don't know.'

'Why not, Rachel?' He dragged her hands away from her face so that he could see her again. 'Why not?'

'What about the children?'

'You can bring the children.'

'And Danny?' She lifted her head to him then, defiant and challenging, and he let his arms drop to his sides. 'He needs me, Kit. Where would he go? How would he manage?' She could not tell him that Danny still wept in her arms in the night, that for all the enmity between them he needed her to cope.

'He would manage.'

'Don't, please don't,' she pleaded. 'I need more time …'

He shook his head in frustration and turned to walk on. The rain began to ease into an insistent drizzle as she hurried to catch up. She linked her arm through his and they walked in silence for a while. All the words that he wanted to say to convince her crowded in his thoughts in violent furious bursts and it was all he could do to stay silent.

'I'm sorry, Kit,' she offered.

He glanced down to her at his side. She was smiling and hopeful and inside him his love for her vied with his rage.

'He doesn't deserve you,' he said. 'He has no right to keep you.'

'I'm the one that's being unfaithful,' she said. 'Whatever else he's done, he never cheated on me.'

'Are you sure of that? Absolutely sure?' he answered. Anger overrode his judgement: he had vowed he would not tell her. 'How can you be so certain?'

They had stopped on the Green on the path that led alongside the tennis courts. There was no one about but the two of them and he could not see her face in the dark. She was silent for a moment, staring at the path at their feet. When she spoke again her words were shaded with a kind of hurt uncertainty.

'We were happy together,' she said, 'before he went away. And if I leave him he'll have nowhere to go. We were happy,' she repeated. 'I owe him that much.'

Kit closed his eyes and swallowed, clenching his jaw against the truth of what he knew, and his anger gave way to a need to backtrack, conciliate. But he had sown a seed of doubt and she would not let it go.

'You think something different, don't you?' she asked. 'You think that he …' She trailed off, her mind still groping to understand the implications.

'Shall we sit down?' he said, taking her elbow in his hand, and guiding her towards their usual bench a little further on. She made no protest, still in shock, and they sat side by side, gazing out into the blackness. Then she turned her head towards him.

'Was it a girl in Italy?'

'No.'

'Did he tell you something?'

'No,' Kit lied.

'Tell me the truth.'

'It was nothing direct,' he evaded. 'Just comments that made me think he might have done.'

He could not tell if she believed him but she asked him no more questions. He put his arm around her shoulders and drew her close and she laid her head against his chest. They sat like that a long time but she made no move to go until finally he said, 'I think we'd better get you home. It's late.'

She lifted her face to his in the dark and with his lips against her cheeks he could taste her tears. He pulled off his glove and wiped them away with his fingers.

'Don't cry,' he whispered. 'It'll be all right. You'll see.'

They kissed, briefly, but they stayed wrapped up in each

other, hidden from the world by the night, the future too distant to care about. It was long past the time she should have been home but she seemed not to care, and he would have held her there till the morning if she had asked him.

Finally, she unwound her legs from his, took her hand from its place above his heart. He shivered, cold suddenly without the close warmth of her body, and both of them hurriedly straightened their clothes as if they had realised for the first time where they were. Then they ambled along the short walk to her house, silent, his arm around her, holding her close.

When it was time to say goodbye they both waited, neither of them willing to be the first. In the end they stayed silent, parting only with a touch of hands and a smile. He watched her hurry up the last stretch of the hill and turn in at the gate and when she had disappeared from sight he turned around and began the long walk back to another night alone.

'You're drenched,' Rachel's mother said to her in the living room.

'Am I?' she replied, looking down at herself in surprise, noticing for the first time the dripping strands of hair around her face.

'Go and get changed. You'll catch your death like that.'

Rachel glanced around the room, mind returning slowly to the reality of her surroundings. It felt like she had woken from a dream. 'Where's Danny?'

There was a three beat silence so she knew there had been another row.

'He's in your room.'

'He's been drinking.' Her father did not lift his eyes from the book that lay in his lap. 'Again.'

She said nothing but went upstairs to the bathroom, taking

her time, reluctant to face her husband. By the time she reached the bedroom she was shivering with cold.

'Get undressed,' Danny slurred. He was sitting propped up in bed, a bottle of beer on the bedside table next to him, a half-smoked cigarette between his fingers. In the dim light of the lamp she could not clearly see his face but she knew from the angle of his head that he was drunk. The room smelled like a pub.

She stripped off her clothes, skin chilling quickly after the dampness of her blouse and skirt, and towelled herself with brisk movements, trying to rub some warmth into her limbs. Danny watched her, appraising, and she remembered the first time he had undressed her, the shyness of her wedding night, and the fear she would not please him. Afterwards she had been happy, nothing then to compare against his tender roughness. Now she knew different and in the pleasure that she gave and took with Kit, a new world of intimacy had opened up before her, a different, more marvellous understanding of what it is to be loved.

'Stop there,' Danny said.

She stood by the bed and shivered, letting him look, accustomed now to this game of humiliation, an expiation for her faithlessness.

'Touch yourself,' he said.

'No.'

'Oh yeah, that's right. Nice girls don't do that.'

'Can I put on my nightdress now?'

He shrugged and as he turned away to take another slug of beer, she slipped on her nightdress and climbed into bed. The sheets were cold but she could feel the animal warmth of Danny's body under the covers. The sense of heat confused her, evoking a momentary instinct to move toward its source before she remembered where it came from and was repelled.

'Don't you miss it?' he asked.

'Miss what?'

'It. You know. Doing it.'

'Sometimes,' she answered carefully.

'But you won't do it for yourself then?'

She said nothing: she had only learned how with Kit.

'No. Of course you won't. You'd prefer to get someone else to do it for you. A nice officer perhaps. A captain.'

'I don't know what you're talking about.'

He smiled and the half-laugh came to his throat as a cough. She waited until the spasm had passed before she settled herself under the covers.

'Good night, Danny.'

He said nothing but turned off the lamp and lowered himself so that he was lying next to her, his face close to hers. The stench of drink and cigarettes almost made her heave. Then his hand was on her thigh beneath her nightdress and she froze, paralysed by his touch.

'Don't you like that?'

'Do you?'

'Yes,' he said. 'I like it.'

'It's yours if you want it. I'm still your wife,' she said, but it was hard to stop the tears. She hoped that in the dark he would not notice.

'That's right, Rache. You're still my wife,' he told her. 'For better or worse. And don't you fucking forget it.' He rolled away from her with a laugh. 'But no, you haven't got to worry. I don't want it. I can't do anything with it anyway.' His laughter trailed off into coughing.

Next to him Rachel lay shaking, fighting to control the shudders and the tears that she could not stop from falling. Within minutes he was in a stupor, his snores filling up the silence in the room. She turned away from him, disgusted, wondering how he knew, and her thoughts took her away from Danny and back to the bench at the Green. Then she ran a hand along her thigh beneath her nightdress and, touching herself in the way that Kit had shown her, she thought of him and was satisfied.

'WHAT IS WRONG WITH YOU?' Jane turned to her friend at the counter, the library almost empty on a windswept morning close to Christmas. 'You haven't heard a word I've said.'

Rachel looked up in surprise.

'Actually, come to think of it, you've been in your own world for days.'

Rachel cast her eyes across the library. There was only one customer, apparently dozing over a copy of *The Times.* She lowered her eyes again to the book she was trying to repair. It would be good to tell someone but she was afraid of what Jane might say.

'What's up?' Jane persisted. 'Tell me.'

She gave up with the book and turned to her friend. 'Kit's asked me to marry him,' she said.

Jane grinned, delighted by the news. 'That's wonderful, ' she cried.

Rachel flicked a glance to the sleeping customer but he did not stir. Stepping forward, Jane put her arms round her friend in a hug of celebration, but the embrace was not returned and Jane drew back, pretty features puckered in seriousness and surprise.

'What's wrong? Don't you want to marry him?'

'I'm already married.'

'Yes, I know. But you could get a divorce, if you really wanted to. It's not like you still love him or anything. You told me ages ago that the marriage was all but over before you even started seeing Kit.'

Rachel nodded and closed her eyes against the logic of Jane's argument.

'Danny needs me,' she said. 'Where would he go if I left him? How would he live?'

'That isn't your responsibility.'

'I'm his wife.'

'But if he's beastly to you he can't expect you to stay.'

'He can't help it.'

'It makes no difference. You're still miserable. And you and Kit adore each other. You'd be so happy together. I'd be off with him like a shot.'

Rachel sighed and ran a hand through her hair. 'I loved him once,' she said. 'I loved him enough to marry him and promise to stay with him for better or worse. And even though I had no idea of how bad it could be when I said it, if I bale out now because it's got hard, then what was the point of getting married in the first place?'

She had turned this over and over in her mind until she was exhausted with the thought of it, hoping always to find a way out of such intransigent logic, but the fact remained unchanged.

'Marriage is supposed to be a partnership,' Jane said, 'between two people who love each other. Not a life sentence.'

'If I leave him he'll be out on the street. I can't do that to him. He needs me.'

'No he doesn't. He's a survivor and he's going to be miserable whether you stay or go, so there's no point in martyring yourself over him.'

'And if Roger had come back crippled and bitter? What then? Would you have just abandoned him too?'

Jane stepped back and folded her arms across her chest, eyes lowered as she pondered the question.

'I don't know,' she whispered finally. Her eyes were sad and all the fire and enthusiasm seemed to have left them. 'I can't answer that because he didn't come back and I can't allow myself to think about what might have been any more. It's too painful.'

'I'm sorry,' Rachel said quickly. 'I shouldn't have asked you that. It was cruel. I'm sorry …' She dropped her face into her hands, overwhelmed by the decision she had to make, the war between her heart and conscience.

The door of the library opened with a sweep of icy wind, and two young mothers bustled in out of the cold, chiding their toddlers towards the children's section further back. She half smiled, reminded for a moment of her own children at that age.

'Have you given Kit an answer yet?' Jane lowered her voice.

'Not yet.'

'Then there's still time. He'll wait. He loves you and he'll wait.'

Rachel was silent, but the slam of the office door yanked her attention back to the library and as Mrs Pitman approached she slunk away from the desk with a trolley of returns.

Rachel was at the desk when Andrews came into the library but she did not notice him until he slid his books across the counter and she recognised the hand that rested lightly on the cover of the topmost book. She looked up, made breathless by the pleasure of his presence, and when she saw the smile that was lurking in his eyes, the future faded out of all existence.

'Hello Rachel.'

'Kit.'

Then, looking down again to find his tickets in the box, it

was hard not to be distracted. It took longer than it should have before she found them.

'Is she here?' he whispered, leaning closer.

'She's in the office.'

'I'm not going to get you in trouble?'

'I don't care if you do.'

They faced each other across the counter and their fingers touched as she gave him the tickets, lingering for a moment. She looked away, unable to hold his eyes with the memory of the last time, and the thought that she could not keep him.

A borrower came to the counter and Rachel fumbled with the lady's tickets, unable to find them, and she was so embarrassed by her incompetence in front of Kit that she could barely see for tears. At last she found them, exactly where they were supposed to be, and she handed them over with a small smile of apology. The woman did not return the smile and turned abruptly away.

'Cheerful soul,' Kit whispered when she had gone.

Rachel said nothing, wiping away the tears with her hand. Then Jane's hoarse whisper came from the other end of the counter. 'She's coming!'

They stepped back from each other, the closeness broken as Mrs Pitman approached and Kit wandered away between the shelves, browsing, or pretending to browse. Rachel watched him until he was out of sight then all the force of the knowledge that she could not marry him took her breath away and she had to sit down.

'Are you all right?' Jane asked, squatting by the chair.

'I don't feel well.'

'Go out and get some air,' she said. 'I'll get your coat.'

Rachel nodded and as Jane went off towards the office she stood up heavily, leaning her weight on the table. Then her friend was back and helping her with her coat as she led her towards the door.

'What's going on?' Mrs Pitman's stage whisper cut through the hush.

'Rachel's not well. She's just stepping out for some air.'

The old woman hesitated, narrow lips pursed in disgruntlement, but there was nothing she could say so she turned away without a word and let them go. Outside, Rachel leant against the wall.

'He's coming,' Jane told her, leaning back to check through the door. 'Good luck.'

'Thanks.'

Then Kit was there and he touched his cap in thanks to Jane before she disappeared back inside.

'Are you all right?'

'No,' she replied, and the tears she had fought away till then began to come.

'Come on,' he said. He put his arm round her shoulders and led her up the hill to the Victorian church on the corner. She had never been inside before, though she had passed it a thousand times, and it was cold and bare and dimly lit. Near the front, people were moving about, setting out hymn books and flowers.

'There's going to be a wedding,' Kit said.

'Or a funeral.'

He smiled and they sat on a hard wooden bench near the back. Rachel rested her head on his shoulder as he held her hand and waited patiently. She wanted to weep and rail against the unfairness of it all but the tears flowed silently and she had no energy for more. When finally they stopped, she lifted her face to look at him. Very gently, he smoothed stray wisps of hair back from her temples.

'Tell me,' he said.

She shook her head, afraid to seal the decision she had made.

He looked away from her towards the altar, eyes observing the people's movements as they wandered to and fro.

'I think I deserve to know,' he said.

'Yes,' she whispered. 'Yes, you do, only I keep thinking that if I don't tell you yet that maybe something might happen that will change things, and make it possible to tell you something different.'

He dropped his eyes to the cap he held in his hands, turning it over and over, examining the worn lining with each spin. 'So I take it your answer is no?'

'I'm sorry.'

He turned to her then, fierce with hurt and frustration. 'Why?' he demanded in a whisper through lips drawn taut with anger. A young woman in a threadbare coat entered the church and walked down the aisle and he followed her with his eyes for a moment before he turned back to Rachel. 'Why won't you leave him?'

'He's my husband.'

'You owe him nothing.'

'He needs me.'

'*I* need you.'

'He's the father of my children.'

'I'd be a better father to them.'

She buried her face in her hands. 'He has nothing. Nothing.'

Kit dragged her hands from her face, but she was terrified to look at him, the strength of her decision too frail to withstand his gaze.

'He has everything,' Kit hissed. 'He has everything that I want and he squanders it.'

'He's been through so much.'

'So have I,' Kit countered. 'But I still know how to love you.'

'He can't love me,' she whispered back. 'Not as you can. Not as any other man can.'

'Did he ever love you as I do?'

She said nothing, his logic too perfect to argue against. But though her heart writhed with the pain of her decision, the stubbornness of her conscience did not waver. Kit sat back away from her, turning the cap in his hand again. In his profile she could see the tension in his jaw.

'I'm sorry Kit,' she murmured. 'I wish it could be different. But if I left him I'd come to hate myself and then you'd grow to hate me too and it would all have been for nothing.'

He nodded but said nothing and in her sorrow for his pain the urge to give him what he wanted almost overwhelmed her.

'I'd better get back,' she said, and got to her feet. 'Can I see you at lunchtime? One o'clock?'

He turned to look up at her and his eyes were charged with tears. He nodded.

'You're going to stay here? Watch the wedding?'

'Or the funeral.' He tried to smile.

'One o'clock then.

'Yes.'

She left him there and at the door she turned back but he was already kneeling and as she hurried back down the hill to the library she wondered what prayers he was saying, and if God would answer them.

KIT WAS WAITING at the door when she went out at one o'clock, lifting his feet one at a time in gentle rhythm in an effort to keep warm. His breath condensed before him in small whiffs of cloud. He smiled when he saw her, and took her arm in his as they hurried towards the restaurant.

'Are you all right?' Rachel asked.

'I'm fine,' he replied with a small tight smile that gave the lie to his words. But she understood he did not want to talk about it and held his arm more tightly. It was impossible to believe when she was with him that she could choose to give him up.

At the restaurant they sat next to the window. The glass ran with condensation and with a gloved hand Rachel wiped a small space clear and peered out. Outside, people strode past in the cold and the clear patch quickly clouded over, obscuring the world beyond it. Kit ordered soup for both of them.

'It was a wedding,' he said, when the waiter had gone.

'Did you stay?'

He shook his head.

'Danny knows about us,' she said then. She had meant to tell him earlier, but in the turmoil and the sadness of her refusal of his offer, Danny knowing had seemed almost unimportant. Now, sitting having lunch with Kit in public, it began to matter again.

'You're sure?'

'Yes.'

'What happened?'

She hesitated, embarrassed to describe the details over lunch.

'Rachel?'

'I can't tell you now,' she said. 'But he knows.' She would tell him another time, in the intimacy of their hotel room, when they were in bed together and there were no secrets between them. In a restaurant she could not talk about such things.

Kit's eyes settled on the misted window, intent, as though he would see through it by sheer determination, and she could not guess what he was thinking.

He turned back to her. 'How did he find out?'

Rachel shrugged, still reluctant to lay the blame on Kate.

'Kate?'

'I don't know.' Perhaps she should ask her, she thought, and find out the truth. Perhaps.

'How else?'

'Maybe someone saw us together. Someone Danny sees at the pub. We haven't exactly been discreet.'

'I suppose it's possible,' he conceded. 'But just because we've been seen together doesn't necessarily make us lovers. How could he know that?'

'He isn't stupid.'

'No,' Kit said quickly. 'Of course not. That's not what I meant.'

She looked at him across the table, saw him awkward and uncomfortable and hurt, and wished that she could hold him and tell him everything would be all right. She reached out for his hand and held his fingers so that he looked up at her and smiled.

'But he hasn't confronted you?'

'Not exactly.'

'Well, he must have his reasons.'

The waiter brought the bowls of soup, and it was hot and comforting. When they had almost finished eating Kit looked up at her again.

'Let's talk about something else,' he said. 'Let's forget about Danny and Kate and the future.'

She smiled. 'All right.'

Then they sat in silence, both of them searching for something to say until they started to laugh with the absurdity of it.

'I've got something,' Rachel said.

He smiled and gestured with his hand, inviting her to speak.

'Have you got any brothers or sisters?' It seemed such a trite thing to ask but there was so much she did not know about him, so many questions she wanted to ask that it was hard to know where to begin.

He laughed. 'Yes, Rachel. I have one brother.'

'Tell me about him.'

'What would you like to know?'

She laughed too, exasperated by his teasing. 'Oh come on, Kit.'

'I'm sorry.'

'So?'

'His name is Edward and he's three years older than me.'

'Is he in the forces?'

'He's an army chaplain.'

'Your father must be proud.'

He smiled. 'Yes, he is. And all the more so for it being so unexpected. Everyone always thought it would be me who went into the church. Edward was the wild one when we were boys.'

'Why didn't you go into the church?' She remembered seeing him kneel to pray and realised she knew nothing of his faith, what he believed.

'It just wasn't what I wanted to do.'

'But you believe?'

'Yes. And you?'

'I don't know any more. What with the war, and Danny, and you. None of it seems to make any sense any more.'

'I understand.'

'When I first met you,' she said, 'I used to pray for the strength to forget about you, and then, later on, when I knew that to forget you was impossible I prayed for the strength to resist you. I was terrified of what I felt for you, of what it meant. But even as I prayed I hoped that God wouldn't answer because I wanted you so much that the rules didn't seem to matter so much any more.'

All the laughter had left his face, serious now, observing her. 'And now?'

'And now I think that perhaps I'm wicked because what we're doing doesn't seem to be that wrong to me. Beside all the killing and the hatred and brutality, how can truly loving someone be so wrong?'

'It isn't.'

'So I don't feel guilty about God but I do about Danny. Silly, isn't it?'

'No,' he replied. 'It's not silly. You made promises to Danny that you feel it would be wrong to break. I understand that. I don't want to. I want to persuade you to break all your promises and come with me, give yourself a chance at happiness.' He fixed his eyes on hers so that she could not look away, pinned by their intensity. 'You know,' he went on, 'that if you got divorced from Danny and married me, that in the eyes of God you'd be doing nothing wrong? You know that, don't you?'

'Yes,' she answered. 'I know that.'

He nodded and the brightness of his gaze ebbed a little. 'But you have to live with your conscience,' he said. 'And in the end I have to accept that.' He reached across to take her hand, turning the wedding band gently to and fro between his fingers. 'Take it off,' he whispered. 'Please? Just for a moment let me imagine that it doesn't exist.'

She slipped the ring from her finger with surprising ease. Her hand looked strange to her without it, someone else's hand, the woman she wished she could be, and the ring sat accusingly bright on the whiteness of the tablecloth. Both of them looked at it, drawn to its power as all that stood between them. Then quickly, afraid of the freedom its absence from her finger gave her, she took it up again and put it on.

Kit smiled wryly. 'For a moment there, I thought I almost had you.'

'I've got to go,' Rachel said. 'Mrs Pitman will kill me if I'm late again.'

'Do you care?'

She laughed, considering. 'No, I don't. Not really.'

They stood up and Kit helped her with her coat and the touch of his fingers against her neck almost brought her to her knees. 'When next?' she asked.

'It'll have to be tomorrow or Saturday. I'm going home over Christmas for a few days.'

She had quite forgotten about Christmas and she remembered now with a jolt – the library closed for the holidays, all of them at home, and no chance for escape to the sanctuary Kit's company offered.

'Tomorrow then. I finish at one.

'I'll be there.'

They left the restaurant arm-in-arm and walked back in comfortable silence to the library.

Chapter Sixteen

It was strange to be home for Christmas, the first time in three years, and Kit stepped off the bus in Marlborough High Street with a sense of unreality, everything so familiar, just as he remembered it, but no longer where he belonged. The town was still unchanged, unchanging over generations he supposed, the same tea room still behind the bus stop; the pub, the town hall, the church. Everything exactly matched his memories but he felt a calm indifference to it, no awakening sense of affection or nostalgia, no feelings of belonging: it was as though the town had never had a claim on him. He shivered in the bitter wind, shouldered his kitbag, and began the long walk towards home.

He walked along the well-known lanes automatically, head down against the cold, and hardly noticed his surroundings, the bare winter fields behind the hedgerows, rutted mud frozen hard beneath his boots and difficult to walk on. He allowed his thoughts to wander idly and afterwards he could not have said what had occupied his mind.

It was late in the afternoon when he got to the village, early winter dusk beginning to settle, and no one about. A redpetalled poppy wreath stood propped against the war memorial and he paused as he passed it to look for a moment. There would be more names to add now, he thought. More mourners each Armistice Day. He turned away, tried to force his thoughts to something else, and they came to rest on Rachel, their last conversation. He would never bring her here, he thought, looking around him at the low brick cottages, the village green, the horse chestnut trees, all a part of him, however much he changed. Depressed, he walked on through the village towards the little church and the vicarage beside it.

His parents were delighted to see him: an emotional embrace from his mother, a hand warmly shaken by his father. They had seen him only once since his return from Italy.

'It's wonderful to see you, Kit,' his father said. 'And looking so well. How's the leg?'

'Not too bad,' he replied, as he dropped his cane into the umbrella stand by the door. His knee was paining from the long walk and the cold. 'Not too bad at all.'

'Splendid, splendid. Well, come in and have some tea. Your mother's been on tenterhooks all day.'

His mother smiled, embarrassed, and ushered him through to the kitchen, warm from the stove, the kettle hissing on the hob.

'We spend most of our time in here now,' she told him. 'It's the easiest room to keep warm.'

Kit sat at his old place at the table, rubbed the worn warm wood with his fingers. An aroma of something baking, familiar from childhood, filled the air, and brief images of boyhood passed through his mind, fleeting and intangible. For a moment he was moved by a vague nostalgia, but the memories quickly faded and he sensed the distance between the boy he had been and the man he had become.

'How long have we got you for?' his father asked.

'I go back on the twenty-seventh.'

'So short?' His mother turned from the stove with the teapot in her hand, swirling it gently to help it brew.

'I'm afraid so.'

'Never mind,' his father consoled. 'It's lovely that you could come at all. Far more than we expected.'

Kit nodded and took the tea his mother gave him, strong and bitter, how he remembered, but good anyway for being hot. He sipped it, fingers warming against its heat, and wondered how Rachel made her tea. He remembered she had given him tea the first time he met her at the house but his mind had been on other things that day and he had no memory of how it had tasted.

'How was the trip down?'

His mother sat at the table across from him and smiled. She had aged since the image of her he carried in his mind in Italy, the bun at the nape of her neck smaller than it used to be, greyer, but the light in her eyes was still kind and shrewd, and he was reassured by it as he had always been as a boy.

'The trip was long,' he replied. 'And cold. I'd forgotten how many places the bus actually stops between here and Bristol.'

'Yes. It's quite a few isn't it.'

A dog barked at the back door and Mrs Andrews got up to open it. Two large golden labradors bounded in, delighted to see their old playmate. Kit bent to make a fuss of them.

'Sherpa's getting old.' He turned to his father, still rubbing the grizzled head of the older dog. 'He's going grey.'

'Aren't we all,' his father smiled. 'Aren't we all.'

There was a comfortable silence. The younger dog moved off to settle himself in the warmth of the basket in the corner but Sherpa stayed, resting his head on his old master's knee. Kit rubbed his ears fondly, remembering him as a puppy, chewed books and shoes and mess everywhere, all forgiven with a tilt of the head and an offered paw. Time was when they were inseparable, boy and dog, but it was years since he had even thought about him. A rush of affection welled with regret and, fighting against it, he turned to his mother with a determined smile.

'Is it open house for Christmas Eve as usual?'

'Of course.'

'All the regulars?'

'Mostly just the regulars' wives,' Mr Andrews said. 'The regulars are still away, by and large.'

'And we see a lot less of the wives than we used to. Most of them have volunteered for one service or another…'

'Quite right too,' her husband interrupted.

'Of course,' Mrs Andrews agreed. 'Only it makes so much work for your father, with no one to help him any more.'

'We manage,' Mr Andrews told his son. 'Can't complain.'

'It's too much for him really,' Kit's mother said. 'But he'd never admit it. You know what he's like.'

Kit smiled and took another mouthful of tea. His father shot him an amused and long-suffering glance.

'I'm perfectly all right. You know how she fusses.'

'She's just trying to look after you.'

'Don't you start.'

Kit observed his parents, their affection for each other still undimmed across the years, his mother's gentle chiding of his father's efforts in the parish. The vicar would have worked himself to skin and bone without his wife to make him eat and rest sometimes.

'So you see, Kit,' his mother said. '*Plus ça change …*'

'So I can see.'

'Everyone's looking forward to seeing you,' Mrs Andrews told him. 'They all ask after you. And Edward.'

'How is Edward?' It was a while since he had heard from his brother.

'He's still in France,' she replied. 'He seems well enough

but he never really tells us very much. Not like your letters. We always used to so enjoy your letters.'

'I know. I know. I should write more often.'

'Only when you have time.'

He finished his tea. His mother took the cup to the sink and washed it out, and the silence seemed heavier, less comfortable than it had ever used to do. He could think of nothing else to say.

On Christmas Eve he stood in the large front reception room that was used only for visitors. Two girls he did not recognise were attempting a duet on the dusty grand piano that his mother sometimes played, giggling loudly with each mistake, and Grace Whitlow moved around the room with a tray of sandwiches while her sister Alice tried to restrain an unruly toddler. He had known the Whitlow girls all his life – they lived just along the lane – and in their childhood they had been constant companions, two brothers and two sisters, a little gang with their own rules and codes, intricate games developed from one school holiday to the next.

Grace caught his eye across the room. She was caught with an elderly neighbour well-known for his long reminiscences. Kit gave her a sympathetic smile. The old man wittered on, a story Grace had heard a hundred times before no doubt, until finally she managed to make her excuses and ducked hurriedly away. She crossed the room towards Kit.

'Hello stranger,' she smiled.

'Hello Grace.'

'Sandwich?'

He took one, fish paste, and, after a short pause, ate it out of politeness.

'Very good,' he said.

'Really? I'm sure you're used to much better fare.'

'It's the company that counts,' he said.

'Of course it is.' She smiled, pleased by the compliment. 'How are you? It must be very strange to be back after so long.'

'It is,' he agreed. 'I'm finding it all very strange. But pleasant,' he qualified, 'very pleasant.'

She smiled, lighting up the plain, placid face. 'It must be lovely to see your family. They miss you very much. We all do. We talk about you often. And Edward too of course.'

'Thank you,' he answered automatically. 'Of course it's lovely to be here, lovely to see you all.' Then, 'And how have you been, Grace? Are you keeping well?'

'I'm fine. You know me, I keep busy.'

He nodded but said nothing, wondering what a girl like Grace would do with herself all day beyond the household chores. Despite the long acquaintance, he barely knew a thing about her: they had rarely spoken since their childhood. What went on behind that patient smile, he wondered. Was there a deeper secret self? Dreams and passions he knew nothing of? He thought it seemed unlikely.

'Your mother said you're based in Bristol now?' Grace kept the conversation going.

'That's right.'

'I went there once a long time ago, as a child. I've forgotten why now, but I remember it seemed very large and very busy. I didn't like it much. I suppose it's even busier now.'

'I should think so.'

She smiled again, and they stood in amicable silence; long years of familiarity had made them comfortable together. His mother came over and, touching her son's arm with a gentle reassurance, she took the tray of sandwiches from Grace.

'I'll do that,' she said. 'So you two can talk. I'm sure you must have lots to catch up on.'

'We've been talking,' Grace replied, stepping away from Kit. 'And I like to help. Really I do.'

Mrs Andrews drew back. 'I insist. You've done far too much already.' She gave her son a quick small smile and turned away to offer the tray to an elderly couple by the window. Kit watched her go, and his gaze was drawn out through the glass behind them towards the dark winter landscape beyond.

Fifty miles away beyond that frozen garden, hidden within the room's reflection, was Rachel. She would be with her children now, he imagined, preparing for their Christmas; wrapping presents, filling stockings, sharing all the magic of a family at this time. And Danny would be there, reluctant perhaps, ill-tempered, drunk, but part of it just the same.

He drew his thoughts back to the room around him, let his eyes graze his mother's decorations, unchanged since he was a boy. He could remember the rituals each year of collecting the holly and making the wreathes, climbing trees for the mistletoe to hang from the lampshades, the time he caught Edward kissing a girl underneath it, secretly in the dark. He wondered what his brother was doing now, if he would spend this Christmas safe and in peace. He tried not to remember last year, a cold Italian hillside.

Once, he thought, the mystery of Christmas had moved him, a magical mystical time of wonder, but now it left him cold, an irrelevance, and his indifference made him sad. Perhaps at church tonight, he thought. Perhaps communion could penetrate the walls.

'Kit?' Grace was speaking at his side, and he had heard nothing of what she said. 'Kit? Are you all right?'

He gave her a half-smile that Rachel would have known was a lie.

'I'm fine,' he said. 'Just thinking.'

'You were miles away,' she said. 'Staring into space.'

'Was I? Yes, I suppose I was. I'm sorry.'

She smiled again. 'Well, it's lovely to have you home at last.'

'Thank you,' he murmured. But his mind had already wandered back to Rachel, and he did not know how he would get through the days without her.

Chapter Seventeen

She had always loved Christmas before: she remembered the sense of wonder as a child, the carols and the presents and the magic of it, the church transformed, the house pretty with its garlands of holly and ivy and streamers. Dressing the tree had been her special job as soon as she was old enough and she had always spent hours placing each decoration in its perfect place: the scent of pine could still evoke those memories of childish innocence. After she was married, she had kept up the tradition, planning the decorations for weeks, the flat bedecked and beautiful in celebration. Danny had teased her at first, gently, with affection, and when the children came along he had begun to understand the joy of it, offering his help to hang the higher garlands, to set up the tree. They were memories of a happier time, an innocence the war had shattered.

She tried to make it special again this year, picking out special presents and wrapping them with care, searching out the prettiest holly with reddest berries, but her heart wasn't in it. It seemed a hollow imitation of the joy of earlier years and only the children showed any interest. So she did it for them, hoping to make up somehow for all that had gone before.

But the tension in the house was almost tangible, all of them at home and nowhere to escape. The ill-feeling simmered, unspoken, all of them skirting Danny's moods with care. George for once held his peace, a concession, she supposed, to Christmas good will to all men, but the days until Kit's return seemed endless. She thought about him constantly, imagining his days in Marlborough, the life she was choosing to give up. The images turned in her mind over and over, trapping her in an endless repetitive loop that sapped her spirit and wearied her.

Danny had said nothing more about Kit but she caught him watching her often, observing her in a different light as if the new knowledge about her made him curious, searching her for some quality he had not seen before. Once or twice she met his look with defiance in her eyes, a dare which met with a knowing smile, but mostly she just turned away from him, no energy for the game he seemed to want to play. Always in the back of her mind was the question of how he knew, and however unwilling she was to believe it, every time she followed the path of her thoughts, it only ever led to Kate.

KATE'S DIARY was hard to find, no longer tucked beneath the books in her bedside cabinet as it had been when they were children. Momentarily thwarted, Rachel sat on her sister's bed and tried to think where it might be. She knew without doubt it was here, somewhere – her sister had kept a journal always, so she could remember her life when she was old, she once said. But where?

Rachel let her gaze travel slowly across the room, searching for possible hiding places. Then, suddenly impatient to get it over with, she stood up and began to rummage in Kate's drawers, turning over clothes and underwear, searching through the odds and ends of make up and ribbons and hair clips that filled up the dressing table drawers. Nothing.

She closed the drawers and turned to lean against them, still searching. It was hard to remember that this had been her room for all those years: there was no trace of her presence left, Kate's stamp was on everything. Even the pictures had changed, the walls hung now with photographs of American movie stars. If the diary were hers, she thought, where would she put it?

Carefully, she lifted each picture off its hook to look behind it. She picked up the corners of the carpet. She knelt to peer under the bed. Still nothing. Then, as she sat back on her heels to think again, inspiration lit. Slowly, almost reluctant now to find it, she edged her hand beneath the mattress, fingers sliding across the rough surface of the divan, the mattress pressing heavily on the back of her hand until her fingertips brushed against something hard. With one swift movement she caught hold of it and drew it from its place, her heartbeat quick with guilt and nerves even though there was no one else at home, everyone back at work now after Christmas and the children playing with the neighbour's kids next door.

The cardboard covers were rough to the touch and on the front Kate had written her name in neat tiny handwriting.

KATE ANN KIRBY.

Rachel swallowed, afraid of what she might find and of the person she had become that would read her sister's diary. Then she held it close to her body and ran downstairs to the privacy of her bedroom.

Flicking through the close-written pages she saw it covered many years. The entries were sporadic, months missing at a time, then pages filled with details of people Rachel did not know, and the minutiae of Kate's days. She tried to find pages that covered the last few weeks but the dates seemed to be jumbled and she could not at first find what she was looking for. Then she saw her own name amongst the words, and Danny's, and though the year was 1939 and she had promised herself she would only look as far as she needed, her eyes were inevitably drawn. Slowly, she sat down on the bed and began to read.

7 December 1939

It all began three weeks ago. I've been too afraid to write till now because committing the words to paper makes it real and I'm not quite sure that's how I want it to be. Well, here goes. Three weeks ago I went to bed with Danny for the first time, and now I'm my sister's husband's lover. There. That wasn't so bad and it hasn't changed a thing.

What's surprised me is just how easy it's all been. I've seen him almost every day – Rachel's so tired with her pregnancy that it's no trouble for us to get away together. We've used the shed, out the back of the shop, their bedroom, my bedroom: we laughed about that and said we ought to keep count of how many places we've 'christened.'

Yesterday we talked about Rachel and he told me that he loves her, as a wife and as the mother of his children, but that she doesn't excite him like I do. He said that I satisfy him completely, that she won't do for him the things that I do. It hurt to hear that he loves her – I want him to love me, not Rachel, but perhaps in time. Strange, now that it's happened I don't even feel that guilty about it – like we're meant to be together and so there's nothing wrong. I felt worse about it all when I was still chasing him, trying to get him to notice me. All the same, I've avoided Rachel as much as possible and she's so very very pregnant I don't think she's noticed. We've arranged to meet again tonight and I can't wait…

Horrified, Rachel stopped reading for a moment, the shock of the words before her too terrible to grasp. Then, consumed by a need to know more, she lowered her eyes again to the page and read on.

January 20, 1940

Rachel's baby was born last week, a little girl called Jean. Rachel's still in hospital so I've spent lots of time with Danny. He's thinking about volunteering and I'm trying to talk him out of it. I don't want him going off getting himself killed when we're having such a good time.

Last night we went to visit Rachel at the hospital together. She's so wrapped up in the baby that she'd never suspect and afterwards we went to the pub. Danny tried to pretend that he wasn't moved by his daughter but I could see when he held her that she meant the world to him. Then he smiled at Rachel like she was the only woman in the world and I had to go out. It hurts too much to see them as a happy family when I want to believe that he hates her, that it's only me he loves. But I know that isn't true because he and Rachel are great friends and I suppose that's more important in a marriage than the other, but I wish it were true and then he'd need only me.

She stopped, the years of happy marriage ripped away as though her life had been rewritten, her memories no longer to be trusted. Trembling now, she flicked forward through the pages towards more recent entries, forcing herself to search for confirmation of what she knew now must be true. This time she found it easily.

December 3, 1944

I told Danny today that Rachel's having an affair with Andrews. I don't know why I did it, really. I think I just felt he had the right to know. But he didn't react how I thought he would – he seemed far angrier with Andrews than he did with Rachel, and said he wouldn't confront her. That's up to him, I suppose. Then he seemed to have some sort of nervous episode so I left him to it.

Rachel dropped the book to her lap and sat motionless, unable to will her limbs to move. She had wanted only to know what Kate had told her husband but she had stumbled on knowledge that sickened her, her world crumbling under her feet. Her own fault, she thought; the fate of those who pry. But what her sister had done was worse.

She sat in silence and the tick of her watch grew louder in the quiet afternoon until her eyes were drawn at last to its face. It was after twelve and she was due to start work at one. She swallowed, nausea lurching in her stomach. She could not work. She could not face the world. Slowly, like an old woman, she heaved herself up from the bed and the light of her reflection in the mirror caught her eye. She stood and looked at it, and the face that peered back was so plain and sad that she could almost understand why Danny had preferred to love Kate, with her prettiness and vivacity. She scowled at the face in the mirror, wishing she could see herself through Kit's eyes and believe that she was beautiful.

She left the house as though for work but went instead to the phone box and rang through to the library. Mrs Pitman answered and in a voice that shook with held-back tears, Rachel told her she was ill. The old woman coldly thanked her for ringing but Rachel did not care: she could have been fired there and then and it would not have mattered. Then she rang Kit on the number he had given her.

He took an age to come to the phone and she could hear the muffled voices in the background as she waited for him to come. It was the first time she had rung him and she hoped he would not mind. Then his voice came on the line and with the sound of him all doubts vanished.

'Andrews.'

'Kit. It's Rachel.'

'Rachel.' He lowered his voice and she imagined him turning his back to the other men in the room, cupping his hand over the receiver so that they could not hear. 'Are you all right?'

'I need to see you.'

'Where are you?'

'Home. I've rung in sick to work.'

'I can finish at three,' he said. 'I'll meet you at the hotel.'

'Thank you,' she whispered. 'Thank you.'

She put down the receiver and left the phone box for the impatient old woman who had stood close to the glass as she talked, foot tapping the pavement. Above her the clouds hung low and full, heavy with their burden of rain, and she wished that she had an umbrella.

She walked slowly across the Green, resigned to the coming of the rain, and at the bench she thought of as theirs she sat for a while staring at nothing, thoughts still numb from what she had learned. A few first drops of rain began to fall and she got up and walked on, taking the back streets off Whiteladies Road that led amongst the grand Georgian houses so she wouldn't have to pass the library. She went past the pub she had gone to with Kit but she got no pleasure from the memory as she would have done another day and she walked on with her head down against the worsening rain.

She was near the hotel when the downpour began to fall heavily, lashing the road at her feet, blinding, and there was nowhere for her to shelter so she walked on through the deluge, her clothes clinging to her cold and wet. She needed Kit, and did not know how she would last the next two hours without him.

She was in the room when he got there, huddled in the cold semi-darkness, the fire unlit. She was still wearing her coat, shivering as she lifted her eyes across the gloom towards him, and the look in them was desolate. Hurriedly, he squatted down to light the fire, fumbling for the sixpence, the match snapping loud in the silence. Outside, rain gusted hard against the windows. The flames caught in the rush of gas and he turned from it and went to sit beside her on the bed. She moved into him immediately, curled up like an upset child, and he held her, without words, though the urge to ask her what was wrong was almost desperate. He could only guess that she had fought with Danny, that he had confronted her at last.

Minutes passed before she shifted and with her movement he touched her face with his fingers, lifting it to look up into his. Her eyes were washed with tears, eyelashes silky and dark and he thought how beautiful she was, even in her sadness. He wished he had the talent to paint her as she looked now, the tragic heroine.

'What's happened?' he whispered. 'What's wrong?'

She shook her head, the words still too hard to find.

'Come to the fire,' he said. 'Come and get warm.'

With his arm round her shoulders he took her to the fire and helped her to sit on the rug before it. She reached her hands out to the warmth, and half smiled at him as he sat on the chair to one side, leaning forward, elbows on his knees, but not touching her, allowing her room. He smiled in return and she turned her gaze back to the flames.

'They were lovers,' she said. 'Danny and Kate. They were lovers. All that time I thought we were happy together and they were lovers. My husband and my sister. They were lovers …' She sighed, the betrayal still too great to comprehend completely, and Andrews said nothing, watching her, waiting for her to go on.

Then she swung round to him and the light in her eyes was different.

'You knew,' she cried, with sudden realisation. 'You knew all along. When you asked if I was sure that he'd been faithful, when you thought it was Kate who had told him. You knew.'

'Yes.'

There was a silence. The hiss of the gas fire grew loud and the splatter of the rain outside seemed far away.

'Why didn't you tell me?' she asked, shifting her body round to face him, skin reddening now in the heat. She was kneeling at his feet, bewildered, and he did not know how he could explain. 'Why?' she repeated. 'I don't understand.'

'There's no one reason,' he said.

He had fought with himself long and hard about it. Ever since the first time he met her, he had wanted to tell her the truth, but each time he decided to tell her it had seemed pointless, and cruel.

'What good would it have done you if you'd known before?' he asked. 'How much has it hurt you? There was no need for you to know and I still think it would have been better if you'd never found out.'

He held her eyes with his own, praying she would understand, that she would not hate him for keeping secrets. She turned away, still uncertain, attention drawn again to the warm orange flames in the darkening room. Watching her, this woman who had saved him, he thought he should be more honest, tell her the real reason for his silence.

'And …' he began.

In the pause she lifted her head, waiting, and he could not read the light in her eyes. He took a deep breath.

'And I wanted you to make your decision about me without knowing.'

Her expression softened. Into sadness? Pity? He could not say.

'How did you know?' she asked.

'He told me.'

'He told you?' He heard the disbelief in her tone. 'Why would he tell you?'

Andrews hesitated, searching for the right words to explain, taking his mind back to a world he preferred to forget. He said,

'You get close to the men you fight with, especially when you spend days in a trench with not much else to do but wait for an attack and listen to the shelling.' He smiled at her, needing encouragement, unsure if he was telling it right. She gave him a small nod as though she understood, and he went on. 'There was a lot of that at Anzio, and sometimes men share confidences in that kind of situation that they'd keep to themselves at home.'

He paused and changed his position, stretching out his injured leg to ease it, but he kept his eyes on her as he spoke.

'He got a letter from Kate when we were there. A Dear John letter.'

Rachel dropped her eyes, and he guessed she was trying to imagine it, to see the two men together in a dugout somewhere, a closeness between them she had not suspected.

'When he showed it to me,' Kit said softly, 'he was crying.'

'You read it?'

'No. There was no need.'

He lifted himself down from the chair and sat next to her on the rug. Her hands were warm between his own cold fingers and she looked down at their hands entwined for a moment before she moved her own away.

'He loved her,' Kit said quickly, anxious that shock was turning into anger, that soon his silence would be the cause of her pain. 'And when she wrote and said she didn't want him any more, it broke him. On top of the war and the deaths of his friends, it was just too much for him to take.'

'He told you that?'

'More or less.'

Rachel nodded and let her head rest against his shoulder. Relieved, he put an arm round her and they sat for a while, uncomfortable, legs and faces scorching in the heat. But he was reluctant to disturb her and so he waited for her to speak again.

'That's why you hate him so much,' she said. She moved back from his embrace to face him again. 'That's why you say he doesn't deserve me. And that's why he hasn't confronted me. Because he doesn't know whether or not you've told me.'

'I would guess.'

She was silent, eyes lowered, still considering, and he could not read her face.

'Are you all right?' he asked.

'I don't know. I think so. I don't really know what I feel.'

'It's been a shock for you.' A thought occurred to him. 'How did you find out?'

'I read Kate's diary. I wanted to know if she'd told him about us and that's what I found. Serves me right, really.'

'You aren't angry with me that I didn't tell you?' He had also kept secrets from her, and he was all too aware of how that must seem to her now.

She said nothing.

'Rachel?'

She raised her eyes to look at him.

'Yes,' she said. 'I'm angry. Of course I'm angry.'

She sat up on her heels then, roused to energy, and he moved back from her, wary of a side of her he did not know.

'How could you not have told me all this time, when you knew how guilty I felt?'

'I thought it was better that you didn't know.'

'I don't need you to protect me, Kit,' she said. 'I need you to be honest with me, to tell me the truth about things. How can I trust you otherwise?'

He dropped his head. 'I'm sorry,' he whispered. 'I'm so sorry. I thought it was for the best. And I didn't want to hurt you.'

She was silent and when he lifted his face again she was watching him, an expression in her eyes he had not seen before.

'I'm sorry,' he said again.

She nodded then and reached to touch his wrist with her fingers, a gesture of forgiveness.

'I understand why you did it,' she murmured. 'But no more secrets, please? I don't care what they are, no matter how much you think they'll hurt me.'

'All right.'

'Promise?'

'I promise.'

They sat in awkward silence, neither knowing what to say. When he could bear the tension no longer he got up and went to the window to draw the curtains against the afternoon. Rain was still gusting along the street, bouncing off the road, cold and hostile. He stood for a moment to watch it before he pulled the curtains closed. Then he turned towards her. She was watching him, waiting, and when he returned to the fire he lay down across the rug and rested his head on her thigh as if nothing had changed. She smiled and stroked the hair from his temples with gentle fingers and he knew he was forgiven.

'Do you have nightmares too?' she asked him.

His eyes flicked up to hers. She was looking down, observing him. 'Sometimes.'

'Danny has them almost every night,' she said. 'That's why he drinks.'

'He drinks because he's full of hate,' Kit said.

She said nothing but kept on smoothing his hair.

He said, 'I love you, Rachel.'

'I know,' she replied.

He laughed and reached up to draw her down to him and they lay together on the threadbare rug in front of the fire. He made love to her, more tender and gentle than he had ever been, losing himself in the peace it seemed that only this could give him. Afterwards, he dragged the quilt off the bed to keep them warm.

'Do I satisfy you?' Rachel asked. She was resting her head on his chest, fingers trailing absently back and forth across his stomach, tickling, the argument forgotten.

He looked down at her in surprise and smiled, but she did not lift her face to look at him.

'What makes you say that?'

'Something Kate said, about satisfying Danny in ways I couldn't even dream of.'

They lay in silence. Then she said, 'You didn't answer the question.'

'Of course you satisfy me,' he said quickly. He was horrified that she could think anything else. 'Of course, of course you do.'

'There's nothing else you'd like me to do?'

'No.'

'I didn't love him like I love you,' she whispered. 'I didn't want him, all of him, like I want you.'

'It sounds like it was mutual.'

'I'd do anything for you. Anything to make you happy or give you pleasure.'

'Except leave Danny.' The words escaped unbidden and he regretted them immediately, knowing they would hurt her. But it was only the truth, after all.

Rachel sat up, upset, and he followed, moving round to sit in front of her. The heat of the fire burned against his back.

'Look at me, Rachel,' he urged. 'Please.'

She kept her eyes resolutely lowered, and he felt her stubbornness beginning to ebb. If he could only get her to look at him. He held her chin with the fingers of one hand and tried to tilt it towards him, but she jerked her head away.

'Why won't you leave him? Why does he have this hold on you? Even after all he's done.'

'He's my husband,' she whispered. 'And he could have left me for her. But he didn't. He stayed.'

'He's lied and he's cheated.' Frustration at her intransigence surged inside him into fury and his voice was raised as he went on. 'He slept with your sister for Christ's sake! For almost two years! He's a drunk, he bullies you. What does he have to do to make you leave him?'

She shrank under his anger, wrapped her arms round herself in defence, but he felt no pity, only rage that she would throw away this chance they had together, that his love was not enough to tempt her. In disgust and disappointment he levered himself onto the bed away from her. Rachel began to cry.

'I don't understand you,' he said. 'You've got every reason to leave him.'

'I know,' she sobbed.

'Then why? Don't you love me? Don't you care about what I feel?'

'Of course I do.' She turned to look up at him, and he got up and moved away, standing by the window with his back to her, peering out through a gap in the curtains. The street was empty and dark and the rain had quietened into a freezing bitter mist.

'But you still care more for him,' he murmured to the glass. 'Why else?'

He turned back into the room and she had not moved, still huddled before the fire, watching him with sad fearful eyes.

'Why else?'

'I don't want to fight with you, Kit,' she said. 'Please? Please can we be friends again?'

'Answer the question.'

She sighed, still unwilling to argue. She said, 'Because he needs me. Without me he'd be on the street, and I could never live with myself knowing that.'

'I need you.'

'Don't, Kit. Don't do this. We've been through this before.'

He swallowed, hesitating, anger struggling with his love for her, his need to cherish her while he could. How could he make her change her mind? How could he make her come to him? He moved towards her, knelt awkwardly beside her next to the fire, touched a hand to her face, her cheek against his palm.

'Rachel, please? I'd make you happy. You know I would.'

'It's not about my happiness, Kit. Or yours.' She was crying now, tears warm against his hand.

'So he gets what he wants and we both go without.'

She closed her eyes and moved her head away from his hand and he knew that he had failed. He let his hand drop to his side.

'Can we stop fighting now?' she whispered. She took his hand in hers, looked up into his face. 'Please?'

He nodded, lifting his arms a little from his sides in a gesture of invitation, then he held her as she clung to him. But always inside him there lurked the shadow of their future separation, and the knowledge that it was in her power to prevent it.

THEY HAD dinner in their room because they were loath to leave its sanctuary. They sat, half-undressed in front of the fire, quiet in its heat on their skin, little to say after all the emotions of earlier, but comfortable in each other's company again. Andrews thought that marriage to her would be like this, a lifetime of peaceful evenings.

Just before nine, he said, 'We should start getting ready. It's almost time to go.'

'Can we stay?' she said.

He stared at her in surprise and she held his gaze. There was no trace of the sad anxious girl of before.

'Can we stay the night here?' she repeated. 'I want to stay the night with you.'

'Of course,' he said quickly. 'Of course we can stay.'

'You won't get in trouble?'

'No. But what about your family?' He was careful not to mention Danny. 'Won't they worry?'

'Let them,' she replied. 'I've always done the right thing. I've never lied; I've never been bad. I've always been conscientious, always reliable. I'm sick of it. Just for once I want something just for me and damn the rest. I want this night with you.'

He nodded, and smiled at the change in her, a feistiness he liked.

'What's funny?' she asked.

'Nothing.' He looked away, into the fire, but he could not stop himself from smiling.

'Tell me.'

He shook his head and turned to her and they both began to laugh. Then they sat next to each other, shoulders almost touching, staring into the flames.

'Are you going to say anything to him?' he asked her.

'I don't know.'

'Danny will think that I told you.' He turned to look at her in the orange light, the line of her lips in profile, the perfect skin of her cheek. She felt his gaze and smiled.

'Does that matter?' she said.

'He told me in confidence.'

'Then I'll tell him the truth,' she shrugged. 'I'll tell him I read Kate's diary.'

'You don't have to.'

'I know,' she smiled at him. 'But you'd rather I did, wouldn't you? Even now, it still matters to you that Danny knows you kept his confidence.'

'Yes.'

'You're a good man,' she said.

He smiled. 'Thank you.'

'I mean it.'

'I know you do.' He turned to her and they moved their faces close together, forehead against forehead, before he moved back a little and brushed his lips across her cheek. Then she tilted back her head and let him kiss her.

THEY LAY awake through most of the night, each moment too precious to waste in sleep, lying wrapped in each other, sharing low murmurs of conversation. In the morning they were exhausted, the pleasure of the night fading with the light of day and the knowledge of their parting. They ate no breakfast but had cups of tea in their room before they packed up and left. It felt to Kit as though he were leaving home and they held hands as they walked down the stairs to the lobby.

Outside, the day was bitter and there was sleet in the air. They walked slowly in silence, arm in arm, and the sorrow of the finished night lay over them like a mantle. At the gate of the Artillery Grounds they stopped and turned to each other.

'Will you work today?' he asked.

'I don't know,' she replied. 'It depends on what happens with Danny.'

'Have you decided what you'll do?'

She shook her head. 'Not yet.'

'Ring me,' he said.

'You don't mind?'

'Ring me.'

She smiled and he bent to kiss her briefly. The cold-looking sentry on the gate looked tactfully away. Then they parted and he stood watching her trudge towards her husband through the sleet. He missed her already, and as her back retreated out of sight the hope that what lay ahead of her might yet change her mind flickered and would not be stilled. He smiled to himself with the memory of the night and turned to go inside.

'A good night, sir?' the sentry grinned.

'Yes, thank you,' he replied. 'Very good.' Shooting one last glance after Rachel, he smiled at the sentry and went inside.

Chapter Eighteen

Half-way home there was a tea room and, cold and exhausted, Rachel went in, needing to delay going a home a bit longer, still unsure of what to do when she got there.

She bought tea at the counter and sat at a small table in the corner at the back, away from the draughts of the door and the windows. The place was busy, workers hurrying their breakfast in a clatter of china and chairs, but the noise seemed removed from her, at a distance, as though in a dream. She watched them all in the midst of their lives, the choices before her circling endlessly through her thoughts, but she could not decide what to do.

Rachel drank her tea slowly. It was hot and it warmed her but it had brewed for too long and left a bitter aftertaste. She was still no nearer a decision when it was gone. She thought of them all at home, wondering where she was, the children surprised not to see her in the morning, her mother telling lies to cover up and, as she wondered what had been said to them, guilt oozed through her like an oil slick.

What could she do? What point could there be in

confronting him? It was ancient history, long ago in a different life for all of them, and now their marriage was so devoid of closeness that the betrayal no longer really mattered. Tit-for-tat, she thought. No wonder Danny had kept quiet about Andrews.

She got up from the table and took the empty cup back across the busy room to the counter. Then she turned her collar up, dug her hands into her pockets and went out to face the morning.

AT THE GATE to the house she paused on the pavement, wishing she did not have to go in, that she could go back to the hotel and be there another day with Kit, that all her days and nights could be with Kit. She took several deep breaths to calm herself then strode up the driveway and into the house. In the kitchen her mother was alone, washing up after breakfast.

'Hello, Mum,' Rachel said from the doorway.

Her mother spun round in surprise and spilled water from the glass that was in her hand. 'Hello love. Where've you been?'

Rachel hesitated, knowing her mother would know the truth whatever she said, but knowing also that the lie would be easier for her to hear. Together they knelt with a cloth each to mop up the water.

'I stayed with a friend,' she said. 'I just couldn't face Danny.'

'Was it Captain Andrews?'

She nodded, eyes lowered. She did not want to see the look on her mother's face. Her mother said nothing but got up abruptly to wring out the cloth in the sink. Rachel stood more slowly and went to stand next to her, leaning one hip against the draining board.

'Did he say anything last night?'

'Nothing.'

'Nothing?'

'Not a word. But you're asking for trouble.'

'It makes no difference,' Rachel sighed. 'He hates me anyway. What's he going to do?'

'How can you look him in the eye?'

'The same way he looked me in the eye all those years when he was carrying on.'

Rose dropped her eyes to the dishcloth in her hands, lips pursed with tension. Rachel studied her mother's profile, the hair greying now in bands at her temple, lines deepening at the corners of her mouth.

'You knew, didn't you?' Rachel said then, and wondered if everyone had known but her.

Rose let the cloth fall with a wet thud into the sink. Then she turned to her daughter and sighed. She seemed aged, and weary of life.

'I suspected,' she said. 'But I didn't know for certain. So he was unfaithful?'

'Yes.' For a moment it was in Rachel's mind to say who the other woman was, to hold up Kate's crime as so much worse than her own, but she was stopped by the tiredness in her mother's eyes. It was a burden the older woman did not need to bear.

'You never should have married him,' Rose said. 'We tried to warn you…'

'Yes. And apparently you were right. But that's not much help to me now.'

There was a silence and she remembered all the arguments, all the tears and recriminations and the heartache. He must have loved her once, she thought, to go through all of that. He must have loved her once.

'Still,' Rose said. 'That's no excuse for last night.' She

reached down into the sink for the cloth and wrung it out before draping it over the taps to dry.

'Where is he?' Rachel asked.

'Still asleep, I think.'

She moved away towards the door, thankful that she did not have to face him yet, that she could slide into bed without waking him and sleep away the weariness of the night.

When Rachel woke the house was quiet and in the half-light that filtered through the heavy curtains she had to squint at her watch to make out the time. It was just after ten, and Danny had long gone. She lay in the warmth of the bed a while, waking up slowly, remembering the night before in another man's bed that had felt more like home. The room was cold and cheerless and it was hard to get up to face the day. In the end, a need for the bathroom forced her up.

Washing herself in cold water, she wiped away the smell of Kit with reluctance, and the shock of the icy water startled her into wakefulness and brought her back to the life she had chosen. On the way back down the landing she passed Kate's room and on an impulse went in. The diary was still in its place on the bedside table and for a moment she let her fingers linger on its spine but she had no real desire to read more so instead she lay back on Kate's bed.

Above her there hung three small silver stars on cotton threads stuck to the ceiling, still left there from a Christmas years before when she and Kate had shared this room as girls, decorating it together each year. She could still remember putting them up and how afraid they had been that their father would see the glue on his paintwork. He had never noticed them though, and one by one over the years they had fallen down until only three remained. They swung gently on their threads on the air currents in the room and Rachel wondered when it had all begun to change. With Danny, she reflected. It had all changed with Danny.

She thought of them together, her sister and husband, unwelcome images of their bodies entwined in bed, her marriage bed above the shop, her husband still in love with Kate even now. She sat up but the image remained: the old Danny, strong and physical, his naked body beautiful, his hands on Kate's slender form, kneading and caressing, mouth against hers.

Fury filled her, a bright hard rage as though she had just discovered the two of them together. She grabbed the hateful diary and hurled it across the room. It hit the dressing table, scattering pots of precious make up and face-cream to the floor. She heard the sound of shattering glass as something hit the stool but she did not stop to check as she stepped hurriedly over the mess and out of the door, unable to be in Kate's room a moment longer.

She would say nothing to Danny, she decided. He had suffered enough. Soon the war would end, and Kit would leave her to her unhappy marriage with a past they never mentioned. Was it worth the confrontation, the damage it would cause? Charlie already refused to go to his father, seeing anger and instinctively avoiding it. And Jean, born as her father was sleeping with her aunt. What would she make of it all with her sad eyes and quiet ways? It would be too hard for all of them to drag such secrets out.

She would tell her husband that she spent the night at Jane's, and though he would know that she was lying, she was sure he would not challenge her. He had his own guilty secret to keep him quiet. But Kate? Kate was different. Kate deserved to answer for what she did.

Made strong by her decisions Rachel wrapped up warm and went out into the morning to telephone Kit. He would meet her later, he said, and walk her home from work. It was good to hear his voice.

RACHEL FOUND her sister that night in her room, lying in bed, reading. The diary was still on the floor where she had thrown it but the pots of make-up had been picked up and stood in tidy rows again on the dressing table. Kate sat up, startled, and pulled the bed covers up around herself as a shield. Rachel sat on the stool at the dressing table and though she was brimming with anger and recrimination, she did not know how to begin. So they were silent for a while and it was Kate who broke it in the end.

'So Andrews told you.'

'No, he didn't.'

'No?' Kate was unconvinced. 'Then why did you read my diary?'

'I wanted to know if you'd told Danny about Andrews. I wanted to know how he knew.'

'Why didn't you just ask me?'

'Because you would have lied.'

Kate pulled her knees to her chest and rested her chin on them, cradling her legs with her arms. 'Probably,' she agreed, looking up at her sister through lush dark eyelashes. 'So did you find what you were looking for?'

'Yes,' Rachel replied. 'And a lot more besides.'

'Serves you right.'

'Perhaps,' she said, but she was appalled by Kate's lack of remorse or contrition, as if there were no strands of guilt in her at all. It seemed she was indifferent to being discovered, her sister's feelings as nothing to her.

'I'm not proud of myself for it,' Rachel said. 'It was wrong of me. But considering what I found there I don't really think you're in a position to criticise.'

Kate lowered her eyes and watched her hands as they smoothed the bedspread across her knees and shins.

'It's in the past,' she shrugged. 'Ancient history now. What does it matter?'

Her nonchalance lit Rachel's temper. 'How could you?' she whispered. 'How could you have done what you did? You chased him. You went with him when I was in hospital having Jean. How could you?'

'I loved him,' Kate said, lifting her head, eyes boring, defiant, into Rachel's. 'I loved him more than you ever did. And he loved me back with a passion you can't even imagine. I satisfied him, made him happy.'

'You're my sister!'

'And you're Danny's wife and the mother of his children. For so long you had everything I wanted and I hated you.'

Rachel was silent, stunned by the knowledge of such hatred all the years she had believed them close. She searched through the memories for some sign she had missed, an inkling of the truth, but there was nothing. The deception had been flawless and she felt like such a fool.

'Would you care if Andrews was married?' Kate spat then. 'Would that stop you seeing him?'

'Yes,' Rachel answered, without hesitation. 'Especially if he were married to you.'

'It doesn't seem to bother you though that *you* are married, to one of his men.'

'This isn't about Andrews and me.'

'Isn't it?'

'No.' Rachel drew in breath, pulse beating hard with the adrenalin of the fight, and anger that Kate had changed the argument. She had not come here to defend herself over Andrews.

'So you think it's different for you, do you?' her sister sneered. 'That your love affair is different somehow – purer, more special. That you're off the hook somehow because you're husband is a cripple?'

'My love affair is different because my husband hates me, and because my marriage has been over ever since he came back from the war. No. Before he even went to war. You saw to that. My marriage has been a sham for years.'

Kate shook her head, throwing the bedcovers off her legs to the end of the bed, turning her body to face her sister, warm now with the passion of their argument.

'We're the same, you and me,' she breathed. 'So don't deceive yourself into thinking otherwise. You're just as deceitful, just as untrue. How many lies have you told? How many times have you betrayed your husband? Go on, ask yourself. At least *I* wasn't married and betraying a husband and my children, like you are now.'

Rage took Rachel's breath away, vision growing red and dark. 'You broke his heart,' she shouted, and suddenly she realised the reason for her fury. 'It was you that broke him. You that made him the way he is. Not the war. Not his legs. You. You were that last straw that tipped him over the edge.'

Kate stared. 'What are you talking about?'

Rage filtered into weary sadness. 'He loved you,' she whispered. 'And when he lost you he just gave up.'

'How can you know that?'

'Kit was there. He told me. He was there when Danny got your letter.'

'So now you're angry because I ended it?'

Rachel wiped the hair back from her forehead with her palms. All the certainty had left her and she no longer knew exactly what she felt. She only knew that Kate had wronged them both and that she hated her. 'It should never have started in the first place. It should never have been.'

Her sister shrugged. 'It's a bit late for that.'

'Don't you feel any remorse?'

Kate smiled. 'Do you? For having it off with Andrews?'

'Yes,' Rachel answered. 'But we aren't talking about Andrews. We're talking about you and my husband, your brother-in-law, the man you were …' she trailed off; it was too hard to say the words.

'The man I was fucking?' Kate supplied.

'Yes. The man you were … fucking, as you put it, while I was in hospital having his children and thinking he loved me. You're my sister and I trusted you. I trusted both of you.'

'As your husband trusted you. He knows better now.'

Rachel was silent. Perhaps she was right. Perhaps it wasn't so different after all.

'And doesn't it bother you that Andrews didn't tell you?' Kate said. 'That he knew all along and kept it secret?'

'He had his reasons.'

'Doesn't it make you wonder if there are other things he isn't telling you? Doesn't it make you doubt him? For all you know he might have a wife tucked away somewhere. Where is it he's from? Marlborough? Are you sure he doesn't have a wife and family in Marlborough that he's keeping secret? I'd be worried if it was me.'

'It isn't you,' Rachel replied, but she remembered how her trust in him had wavered when she first found out, how she made him promise to be truthful. 'It isn't you.'

'So you still trust him?'

'Yes,' Rachel answered, because she did not doubt his love for her and in the end it was that that really mattered. 'Though I don't see what it matters to you.'

'Well, I'm surprised,' her sister said, with a half-laugh, 'because if all this should've taught you anything, it's that you can't trust anybody.'

'I think that's a terrible thing to believe,' she whispered.

Then she shivered, noticing the coldness of the room for the first time. She rubbed her hands together between her knees, goose bumps spreading up her legs, and remembered the heat of the fire at the hotel, Kit's body next to hers, warm and orange in the glow, drawing strength from the thought of it. She looked across at her sister, huddled once more under the covers of her bed, pretty with her hair tumbling round her face, and cruelty beneath the prettiness.

'So why did you tell him?' Rachel asked. She was calm now, and curious, and all her sister's power to hurt her faded into the shadows now the truth was in the open air. 'Why tell him something that could only hurt him? What good did you think it would do?'

'I thought he had a right to know.'

'The good sister-in-law.'

'I thought if he confronted you about it that you'd stop …'

'… and Andrews wouldn't get the chance to tell me the truth?'

Her sister's face tautened into resentment, the pretty features turning ugly: growing old would give her bitter lines around her mouth and eyes, Rachel thought: that face held nothing kind.

'So, are you going to leave Danny?' Kate asked.

'No.'

'Still the good wife. So stoical. Such a martyr to her conscience. Danny always hated that about you.'

She said nothing, stung by the depth of Kate's malice. She had never known her sister at all, she thought. All those years of loving Kate and she had been someone different all along. But Danny had known the truth about her and had loved her all the same. She should have hated both of them but instead she felt a detached and weary sadness.

'Are you going to speak to him about it?'

She shook her head.

'Why not? Why me and not him?'

'Because he's paid enough already and, besides, what possible good could it do?'

'So you'll pretend you don't know about his affair and he'll pretend he doesn't know about yours. How can you live like that?'

'What choice have we got?' Rachel said. Then she got up from the stool, squatted to retrieve the diary from the floor by her feet and tossed it on to the bed. Kate watched it fall and did not look up again as her sister went out of the room.

KATE TOOK to staying out of the house with friends or, as Rachel and her mother suspected, with another man she had met. Rachel was glad of her absence, the tension between the two women almost unbearable, but it irked their father that she was so often gone and he complained bitterly about the morals of the younger generation.

'In my day, only girls who were no better than they should be stayed out like she does.'

They were sitting at the dinner table, the daily battle-ground. George looked across the table to his wife for confirmation. She lowered her eyes and stayed diplomatically silent.

'Imagine what your parents would have said, Rose,' he went on, 'if you'd carried on like she does. Just imagine.'

If he only knew the half of it, Rachel thought, but she kept her eyes on her plate.

'Carry on like what?' Charlie asked through a mouthful of mashed potato.

'Don't talk with your mouth full,' Rose scolded.

Charlie swallowed hurriedly and asked again. There was a moment of silence, the grown ups unsure how to answer until Danny lifted his head and turned to the boy at his side.

'Your grandad doesn't like your Aunt Kate going out and having a good time with her friends,' he said. 'He thinks she should stay at home, and be miserable like the rest of us.'

'Oh,' Charlie said, turning puzzled eyes to his mother.

Rachel smiled at him, gesturing with her eyes that he should shush and eat his dinner, and she was torn between reluctant admiration for Danny's defiance of her father and an inward cringe at the tension it provoked.

George half threw his knife to his plate and dropped a hard clenched fist onto the table. 'For God's sake, Daniel!' he spluttered. 'Why must you always contradict me?'

'It's only the truth,' Danny answered with a shrug and glance at his wife. 'Nice girls don't have fun. Isn't that right, Rachel?'

'Danny, please,' Rachel murmured.

The children's eyes came to rest on their mother and she took another mouthful of cabbage, face lowered to hide the flush there.

'Am I nice girl, Mummy?' Jean's voice was small in the silence. 'Am I allowed to have fun?'

Rachel closed her eyes in pity and Danny touched his daughter's shoulder with a gentleness Rachel thought he had forgotten. Jean looked up at him with deep expectant eyes.

'Of course you are, my love,' he said. 'You can do what you damn well please. And don't ever let anyone tell you different.'

Jean nodded as though she understood completely, and George's fist clenched and unclenched where it rested on the table, impotent and itching.

'Isn't Aunt Kate a nice girl, then?' Charlie asked.

For the briefest instant Danny and Rachel touched eyes in a moment of complete understanding. Then Rachel said quickly, 'Of course she's a nice girl.'

'Then why are you cross with her, Grandpa?' Charlie turned to George, who swallowed hard and cleared his throat.

'I'd just like for her to be at home a bit more,' he said. 'With her family.'

Charlie nodded and turned his attention back to his dinner where the cabbage remained uneaten. He pushed at it with his fork then looked at his mother to see if she had noticed.

'If you don't want it leave it,' Rachel said. She had no energy for a fight with her son about vegetables. Her mother's eyes flicked to her in surprise.

'Me too?' Jean asked.

'All right.'

'Can I leave the table then?'

'Go on,' she said. 'But take your plates out first.'

The children slid from their chairs, holding their plates with exaggerated care as they went out to the kitchen. Then they raced back through and into the hall, their feet loud and quick on the stairs, Charlie taking two at a time. The rest of the family sat quiet, dinner finished.

'So where is she this time?' George wanted to know.

No one answered.

'Well someone must know!'

'We see her as much as you do,' Rachel said. It seemed to have escaped him that his daughters no longer spoke to each other.

'She isn't waiting for Paul, that's for sure,' Danny said. 'So that's something to be grateful for, eh, George?'

George ignored the taunt. 'Rose?'

'She stays with the other nurses. A lot of the girls have got digs at the hospital. It's easier with her shifts and everything.'

'Well I don't like it. She should come home at night,' George insisted.

'She's young, George,' Rachel's mother said. 'And things are different now. Girls these days have far more freedom than in my day. You can't blame her for wanting to have a bit of fun with her friends. She works terribly hard the rest of the time.'

George grunted and pushed his plate away. 'Any dessert?'

'No,' Rose said. 'I'm sorry, there wasn't time.'

He sighed and got up from the table, moving to the chair in the corner with the newspaper.

The two women said nothing as they cleared the dishes from the table and went out into the kitchen to wash up.

Chapter Nineteen

As the days lengthened and the sun began to warm with the coming of the spring, Andrews grew more brazen at the library, touching his cap with a smile to Mrs Pitman that she could not completely ignore. He knew that it incensed her but it made Rachel laugh, and that gave him a childish delight. The old woman returned his greeting with a curt, bad-tempered nod then moved away to breathe her ill-grace over the elderly gentleman who was next in line. The poor man seemed to shrivel beneath her glare and slunk hurriedly away.

Andrews passed his books across the counter to Rachel without a word, and she took her time to find his tickets, each moment of their nearness precious. He watched her as she worked, her head bent forward, errant strands of hair falling against her face, and he itched to reach across and tuck them back behind her ear as he would when they were alone. When she finally passed him the tickets, he caught her hand with burning fingers for a forbidden moment of contact. She looked up at him quickly and smiled as he let her hand go, and the warm blush brought the carefree youth back into her face, a forgetting of a lonely future. He smiled in return then wandered away to browse the shelves, waiting for the chance to speak to her. But Mrs Pitman remained obstinately at the desk and in the end he returned regardless, leaning a nonchalant elbow on the counter and refusing to drop his voice in deference.

'I was wondering if you would be free for lunch today, Mrs Lock?'

Rachel flicked guilty eyes in the old woman's direction, laughter barely suppressed. 'I would be, Captain Andrews.'

'At one o'clock?'

'Yes.'

He glanced at his watch. It was ten to the hour. 'Then I'll wait for you,' he said.

'If you like.'

Smiling, he moved away towards the reading room and took a copy of *The Times* from the rack, but it barely held his interest, his eyes always drawn towards the desk. Rachel worked with a smile, aware of his attention and happy because of it, her movements light and animated. The minutes to one seemed to drag with agonising slowness. Then finally the clock ticked round to the hour and they stepped out together arm-in-arm into the pale spring sunshine.

'You're wicked,' Rachel laughed as they moved away from the library. 'You shouldn't provoke her. She's going to be hell for the rest of the day.'

'I enjoy it,' he replied. 'Don't you?'

'Yes. Very much,' and they laughed together.

They ate soup as always at the restaurant, comfortable in their habit of being together.

'The Canadians have taken Arnhem, finally,' he said.

'I heard.'

'I don't think it's going to last much longer now.'

'No. A few weeks perhaps?'

'Thereabouts.'

They ate then in silence, the shadow moving closer, darkening, the end of the war a time they had not dared discuss again. He was afraid to spoil their time together, scared that if he pressed her too hard, he might lose her sooner. But each time he saw her he had to bite down the words, desperate to make her change her mind.

'How are things with Danny?' he asked.

'The same,' Rachel answered. 'The same awful nightmares.'

'Poor fellow,' he said, and meant it.

'And there's nothing I can do to help him. He used to let me hold him, when he first came back. But not any more. He just shoves me away.'

Andrews dropped his eyes away from the image of her cradling her husband in the night, the thought of it rousing shards of jealousy. He shifted in his chair, trying to dislodge the sharpness of the feeling.

'You can't blame yourself for that.'

'But perhaps if we still had a marriage worth the name…'

'Whose fault is it that you don't?' he said quickly, angry with her sense of guilt, that she had taken on herself the burden of her husband's self-hatred.

She shook her head, the words to explain beyond her reach.

'You tried,' he insisted. 'Long after he'd given up, you kept trying. You can't blame yourself.'

'But I should be a better wife.' She raised her eyes to meet his and he saw the tiredness in them, the lack of hope. 'A better wife, instead of…' She trailed off and looked away, fingers absently caressing her glass of water.

'Instead of what?' he asked.

She watched her fingers moving up and down the glass, hesitating. Then she said, 'Instead of carrying on with you.'

He was silent but ran his tongue across his lips and looked

away from her, through the window to the street outside. There was nothing he could say. On the opposite side of the road an RAF officer was kissing his girl and the two of them were oblivious to all but each other. Instinctively he smiled.

'They look happy.'

'Yes. Don't they?'

'Perhaps we should go out and do the same,' he suggested.

'At the library.'

'Give Mrs Pitman a heart attack.'

They laughed to cover the sadness and after a little while they left the restaurant and wandered back up the hill, arms linked again, no longer caring who saw them or what they thought. The kissing couple had moved on out of sight.

When they got to the library steps, Andrews put his arm round Rachel's shoulders and turned her to face him. Then he bent to kiss her.

'I was joking!' she whispered, breathless, when he took his mouth from hers.

'I wasn't,' he replied, and pulled her harder into him, kissing her again. He felt her slight reluctance in the pressure of her body against his arms but did not let her go until he had filled himself with the taste and scent and feel of her in his arms. Then he loosened his hold and she backed away up the steps, smiling and flushed, so that he was almost tempted to drag her to him again, to take her to the hotel and to hell with everything else.

'Tomorrow?' he asked.

'I finish at lunchtime.'

'Can I see you in the afternoon?'

She nodded.

'I'll be here.'

'See you then,' she replied. Then she turned and raced up the last two steps out of his reach and disappeared into the dim light inside.

He smiled as he turned away to walk back to the Artillery Grounds and all the way there he was aware of the taste of her on his lips.

'Tell me about Anzio,' she asked him.

They were sitting half-dressed together at the open window of their room at the hotel and the spring evening air was cool on skin still flushed from their lovemaking. Beyond the rooftops a moon waxing close to the full had begun to rise in a sky that was not yet fully black with the oncoming night. Kit touched her thigh with his fingers and she smiled. She was not self-conscious with him as she had always been in front of Danny, and the roundness of her thighs and stomach did not embarrass her.

'What would you like to know?' he replied.

'Anything,' she shrugged. She had not thought he would tell her. She had assumed he would prefer to keep it locked inside, unspoken.

He hesitated before he lifted his eyes from the floor by his feet. His face was pale in the half-light, his eyes dark.

'Anything at all,' she said.

He half smiled and his fingers rubbed absently against her thigh.

'I have a recurring nightmare about it,' he said, turning his head away from her to stare out into the evening. Rachel shifted closer to him so that she could catch his words more clearly.

'I dream that I'm marching in a column of men in utter blackness. I'm holding onto the pack of the man in front of me to find my way and I can't even make out so much as his outline. I have no idea where we're going and no memory of where we've been. The march seems endless and pointless and it always strikes me as strange that our boots make no noise on the dirt below them. Then there's an explosion that comes from nowhere. It's not the sound of a gun or a mine or shell that I recognise; it's something else entirely, but somewhere in the column I hear a man scream and fall. I don't know who it is. Then there are more explosions and more men scream and fall but in spite of the bombs there's still no light, only the spatter of blood against my uniform and against my face so I can taste it on my lips. There's no pause in the march, no change in pace, no ducking for cover or screams for a medic, just this awful inevitability, a knowledge I can do nothing to prevent the dying so I trudge on and wait for the explosion that is mine.'

He turned to her and sought her eyes with his. They glittered with a darkness she had not seen in them before, witness to horrors she could never know or understand.

'The hardest thing about Anzio was that there was no respite,' he said. 'Even off the line in the rest areas they could still get you. My batman was blown up fetching water for me to shave one morning; nothing left of him to bury. The hospital tents were right next to the ammunition dumps and nowhere was safe from German shells: the men used to joke that they were safer in the line than in the hospital.'

Rachel said nothing but she took his hand, still resting on her thigh. He let her take it but did not return the pressure.

'I'm sorry,' she said.

He shrugged and tried to smile. 'It's in the past. I survived. And it's natural that you should want to know. What happened there broke your husband and damn near broke me.'

'But it didn't break you.'

'No.' He gave her his wry crooked smile. 'Not quite.'

'I'm glad.'

They moved closer so that their bodies were touching and she could feel the coolness of his skin against her as they sat in silence, watching the slow darkening of the twilight and the stars lighting up one by one.

'How long do you think we've got left?' Rachel said.

'Of the war?'

'Of us.'

'I don't know,' he whispered. 'Till the end of the war, I suppose, and then however long they want to keep me here.'

'I wish the war could go on for ever,' she said, moving into him, resting her head against his shoulder where she felt safe. He put his arm round her and touched his lips to her hair.

'No you don't,' he said. 'Not really.'

'No. I suppose not,' she replied, but there with him holding her it was impossible to imagine that they could ever be apart, that soon he would only be a memory. 'But I wish you didn't have to go.'

He drew back from her and stood up, staring out into the darkness. Then he moved across to the bed and sat down, lowered his head into his hands.

'I'm sorry,' she murmured, going to him, kneeling before him, trying to take his hands from his face. But he tensed his arms against her grip and would not look at her.

'It's your decision,' he whispered. 'Your decision.'

She was silent because there was nothing she could say to deny it and Kit kept his face in his hands so that he would not have to look at her. A gulf opened up between them and Rachel moved away, back to the window to stare out at the moon.

The parting had begun, she thought, and she had only herself to blame.

ANDREWS WOKE from the nightmare sweating and startled. He sat up, breathing hard, chasing the images with his conscious thought, searching for what was different from the usual dream, to identify the new source of terror. He rubbed his hands across his face, and his palms were wet with sweat. Wiping them dry on the sheet, he tipped himself out of bed and padded across the floorboards of the spare tiny attic to the window, but all he could see was the backs of other houses, their windows dark and blank. He sighed, heartbeat slowing, agitation giving way to tired but wakeful restlessness. Turning from the window he went to the bed and sat on its edge before the answer sliced across his thoughts with precise and awful clarity.

Rachel. Rachel had been in the column of men and there was nothing he could do to keep her safe. He lay back, cradling his head in his hands, running his mind back over the dream before he remembered the truth that lay behind it.

No one on the beachhead moved in daylight: the Germans held the high ground, as they always did in Italy. It was a defender's country, the attackers slogging up the boot from the country's toe one hill at a time, the Germans in their brilliant retreat destroying each place as they left it, leaving mines and booby traps that killed the wary and unwary alike. He learned to trust nothing – even the corpse of a friend could hold some kind of trap so that there was no rest even after the battle was over, the fear always there, relentless.

They had been at Anzio almost a month, pulled out of the bitter trudge north to reinforce a beachhead where the weather teemed hard and icy into the gullies where they sheltered, heads kept low until darkness. Little rest and scant supplies, and endless patrols through the night left them drained and exhausted, nerves worn ragged by the months of war. Old hands started to crack, fear held at bay for too long, stretched too thin to last.

It was his own stubborn pride that kept him going, and the dark aloof detachment that he taught himself to feel: in the middle of insanity, normal rules did not apply. He could think of none of them as men, just as pieces won or lost. He had never thought it possible to be so cold, to take a human life deliberately, without remorse, or watch the deaths of men he knew without a flicker of emotion. He told no one what he felt, even in the letters to his brother, ashamed of his indifference, of the man he had become. But to unearth the buried feelings now would be the end of him, and so he dug them deeper in the corners of his mind, left them there rejected and unvisited. Only the fear of death remained.

The patrol moved out beyond the wire that marked the safety of their lines, and into no-man's land, where the night became more dangerous and uncertain. Behind the fleeting clouds a sliver of the moon cast lurid shadows that flickered at the corners of his eyes and made him jumpy. Behind him he could hear the others, moving carefully in single file through the darkness. A reconnaissance patrol, they travelled light – no kit or helmets that might rattle in the quiet and give away their presence. But they had their rifles ready, each man peering into the night, each man hoping there was nothing there. The air around them was foetid, the stink of unburied bodies on the breeze, and away to their right desultory enemy shells fired into the American lines. Hidden frogs croaked in intermittent chorus, apparently undisturbed by their passing.

Andrews was still uneasy, the well-known fear acid in his stomach, sweat in streams along his back. For a while he would be frightened, touched by the nerves of anticipation, but time would slowly wear the trepidation down, and the movement make him calm. Like going out to bat, he thought, the first few balls the worst, until he got his eye in and started to relax. Beforehand was the hardest, waiting to go in.

The grass underfoot gave way to mud that was slimy and treacherous. He skidded slightly and swore beneath his breath, stumbling to regain the rhythm of his steps. Near the river he slowed, waiting for the others to catch up. It was easy to lose people in the dark. Then the group stood and waited, eyes lifted skyward as two light planes flew above them. German, he guessed, though it was too dark to know for sure. Behind them an anti-aircraft gun opened up, too late, and the planes banked away untouched towards the German lines, going home for the night. Lucky fellows. The men were silent, nothing to say, each in his own private world.

At the river they could hear the voices of the German troops across the water. He listened hard, trying to pick out words he might remember from German lessons at school, but he could only hear the pattern of their talking. He moved up the bank a little way, checking the approaches, the possibility of crossing. Steep banks, little cover, a German gun nest on the other side. Not a very likely choice.

Then he led them back a different way. He had memorised the maps that day, hours spent poring over them in the half-light of his dugout, sure by nightfall of where the mines were laid, their positions set out clearly in his mind. But Danny argued with the route, the two of them face to face amongst the trees as Danny hissed out his objections.

'There's mines everywhere. You can't know all of them. We should go back the way we came.'

'Two nights ago a patrol was ambushed doing that – four of them were killed. I'm not taking that risk.' There was no time for argument, too close to Jerry for discussion.

Danny scowled. Since the death of Peter Lewis he was harder to command, arguing all the time, always questioning orders. Kit knew it came from fear and grief, the slow erosion of his courage, but he was tired of it: it damaged the other men's morale and made them doubt him too. Life was hard enough already.

'Follow me,' Andrews breathed. 'And yes, that's an order.'

He stood and walked away and heard the others follow on behind. He was rattled now, breathing hard with anger, his mind less focussed than before. They crossed some open ground, pasture once, he supposed, for animals that had not survived the first few days of fighting. He tried to picture it how it must have been before, peaceful and bucolic, traditions unchanging through the generations. The birthplace of Nero and Caligula. All the peasants were gone now, evacuated to Naples, their communities destroyed, probably eking out a living in some city slum. Shaking his head to clear it of distractions, he strove to fix his thoughts on the patrol.

Nothing moved in the dark. The shelling had ceased for a time, and he could no longer hear the frogs: the silence was unnerving. He scanned the skyline, the trees ahead a deeper black against the sky above them. For a moment he was disorientated, unsure of their position. He stopped to get his bearings, heard the others halt behind him. Glancing round, it took a minute to be sure again, to trust himself. There was a glint of moon between the clouds.

'This way,' he heard himself whisper, and the trudge of boots had just begun again when an explosion ripped the silence and lit the night, hurling him forward to the ground. Stunned, it was several seconds before he could haul himself over onto his back to see the carnage, ears drumming so that it seemed as though everything was in the distance. He blinked, trying to force himself to clarity, stumbled to his feet. Private Slade was crouched above the body of another man.

'Perkins is dead, sir,' the Private said.

The scene drew sharply into focus. Andrews rubbed his hands across his face and hair, felt the grit and mud, pulled himself together. He went to Slade and grasped his shoulder briefly to show he understood. Then he heard the other man, a stream of murmured curses. He spun, searching in the blackness.

'Danny's been hit, sir. Over here,' he heard. 'His legs, sir.'

Andrews swore. One stray mine that should not have been there. Probably American. He squatted down.

'You're going to be all right, Danny,' he said. 'We'll get you out of here. Just hold on.'

The other man was silent, but through the sliding moonlight the accusation in his eyes was clear. Even in such extremity of pain his hatred burned more brightly. Andrews turned his face away from it.

'Get the medical kit from Perkins,' he said to Slade. 'Get the morphine.'

In his haste and shock, Slade fumbled with the bag, fingers rummaging blindly to find the precious syrettes of morphine.

'The morphine,' Andrews repeated. 'Now.'

Slade found it at last and Andrews gave Danny the shot. Then together they heaved up the wounded man, who cried out with the movement.

'Hold on, Danny,' he said again. 'Just hold on.'

Their lines were close: calls for a medic and a stretcher. As the first grey of dawn touched the beachhead, Andrews watched the medic bind the damaged legs and hurry the injured man away towards the aid post further back.

After they had gone the look in Danny's eyes stayed etched in Andrews' mind, acid burning through the shield of his indifference.

Chapter Twenty

In May the war in Europe ended and Rachel felt the ice begin to crack: beneath it the cold of icy water beckoned. But in the general gaiety of the victory celebrations no one seemed to notice her distraction. Standing on the edge of the street party fervour she wondered if Kit was somewhere celebrating, or if he too was hanging in the margins of the day's exuberance. She tried to picture him drinking in a bar somewhere, at the officers' mess at the Artillery Grounds perhaps, or in the pub where he had taken her, laughing, sharing the relief and excitement of men who would not now have to fight and die. But it was too hard for her to imagine – she could only see the face of the man who told her his dream about Anzio.

'Where's your husband?' A neighbour's voice cut into her thoughts. 'Not joining in the celebrations?'

Rachel turned, startled, and looked into the drunken eyes of the man who lived across the road. He was staggering a little, struggling to focus as he waited for her answer. It was not yet two o'clock. Behind him, the children from the street sat at trestle tables, tucking into treats that had been hurriedly baked that day, mothers breaking into carefully hoarded rations of sugar and eggs and butter, pooling what they had together in celebration. Bunting fluttered overhead, flags hung from windows. There was a sense of recklessness in the air, and further down the road a man Rachel had not seen before struck up intermittent tunes on an accordion. Some of the mothers swayed in time to the music as they moved around the children, and a few of the younger women found partners amongst themselves and danced while the music lasted. Rachel smiled at their fun but did not feel a part of it.

'Mrs Lock?' the neighbour said. 'Where's Danny then? Not celebrating?'

'He didn't feel up to it, Mr Prentice,' she told him.

'He should be happy about it,' he replied. 'Glad it's all over at last.'

'It isn't over for him, though,' she said. 'And it never will be.'

The man with accordion stopped playing and accepted a bottle of beer that someone gave him. The dancers clapped, hoping to persuade him to play again. He shook his head, laughing, and one or two of the couples danced on regardless, moving in rhythm to their own songs.

'Any news of his brother?' Prentice asked.

'Nothing.'

'Singapore, wasn't it?'

'Yes.'

'Well, it least it hasn't all been in vain,' he shrugged and walked uncertainly away.

Rachel watched him go and thought with a wry smile of the obscenity that would have been Danny's reply. Prentice returned to the knot of men who stood on the sidelines and found himself another drink, raising it with a loud *cheers* to anyone who would listen. A couple of others raised their glasses in acknowledgment, and Rachel thought of Danny at the pub, trying to wash away the memories, erasing the past in the bitter oblivion of alcohol. He had heard the news in silence, not even the flicker of a smile, and she knew that the end of the war meant nothing to him. So she kept her distance, wary of the feelings that the day might arouse.

It would have been better if that mine had killed him, she thought. Then she shuddered and was ashamed of herself for thinking it.

When Danny returned home that night he was so wretchedly drunk that she had to help him get undressed and into bed. She wondered how he had managed to get there, if someone from the pub had helped him home.

'I'm sorry, Rache,' he mumbled again and again. 'I'm sorry.'

'It's all right,' she told him. 'I don't mind. I really don't.'

And it was the truth. That night she felt only pity for him, the struggle plain in his face as he fought to contain the memories. Settled in bed, he fell quickly asleep until morning, but he twitched and whimpered as he dreamt, and when she placed her arm around him he held it tightly, nestling his body into hers. For the rest of the night she lay uncomfortable and restless, and her mind was filled with the future she would not share with Kit, because she could not leave the man who lay beside her.

THE ELATION WAS SHORT-LIVED. In the Far East the Allies went on slaying their way towards the eventual surrender of the Japanese. Everyone knew of men still fighting, men still imprisoned, their whereabouts unknown, and others worried that men who had survived the war in Europe might yet be sent to fight on in the East. It seemed as though this enemy would never give up, their suicide tactics proving them alien, and bereft of humanity. There seemed little chance of seeing Danny's brother alive again.

Kit did not propose to her again but the question hung unspoken over them always, so they talked instead about less painful things, recounting their pasts, or lying in comfortable silence together, the touch of a hand or a meeting glance their conversation. They saw each other often because Rachel took days off sick, ringing in to the library with phantom illnesses that she could not shake off, and though the guilt left a bitter taste and a constant tension in her muscles, she became more adept at the deception and learned to look her husband in the eye even as she lied to him.

In the warmth of the summer months they would lie half-naked in the hotel room they had come to think of as their home, learning to know each other more completely, reading each other's subtleties with an understanding that became second nature. He told her more about his war, and about the Middle East, digging out old photographs from his foot locker that showed him smiling with other young men who had not made it home. He looked so young in them, so carefree, and there was not the sadness about him that was in the eyes of the man she knew now. He showed her pictures of his family, and the house that he grew up in so she became familiar with his life in Marlborough, and saw more clearly all that she was giving up.

'My mother would love you,' Kit told her.

Rachel took the picture from him to see it better in the low light of the room. The image showed a pretty woman even still, a gentle beauty in her face that would never leave her.

'She must have been very beautiful when she was young.'

'She was,' he smiled. 'And her father thought she was wasting herself when she insisted on marrying the curate. But they've been very happy together. I don't think she has any regrets.'

Rachel smiled and gave him back the picture so that he could put it with the others in the envelope.

'She's an avid reader, like you,' he said. 'The house is full of books. A librarian for a daughter-in-law would please her no end.'

'Even a divorced librarian, with the children of one your men in tow?'

The smile left his mouth and he turned his head away from her towards the window so that she could not read the expression in his eyes.

'I'm sorry,' she said. 'I'm sorry, I didn't mean that. It's just …'

'… that's how she would see it,' he finished, turning towards her again. 'And you're right of course. You're absolutely right. She would be heartbroken.'

Rachel said nothing, wishing she had let him keep his fantasy, wishing it could be as he wanted it to be. She moved from the chair where she was sitting and knelt next to him on the floor, touching his shirt sleeve in caress. He gave her a half-smile that did not reach his eyes, then lifted his fingers to her face.

'I'd still do it though,' he said. 'I'd still take you there as my wife if you'd come.' It was the last time he would ask her.

'I know,' she replied. 'But I can't. You know that I can't.'

He nodded and dropped his hand from her face to the floor.

'I love you,' she said.

He was silent and she knew he was thinking that she should love him more, that she should love him enough to go with him. She touched his arm again.

'Don't be distant,' she said. 'Please. We have so little time.'

She shifted closer to him and lifted her face to let him kiss her. Then he lay her back on the threadbare carpet and made love to her with an urgency that was painful, his face buried in her hair. Afterwards the hair was wet against her neck and she knew that as he loved her he had cried.

They lay a long time just holding each other and her senses were filled with his warmth and his heartbeat and the smell of him. Then she remembered that soon he would be gone, and began to shudder with the grip of the cold. If he had asked her then to go with him she would have accepted, anything not to feel so cold, but he could not know her change of mind and without that knowledge he was too proud to ask again.

'Are you all right?' he asked, after a while.

She moved back so that she could look at him and she made no effort this time to hide her tears. He touched them with his fingers, brushing them away from her eyes.

'Don't cry,' he whispered. 'It isn't over yet.'

'How much longer will it be, d'you think?' she said.

'Who knows? A few weeks perhaps? But it might a while before demob. I don't know.'

'I hope so,' she said. 'I hope they keep you here for ever.'

He smiled and ruffled a hand through her hair. 'It's almost nine,' he told her. 'We should get you home.'

'Yes.'

They got up with reluctance and got dressed, then went out into the soft almost darkness of the summer evening.

Book Two

Chapter Twenty-One

The image of Kit leaving was branded over all of Rachel's thoughts. After that day, wherever she was she could conjure the picture of his face at the window of the Marlborough bus on Prince Street, turned to watch her on the pavement as the vehicle laboured up the cobbled street, crossed the narrow bridge, and disappeared. Every detail was fixed in her mind: the dampness of the morning with the coming on of autumn as they walked hand-in-hand to the bus, the warmth of his fingers entwined with hers as they stopped to watch the ships unload on the floating harbour; the slate grey sky and the rank salt breeze, the raucous squawks of seagulls, the shouts of men. She could still recall the headline on the newspaper that was folded under his arm, and the silence between them as they waited in the cold and busy street still holding hands, time speeding up as they fought to keep the moment. In the city centre now she would walk a long way round to avoid the same sights and sounds, afraid that the memory might overwhelm her.

He wrote to her often, long rambling letters that he sent to her at the library, details of himself revealed on paper he would have found it hard to speak in person. He had seemed to slot back quickly into the old routines of his pre-war life, he said, reclaiming the semblance of his former self with comparative ease. But although the surface seemed to be the same, underneath he felt the hidden burden of the intervening years and knew it was a sham. The man he used to be before the war had gone for good, and in his place there lived the shell of an imposter, going through the motions with a wearisome detachment. Only thoughts of Rachel saved him: storing up the details of his days, framing his impressions in the words he wrote to her, gave a purpose to his life. He felt himself to be an island, connected to the world only through the lifeline Rachel held.

Your letters are the glue that holds my life together.

His letters measured the passage of time for Rachel, the hard monotony of her life with Danny blurring in deference to the clarity in her mind of another life in Marlborough, an imagined life with Kit. It left her with a sense of dislocation but it made her life seem possible: without that other world to escape to she would have found it hard to cope. She memorised every word he wrote, so that when she could not sleep for missing him she could hear his voice inside her head and deceive herself that he was not so far away.

On her days off she wrote long replies when the house was quiet with the children at school and her husband at work, and as she wrote she imagined him reading her words, sitting at the desk in his classroom at school, or in the house he shared with his parents, blue eyes flicking across the pages, his features still with concentration. Then she heard the knock of his mother's hand on the door, saw the hurried hiding of the letter as she brought him tea and toast. He would be a good son, she thought, loving but formal, and she ached to become a part of the world that seemed to be more and more where she belonged. Then she would question her decision again, and regret the rigid conscience that was keeping them apart. Even now, she knew she had the power to save him: every day she had to fight the urge to go to him, knowing he would take her back without a word. But she had made her choice and so they wrote to each other of other things, and drew comfort from their distant intimacy.

In the following summer Kate got married, but not to Paul. Instead, she married a doctor from the Infirmary where she worked. They had not been together for long and Rachel wondered what she wrote to the man whose ring she had worn, still serving somewhere in Europe, if his heart had broken when he read it. It was hard to imagine Kate staying faithful long to anyone: no doubt this doctor's heart would soon be just the latest in the trail of damage Kate seemed to leave behind her.

It was a small wedding at the registry office with a party afterwards in a room above a pub near the hospital: a few friends and family, though no one, it seemed, from the groom's side. Danny and Rachel were reluctant guests, each for their own reasons, and they sat together on the outside, looking in and watching it all. They had reached a tacit truce between them now, an acceptance of the facts and, by treading carefully around his temper, she made sure they kept up their fragile mask of harmony. Kit was never mentioned, a kindness she was grateful for, and they lived inside a bubble of pretence, truths known but not admitted, the only way they could exist together.

'Think it'll last?' Danny asked.

Kate was dancing with the groom's best man inside a circle of laughter and the groom stood watching with an uncertain smile. Danny lit a cigarette and coughed hard, air rasping painfully through his lungs, his whole body jerking in the effort just to breathe.

'You should see about that cough.'

'It's just the fags.'

'Maybe. But you should still get it checked.'

He shrugged and took another drag and she knew he would not go. 'Well, your dad seems to like him.'

Rachel looked across to her father, beaming proudly as his daughter danced with another man who was not her husband.

'Poor Paul,' Rachel said. 'I liked him.'

'Did you?' Her husband turned to look at her for a moment before he dropped his gaze to the empty bottle in his hands, weighing it in his palms, thoughtful.

'Yes, I did,' she replied. 'He reminded me of what you used to be like when I first knew you.'

'Oh?' He looked up at her again. 'How's that?'

'Oh, I don't know. Mischievous, a bit cocky.' How he was when they still loved each other.

'Maybe the war knocked it out of him too, eh?'

'I hope not.'

They were silent a while and Kate began to dance again with her husband. The music changed to a slower tune and bride and groom moved together in more intimate harmony. Danny looked away.

'Are you all right?' Rachel asked.

'I could do with another drink.'

Rachel nodded and took the empty from his hand, then skirted round the outside of the dance floor towards the bar.

Chapter Twenty-Two

Just before the Christmas holidays, when the decorations were hung but Rachel had not yet bought all the presents, a letter from Kit came to her at the library. Jane lifted it from the pile of post she was sorting and presented it with a flourish and a knowing expression. Rachel took it with a delighted smile, tucked it into her pocket for later. She would take it out at lunchtime and savour it, read it at the restaurant while she ate her soup. Then she could imagine he was with her and things were like they used to be. Jane grinned and rolled her eyes.

'More letters? When are you going to go and see him again? Letters don't keep you warm at night.'

Rachel smiled but said nothing, used to her friend's good-natured teasing, and for the rest of the morning her attention was drawn to it often, as though a warmth radiated from it through her body to remind her of its presence. Then she would smile again to herself in anticipation, and Jane would roll her eyes and laugh.

She took her lunch late to keep the promise for longer, and she went to the restaurant where they had always gone, the soup still as good for the memories it evoked. She sat by the window and drew the letter from her pocket, got herself settled and comfortable, ordered her food before she took the knife from the table and slit the envelope open. She felt herself flush as she drew the paper out, paper that his hands had touched and prepared for her, her heartbeat rapid with delight. She smiled at herself, getting so excited at a letter, like a child, but she lived for these moments when she could lose herself in him again, and pretend to herself that they were still together.

Carefully she unfolded it, puzzled to find only one sheet of paper. Usually his letters ran to pages and pages so she knew he had been thinking of her through the days since the last one, recording all the details of his thoughts for her, bringing her close. She opened out the single sheet with a half-formed sense of trepidation, and read:

18 December 1946

Darling Rachel,

This letter will be brief because I have news to give you that will bring you pain, and I cannot bring my mind to bear on anything but what I have to tell you and the hope you can forgive me.

My dearest Rachel, I am to be married early in the spring of next year to the daughter of a neighbour. I have known her almost all my life and our parents have always hoped that eventually we would marry. Her name is Grace Whitlow and though I do not love her, she is kind and sweet and will be a good wife.

I know how much this must hurt you. I can see the tears welling in your eyes as you read. But the truth is, darling Rachel, that I am lonely. Horribly and utterly lonely. I have no children as you do, to nurture and give affection, to give some meaning to my life, and I have not known the touch of a woman since we parted.

Please, please believe me when I say my heart belongs to you: I would break things off with Grace in a moment if I thought there was even just a chance you might one day change your mind. But in the absence of that hope it seems pointless to deny myself some small comfort out of life, some chance at happiness.

If you choose to stop writing to me now, I will understand. I just hope and pray that you will continue because your letters are the sun and moon of my life and I cannot imagine how I might go on without them.

I will stop now because to write more can only cause grief to both of us,

Yours always,
Kit x

The clamour of the restaurant grew silent round her as she placed the letter on the tablecloth, arranging it neatly between the knife and fork. Automatically, she raised her eyes as though Kit were there before her in the place he used to sit across the table, but the chair was empty now and she met only the gaze of the customer at the table beyond, a businessman in a suit who stared at her strangely. She dropped her eyes again to the letter, smoothing it out gently with her fingers, but the words were blurred by tears.

The soup arrived and the grip of shock was broken by the waiter's voice so that the hubbub of the restaurant surged across her thoughts and made her reel. She picked up the letter and stared at the bowl that had taken its place but she was no longer hungry. In a daze, she got up and paid at the register; in her distraction she mistook the money and had to count it out twice.

Outside the restaurant she stood for a moment in the winter air, shivering, undecided which way to go. Then without knowing she had made a decision she turned and headed up the hill towards the church, the letter still in her hand, ungloved fingers growing numb with the cold. Inside the church, she slid into the pew where she had once sat with Kit. Such a long time ago, though the sadness had already begun.

She remembered seeing him kneel to pray and wished her faith was strong enough to help her now.

The choir was standing in rows before the altar, practising the carols, their sweet childish voices filling the air with the hope and joy of innocence. At another time it would have been magical but now the music only filled her with a misery too deep to be expressed. In desperation she lifted her eyes to the wooden painted figure of the Christ above the altar, his arms stretched out in welcome. She was glad it did not show him in his agony. She did not want her Christ in agony. She wanted him to comfort her, to know that if she gave him all her love that he would take her pain away. So she tried to pray, but her love was too bound up with Kit, and there was none left for her to offer Christ.

Feeling like a fraud, she groped her way from the pew and had stepped outside into the cold before she realised she had left the letter behind. Panicking, she ran back inside, eyes searching frantically across the wooden pews for it. It was not there. Dropping to her knees she peered beneath the seats, wondering if perhaps she had knocked it to the floor in her haste to leave, and the stone slabs were hard and cold against her knees when finally she saw it. Relieved, she scooped it up and when it was in her hands again, safe, she folded it carefully, put it back in the envelope and slipped it into her bag. Then she left the church a second time, hurried down the busy road, and went back to start the afternoon at work.

Jane insisted on taking Rachel for a drink when they finished, demanding an explanation for the tears she had not been able to hide during the afternoon. The pub was crowded, the Thursday night before Christmas, and it took a while to find two stools at a table in the corner. They attracted some glances, two young women in the pub on their own, but Rachel was too upset to notice and Jane too defiant to care.

Jane bought them each a double brandy and Rachel thought of the brandy she had drunk with Kit. Then she wondered if he sometimes drank brandy with Grace Whitlow at the pub and if the two of them sat over their drinks in the same quiet intimacy that he had once shared with her. She wished Grace Whitlow were dead.

'So what's happened?' Jane asked. 'Is it Danny?'

'No. It isn't Danny.'

'Then what?'

Rachel hesitated, uncertain what to say, her thoughts still incoherent with emotion.

'Come on.'

'Kit's getting married,' she said.

'Oooh,' Jane replied. 'That didn't take very long.'

'It isn't like that,' Rachel snapped. 'It isn't like that at all.' She took a swig of the brandy, and the unaccustomed heat against her throat made her cough.

'Calm down. I didn't mean anything by it. So, goodness, that's awful news. You poor thing.'

They sat in silence for a minute. Rachel drank more of her brandy. It felt good and warm inside and she began to understand why Danny drank to dull his pain.

After a while, her friend spoke again. 'What did he say?'

'He's lonely,' she said. 'She's a friend of the family. Grace Whitlow. He doesn't love her, but why not? If he can't have me, why not?'

'Because you love each other.'

'But we can't have each other.'

'It makes no difference. You've got to stop him.'

Rachel stared in astonishment. It had not even crossed her mind to ask him not to do it. 'Why?'

'You're asking me why? Honestly, Rachel, sometimes I

worry about you. Look. At the moment he's single and so there's hope. All it would really take at the moment is a change of mind from you and he's there waiting, isn't he? Once he's hitched … well … then it's out of your hands.'

'Perhaps that would be for the best,' Rachel said. She was weary of it, tired of the time she spent each day fighting the desire to go to him, forcing herself to stay with a husband she did not love. It would be so much easier if he were completely out of reach, if the decision were no longer hers to make.

'Do you want to lose him for ever?'

'I already have.'

Jane shook her head in exasperation and there was part of Rachel that agreed, that was desperate to beg him not to. One word from her and he would call it off, she knew for certain: he had said as much. But what right had she to deny him a chance at love and happiness, a wife, a family?

'When's the wedding?' Jane asked.

'Early spring.'

'So you've still got time. It isn't too late.'

Rachel shook her head.

'You were so full of life when he was here,' her friend said. 'So happy. So full of fun. Now look at you. You've been wretched for months. Do you want to live your whole life like this?'

'I'll get over him eventually,' she replied. 'If he's marrying someone else, I shall have to.'

'What? And go back to being happy with your husband?'

'That's unfair.'

'It's only the truth.'

But Jane did not know even half the truth and Rachel could not tell her. They sat in silence then and finished their brandy.

'I'd better get going,' Rachel said.

They left the warmth of the pub and stepped out into the night. It was clear and cold, the moon bright above them, floating on the stretch of sky between the tops of the buildings. Like the night she had stood there with Kit, Rachel thought, the night they were sad for the fliers who would be killed because of the brightness of that moon. Jane cut into the memory.

'You should go and see him. He'd give her up if you asked him. You know he would.'

'Yes, he would. I know that. But how can I ask that of him?'

'It would give you a chance for the future. You never know what might happen. If you're destined to be together then things will work out.'

'It's unfair of me to ask.'

'Why?'

'If I won't marry him, I don't really have the right to stop him marrying anyone else. He's lonely. He wants a family, children.'

'It isn't as though he loves her,' Jane insisted. 'How happy does he think he's going to be with her? He's going to be miserable because he doesn't love her. He loves you.'

'Jane, don't.' Everything Jane said made perfect sense, but still she understood Kit's reasons.

'You've got to stop him.'

'I can't,' Rachel answered. 'I have to let him make up his own mind.'

Jane sighed, defeated. 'Well, it's your decision. But I think you're both completely mad. I thought you were mad to let him go in the first place and now I think you're mad to let him marry someone else without at least trying to talk him out of it.'

'I know. But thanks.'

'You're welcome.'

They turned and walked slowly back towards the main road.

ONE MOMENT of desire for Grace was all that it had taken, the soft warmth of her body against him the day he walked her home. He had wanted her, craved a woman's touch, and with his need the walls that had kept him safe till then began to crumble.

Kit had known her all his life. Growing up together they had been friends: like a sister, she was just a part of life at home. She visited often, a familiar presence chatting to his mother over tea as he supposed she had done during all his time away. In his self-sufficiency, it took time for him to realise that it was actually him she came to see, and that her interest was not sisterly.

With the realisation he began observing her with different eyes, and for the first time noticed she was pretty; the plumpness of her childhood had given way to the gentleness of curves, and there was a sweetness in her smile that reminded him of Rachel, though it lacked the quick intelligence behind it. Instinctively he mentally undressed her and wondered if behind the docile affability there lay a secret passion.

She must have sensed the change in his attention because the chatter with his mother stopped abruptly and she turned herself to face him.

'What is it, Kit?'

He half smiled to hide the embarrassment at being caught, guilty for the picture of her body in his head. 'Nothing,' he mumbled. 'Nothing.'

She laughed and turned her glance towards his mother, and in their quick exchange he saw complicity.

'Why don't you walk Grace home?' his mother said.

He hesitated. Grace came and went alone with ease – she had been doing so for years – so to walk her home could only be construed as interest. But to refuse the direct suggestion would be rude. He had no choice.

'If you like.'

Grace smiled and moved towards the door and on the path she linked her arm through his. Her skin was warm and soft, and his loneliness was tempted by the touch of her. He kissed her in the lane outside her house, hidden from the windows by the hedgerow with its load of ripening blackberries. As children they had often picked the fruit together – he could reach the higher branches now.

The kiss made her breathless and it occurred to him that it might have been her first. Standing together in a loose embrace her head was lowered, made shy, he guessed, by what had happened. He lifted a hand to her chin and raised her head. Then he kissed her again, closed his body tighter in to hers. She let him do it without resistance but there was no hint of answering desire, no appetite for him in her caress.

He thought of Rachel and in an instant was disgusted with himself. He drew back from Grace, disconcerted, aware that he had crossed a line it would not be easy to retreat from. She watched him, an amiable smile around the mouth he had just been kissing, and he wondered what it would take to move her into passion.

They stood in silence. In a sycamore tree across the lane, a blackbird broke into strident voice, and somewhere near the river a dog was barking. The sound carried easily across the open fields. It sounded like one of the Labradors.

'I'm sorry,' Kit said.

'Don't be sorry,' she replied. 'I enjoyed it.'

'Did you?'

'Couldn't you tell?'

He gave her half a smile.

'Shall I see you at church tomorrow?' she asked.

'Of course.'

'Perhaps we could go for a walk afterwards?'

He nodded, caught.

'Tomorrow then?'

'Tomorrow.'

He stood and watched her walk the last few yards to the gate without turning back. When she was gone he stood in the lane in the late summer sunshine, rubbing the back of his head with the palm of one hand, contemplating what on earth he had begun.

Now Kit waited daily for the post, half-desperate for Rachel's blessing, half-hoping she would ask him not to do it. Already he was having doubts, growing afraid of tying himself to a woman he did not love. But the rest of his life alone, no human touch, without the love of children, was more than he could bear to think of.

When Rachel's letter came he was careful to open it in private, in his room, so no one would be there to see him weep.

January 2nd 1947

Dearest Kit,

I do not know what I should say in this letter. I can think of nothing but the fact that I am losing you to someone else. Soon you will share your life with Grace and she will come to know you better than I ever could, living with you in the intimate familiarity of marriage. And in time, she will come to mean more to you than me, because you will be partners in this world. You will have children to share and a life in common that was always beyond our reach to enjoy.

I wish you every happiness in that life but I can no longer be a part of it. I am only a memory from your past now, a dream that made you happy for a while. And like all dreams, Kit, it could only be a passing shadow.

I love you Kit. I always will. Thank you for everything.

Yours always

Rachel x

The page was stained with tears before he opened it, fingers shaking at the blow of losing her again. His own fault this time, his heart exposed and gaping with her loss.

He sat a long time in his room, growing cold in the winter morning, everything forgotten but what he felt for Rachel.

Chapter Twenty-Three

Danny began to cough up blood in secret. It was easy to keep it from Rachel – they barely spoke any more, only what they had to, enough to maintain the lie that they were friends and not enemies. She was even with him now, both of them unfaithful. A level field.

Danny had watched her fall in love with Andrews, aware of the attraction straight away, and knowing that the usual rules held no sway. Andrews knew too much, the husband's infidelity an excuse to take the wife. And they were suited to each other, Andrews the sort of man she should have married, the sort of man to give her what she wanted out of life. A better match than a barrow boy.

But they had loved each other once. Enough for them to persist against the odds. The early years were happy; Charlie's birth, the closeness of his parents in the shop, good friends. Simple pleasures. Until Kate had come along and worn down his resistance. She had won him with persistence; teasing, clever, until finally he fell. Hook, line and sinker. Head over heels in love. But still he kept it secret, Rachel still the mother of his his children, still his wife and partner, a bond too strong to break.

But there was nothing left now of what he used to feel for her, no trace of the affection her sweetness once aroused, just resentment of the sense of duty that kept her with him, the martyred spirit that had stopped her going with Andrews.

He had known the day that Andrews was demobbed, the day that he left Bristol and went back home to live a life without her. He had seen the marble stillness of her features, the setting of her heart against the pain, and recognised the symptoms. It raised a sense of pity in him briefly, a recognition of what she had given up to stay with him, and it crossed his mind to tell her she should go and grab her chance while it was offered, that he would rather take his chances on his own than have her pity. But then the dreams had shaken him awake that night and she had held him in her arms and for all that he despised her he was afraid to be alone.

He coughed again, pain wracking through his chest, the handkerchief flecked with blood. He would wash it in the laundry at the pub, dry it with the tea towels, and she would never know. He did not want her fussing. It was just a cough, he told himself, a bit of an infection, and time would sort it out.

When he could no longer propel the wheelchair up the hill to work for the weakness in his arms, Rachel was insistent.

'I'm taking you to the doctor,' she said. 'You're ill.'

Too weary to protest he let her take him, the first time she had walked with him like this, and it must have looked to passers-by as though they strolled for pleasure in the April sun, the gardens bursting with new life, bluebells brightly reminiscent of his childhood, and petals from the cherry trees floating down in showers with the breeze.

At the surgery he sat embarrassed amongst the old dears in the waiting room, eyes averted from their sidelong looks at the wheelchair, at the space where his legs used to be. He could almost taste their pity and he hated them. This was no way to end a life, surrounded by the old and sick, no mates to mourn his passing. He had no illusions about what he would find out today – he knew enough to know that he was dying. He had put it off as long as he could, more afraid to hear the sentence in a doctor's room than to face the haphazard lottery of battle. He was trembling, the waiting the worst, and ashamed of being scared. Rachel caught his eye and out of instinct squeezed his hand. Grateful, he returned the pressure.

Rachel sat with him in the doctor's room, surprised that he wanted her there. The doctor said little, just murmured commands as he tapped his patient's chest over and over, listening through his stethoscope. Danny coughed obediently, unusually subdued, and Rachel had to fight a rising sense of panic, a wave of guilt. She should have brought him earlier. She should have made him come.

The examination ended and the doctor took his seat behind the desk as Danny buttoned up his shirt and shrugged his jacket on. Rachel sat quietly beside him, waiting: he did not need her help.

The doctor waited, steepled fingers by his lips as if in prayer, and observed the man before him. Rachel flicked a glance to Danny who sat impassive, just a single muscle working in his jaw to betray the tension, until he broke the silence, forcing the question to his lips.

'Is it cancer then?'

'We need to do more tests,' the doctor answered gently. 'To be certain. But yes. I think it's probably cancer.'

Danny nodded but there was nothing to be said.

She should have brought him sooner.

WHEN THE DIAGNOSIS WAS CONFIRMED, Rachel spoke to Mrs Pitman.

'May I have a minute?' she asked.

Mrs Pitman took her time to finish the sentence she was writing and lifted unclear eyes slowly from the desk.

'What is it?'

Like a schoolgirl before the headmistress, an automatic sense of guilt took hold of Rachel, and the words she had rehearsed failed to come.

'It's my husband,' she blurted. 'He's got cancer. He's dying.'

The older woman said nothing, watery gaze steady above the half moon spectacles, waiting.

'I need to take some time off,' Rachel said. 'To look after him.'

'How long?'

'Until the summer,' she replied. 'The doctors said he's got until the summer.' She stopped, closing her lips against the conflict of emotions. She could say no more for fear of crying.

'Perhaps you should sit down,' Mrs Pitman said, with unexpected sympathy.

Rachel slid round the chair she stood behind and lowered herself to the seat. They sat in silence until Mrs Pitman judged they had waited long enough.

'And how are we going to manage without you?'

Rachel stared, unprepared for such a question. 'I … I … don't know.'

Mrs Pitman sighed. 'I suppose we'll have to get someone in. There's nothing else for it. He's your husband and obviously you've got to look after him so I suppose we'll just have to cope the best we can, won't we. When were you thinking of stopping work?'

'I was wondering if perhaps I could reduce my hours first of all. He doesn't need me there all the time just yet.'

She was reluctant to stop work at all, dependent on the money and scared of being at home all day with Danny. Such confinement would be hard to stand.

'If you like,' Mrs Pitman replied. 'That'll give us some time to find a replacement for you.'

'Thank you.'

'Leave it with me then, and I'll work out a new roster. We'll see how it goes from there, shall we?'

'Yes.'

Mrs Pitman took her spectacles from her nose and wiped one eye with the back of the hand that held them. 'I know what it's like to look after someone who's dying,' she murmured. 'That I do know.'

Rachel nodded. 'I'd better get back to the desk.'

'Yes. Off you go.' She replaced her glasses on her nose and resumed her steady writing in the ledger. Rachel turned and left her to it.

'What was all that about?' Jane asked in a brief lull at the desk, flashing such mischievous eyes at Rachel that in spite of everything she smiled. 'What've you been up to this time? Not another army captain, is it?'

The smiled turned sad. 'Danny's got cancer,' she said. 'He's dying. Another couple of months maybe.'

'D… d… dying?' Jane faltered. Then, 'Have you told Kit yet?'

Rachel shook her head, close to tears again. 'Not yet. We only found out yesterday for sure.'

Jane was silent and Rachel knew all that she was thinking but it was too hard to talk about, regrets wrapped up too closely in her sense of guilt.

'It's his lungs,' she said, to fill the silence. 'There's nothing they can do.'

'Oh, you poor thing. Especially with the timing. If only you'd found out sooner, before the wedding.'

'It could be worse,' Rachel snapped. 'I could still love him. That would be worse. Don't you think?' She rubbed an angry hand across her eyes, smudging tears across her cheeks, furious at the injustice of it all.

'I'm sorry,' Jane said. 'I just don't know what to say.'

'There's nothing you can say, except that you told me so.'

'Will you write to him?'

'What good would it do?'

'He'd want to know.'

She was right, Rachel thought, but she did not want to hurt him any more. She wanted him to have his chance at being happy.

'You will write, won't you?'

Rachel nodded briefly before a group of children from the local school filed in with their books, reaching up in turns to put them on the counter, and they spoke no more about it.

'Think you can cope?' Danny asked, when Rachel told him what she had arranged. They were in the living room after dinner, the children in bed and her father working in the garden, enjoying the long evening light of spring. Danny stubbed out his cigarette in the ashtray that was balanced on the arm of his chair. He had lost a lot of weight, she noticed, barely eating any more, the hard strength of his upper body leeching out of him.

'I'll have to.'

'Should have been a nurse, eh?'

'Like Kate, you mean?'

He shrugged and dropped his eyes, staring at the crumpled bloodstained handkerchief he always held now, and she was sorry she had said it.

'We'll manage somehow,' she said.

There seemed to be no anger in him then, just the sadness of a disappointed life. Perhaps to die would be a blessing, an escape from the prison of his body.

Rose looked up from the sock that she was darning. 'I'll help too,' she said. 'I'll do what I can.'

Danny gave a curt nod of thanks but it was hard for them to talk about and they were uncomfortable together.

'Have you told the children?' Rose asked.

'They know he's ill.'

Danny lit another cigarette then held the handkerchief against his mouth and coughed. Rachel turned her head away: she could not bear to watch.

IN BED she knew he was in pain from the rhythm of his breathing.

'Do you need anything?' she asked.

'New pair of lungs. New pair of legs.'

She smiled. 'Anything else?' She turned towards him and propped herself up on one elbow so that she could just see his profile in the gloom.

'Apart from the lungs and the legs?'

'Yes.'

'I'm not scared, if that's what you mean. I've already had more time than I should have.'

'What do you mean?'

'I should have died in Italy. Andrews should have fucking left me there to die with the others. It would have been better.'

'Is that what you wish?'

He turned his head towards her on the pillow but she could not make out his features in the dark. Lifting a hand he touched her hair, twisting loose strands around his fingers. She tensed, unsure if the gesture was affection or something else.

'Would have saved you a lot of trouble,' he murmured.

'Perhaps.'

'And Andrews.'

She hesitated, uncertain where he wanted this to go. She said, 'He couldn't very well have left you there.'

'That isn't what I meant.'

'What happened, Danny? You've never said.'

'Andrews didn't tell you?'

She shook her head.

'I thought he would have.' He let the strands of hair drop from his fingers and put his arm back beneath the covers. Rachel waited, but he was silent. She lay down on her back so that their shoulders were almost touching.

'Good night, Rachel,' he whispered.

'Good night.'

Sleep took her quickly but she woke many times through the night, disturbed by the cough and the hoarseness of his breathing.

She did not write to Kit.

Danny died in June: three years since the fall of Rome, still spitting hatred. She had hoped it would be different, that with the coming of his death he might find peace or some forgiveness but there was none, and the remnants of his strength were spent in fury at the world.

Rachel nursed him, learning how to give the morphine that took the edges off his rage, her emotions closed against him, the only way that she could cope. Numbed by tiredness, she stumbled through the days and in the wakeful nights she allowed herself to think of Kit, married now, another woman in his bed. But she forbade herself to cry and fought against the tears: she only had herself to blame.

Near the end she sat with Danny and held his hand as he grimaced with the pain that wracked his body, nothing she could give him but her company. He squeezed her hand, still needing her, and she was glad that she had stayed, that he did not have to die alone. He seemed to hover on the edge of his life, still fighting to hold on to it, and she waited, patient, for the end to come. Then with one final effort he locked his eyes on her and strained to speak. She bent close to him, her ear against his lips to catch the whisper of his final words.

'You're free to go now,' he breathed. 'Free to go fuck Andrews.'

She jerked back from him, horrified, but he gripped her wrist so tight she could not move.

'Happy now?' he gasped. 'You fucking bitch.'

His grasp loosened on her arm as he sank back on the pillow in the painful wheezes of his final breaths. She stood and watched him die, gasping till the very last, tenacious in his grip on life until his body beat his will and he was still.

She watched him for a long time after, in shock and disbelief, half expecting him to rise and spit more venom. Twice she raised her hand to close his eyes and lowered it again because she could not bring herself to touch him.

A shout outside, the rag and bone man with his clopping horse, broke the suspension of the moment, and sent her running from the room, desperate to escape from its pollution. She fled into the garden and crouched down by the swing behind the garage and finally allowed herself to cry.

On the day of the funeral it rained, great torrents lashing down from clouds that hung black across the rooftops. The service was at the crematorium, a bare nondescript chapel, functional and without beauty. The church would have been nicer, Rachel thought, with its sombre ancient hush, but Danny had hated the church and all it stood for, so this had seemed more fitting.

She stood at the front between her parents, her father impassive on one side, a rock to hold on to if emotion overtook her, her mother's hand warm and reassuring on the other. Beyond her mother the children stood together, silent, subdued by the solemnity, and twice Rachel saw Charlie touch his sister with a smile. He was a good older brother, she decided; he would look after Jean in the years ahead and take the role of the father she should have had. Catching his eye, she smiled at him and Kit's offer to be their father wormed its way into the forefront of her mind. She let it linger, less painful to think of than Danny's death, and wondered if Kit would see the notice in *The Times*, if he would come. She had not had the courage to write and let him know, and she dared not turn to see, not yet.

The coffin was covered with roses the children had cut from her father's garden. It had been Charlie's idea, his father's death turning him from his hostility to a desire to set things right. He had grown into a serious child, too thoughtful for his age. She worried about him, about the effects of so much anger in his young life. Near the end, when Danny's outbursts became more unpredictable, his language coarse and vile, she had kept them both away from him: it was not what she wanted them to remember.

It seemed impossible that Danny was in the box before them, all the life and energy of his rage and bitterness extinguished. She wondered where he was now, where the dead go who have no faith, but she was not afraid for him. He was free of the body he had hated, and free too, she hoped, of his nightmares. During the days since his death his last words had played like a chorus in her mind, louder than all other thoughts, impossible to ignore. She stared at the coffin, struggling to turn her mind towards memories of a happier life. A movement of her sister's caught her eye, and she remembered that their happiness had only ever been short-lived: Kate had seen to that.

Now her sister bent to whisper to the children and Rachel looked away: her presence was a mockery – in all the weeks of Danny's illness she had not come, too busy and selfish and self-absorbed to say goodbye, unrepentant, though she must have known he still loved her.

The organ slid from one dirge to another, and Rachel knew without turning that Kit was in the room. She could feel his presence behind her, sense the tone of his whisper above all the others. She kept her eyes fixed on the coffin, naming each rose that lay on it in her mind. The clear pink of the *Dorothy Perkins*, the brighter pink of the *American Pillar*, the primrose yellow blooms of *Peace*, each stem chosen with careful solemnity, Grandpa's best secateurs used with reverence. But the urge to turn was hard to stand against. Almost overwhelmed, she began to sway and her mother caught her hand to steady her.

'Are you all right?' her mother whispered.

'Yes. I'm fine,' Rachel lied. She turned her gaze briefly past her mother, over her shoulder, behind her, but he must have been standing on the other side of the chapel because she could not see him.

The minister's footsteps on the wooden steps to the lectern broke the hush. He stood above them, waiting for the mourners' attention to focus on him before he began. Rachel lifted her eyes and forced herself to listen.

'We brought nothing into the world,' the minister said, 'and we take nothing out. The Lord gave, and the Lord has taken away, blessed be the name of the Lord.'

There were mumbled Amens.

'We have come here today to remember before God our brother, Daniel Lock, to give thanks for his life, to commend him to God our merciful redeemer and judge, to commit his body to be cremated and to comfort one another in our grief. Let us pray.'

She bowed her head. There was nothing this man could say about her husband: he had known him only by his absence from his church every Sunday, a perfunctory '*and how's your husband?*' through his years away at war: he had met him only for their wedding. What could he say about a man he did not know? She turned to check on the children, still standing dutifully at attention, still holding hands. Kate saw her look and smiled as their gazes met and Rachel turned away.

'Please sit,' the minister instructed.

Wooden benches creaked as the congregation sat.

'Daniel did not wait to be conscripted,' the minister said. 'He heard the call and answered, fighting for his country first in Sicily and then in Italy …'

Rachel had no memory of telling the minister this. Her mother must have done it.

' … Where sadly he was badly wounded and discharged …'

Her mother patted her arm and tried to smile.

' … Back with his family at last, Daniel quickly found a job …'

She stopped listening, resentful of the reduction of her husband to a bare list of facts, no mention of his suffering, of the love he gave and took, the cheeky smile he used to give her, the elements that made up who he was. He could fix anything, Kit had said, a good man to have in the platoon.

She should have written to Kit, she should have told him. He could have talked about the man he served with, the man he knew, a proper eulogy for a wasted life instead of this bland and boring catalogue. No one in the room was interested in this: each mourner had memories of his own, more personal, more full of life.

'God of mercy, we acknowledge that we are all sinners …'

The bowed their heads in prayer again. She breathed deeply, the room growing warmer and stuffy, the stink of mothballs sickening. She would be glad when it was over.

'Lord have mercy.'

'Lord have mercy.'

'We will now sing hymn number 437, Abide with Me.'

There was a fumbling for hymn books as the organ strains filled the small hall but then strong and emotional voices rang out behind her as the men of his regiment sang their anthem. She had not realised so many had come and as she picked out Kit's voice among them she wondered what went through his mind as he sang, if he sang for all the men he had known who had died.

The final notes of the organ died into silence.

'We have entrusted our brother Daniel to God's mercy and we now commit his body to be cremated; earth to earth, ashes to ashes, dust to dust …'

She watched the coffin slide silently away and had to sit down.

Afterwards, she stood in the porch, sheltering from the rain as various men she did not know came to offer their condolences. She recognised some of their names from his letters and they all told her what a good man he had been, how his humour and his courage had often kept them going in difficult times. She was glad they would never know what he became, that the old Danny would live on in their minds unchanged. She invited them all back to the house for the wake but most of them declined, trains and buses to catch, long journeys to make, and she did not blame them. She was grateful they had come, that Danny's death had not gone unnoticed.

Kit was the last to leave the chapel to talk to her and then she noticed that his wife was on his arm. She was pretty, Rachel thought, in a homely sort of way, the kind of woman she could picture baking cakes for raffles at the church, but she lacked a certain animation, movements slow and docile.

Rachel faced them as they approached, battling with emotion. His wife would think the struggle was with grief, but Kit would know the truth.

'Mrs Lock,' he said, extending his hand. He had not changed, though it was still strange to see him out of uniform. 'I'm so sorry.'

Her hand was trembling as she took the hand he offered and she had to look away from the pressure in his gaze. Nothing had changed between them.

'Captain Andrews,' she murmured. 'It was good of you to come.'

He turned to the woman at his side. 'This is my wife, Grace.'

'It's nice to meet you, Mrs Lock.'

'I'm sorry it's not under happier circumstances.'

A sudden squall spattered rain into the doorway and drenched Grace's legs. She squealed in alarm and stepped closer in to her husband so that he might shelter her more from the weather. Rachel remembered walking in the rain with him, the park bench, the smell of wet wool, and in the glance they exchanged, she knew he had thought the same.

'Are you all right?' he asked his wife.

'Soaked,' she replied. 'Just soaked.'

There was a pause and Rachel's mother came over, stepping carefully over the puddles on the path, the umbrella hard to hold in the wind. The small group moved further inside the porch to make room for her.

'Captain Andrews. Thank you for coming.'

'Mrs Kirby.'

'It was a lovely service,' Grace said, to fill the silence.

'Thank you.'

'Will you come back for the wake?' Rose asked them. 'It's nothing grand. Just a few sandwiches and some sherry, but you're more than welcome.'

'We'd love to,' Kit replied.

'Do you remember where it is?'

'Of course.'

'We'll see you there then.'

'Yes.' He smiled his half-smile as Rachel's mother took her arm and led her across the rutted path to where the funeral car was waiting.

THE MODEST HOUSE seemed crowded even with the few people who came. Men from Danny's company stood by the window in the living room and talked with Kit, catching up, reminiscing. Rachel watched them: Kit's easy familiarity with the men, the pleasure they all shared in one another's company. Occasionally one or other of them would laugh out loud and the others would quieten him down with a reminder of where they were. Rachel wished they would laugh more and louder – Danny would have wanted no solemnity on his account. Grace stood slightly to one side on the edge of the group, cradling her sherry glass and nodding with bored politeness. In a lull in the men's conversation Kit's eyes strayed past his wife to Rachel who caught his look and turned hurriedly away. He saw her whisper to her mother and head towards the door, through the kitchen out into the garden.

'Excuse me a minute,' he murmured, and though he knew that Grace was watching him, that others would see him cross the lawn, he followed Rachel's path and found her sitting on the swing that hung beneath the laurel tree, hidden from the windows by the garage. The rain had settled to a drizzle but the wind still whipped her hair and clothes. She held her skirt against her thighs with one hand; the other hand moved across her hair, vainly trying to stop it lashing across her face.

'People will see,' she whispered, looking up at him.

'It doesn't matter.' He moved closer. 'How are you Rachel?'

'Tired,' she replied. 'And sad.'

'You look tired.'

She smiled. 'So how's married life?'

He gave a wry smile and dropped his eyes. 'Fine,' he lied.

'She seems … nice,' Rachel offered.

'Yes. She is,' he nodded. 'We get along all right.'

There was a silence and a gust of wind spattered them with spray of water from the leaves above. Rachel smiled and wiped the water from her cheek.

'It must be good to catch up with the men,' she said.

'Yes, but it's very odd. This is the first proper funeral we've been to together, even though we all know so many men who've died.'

She was silent, nothing she could say, watching him, and in another time they would have spoken with their bodies, fingers talking against each other's skin. Instinctively he turned to look behind him, to check they were still alone. There was no one but the moments were too short to tell her what he felt.

She lowered her face into her hands.

'Are you all right?' he asked, squatting down to her, his bad leg paining. He laid a hand against her back as she sat hunched over and at his touch she lifted up her face. It was hard to be so close to her, the scent of her so familiar. She wiped at her eyes with the heel of her hand until he reached in his pocket for a handkerchief.

'Here,' he said. 'Take this.'

'Thank you. I'm sorry,' she whispered. 'It's all been very hard. I'll be all right in a minute.'

'Take your time. I'm not going anywhere. Not yet.'

She nodded and dabbed at her face with his handkerchief, his hand still against her back, lifting and falling with her breath. Then her mother appeared, tentative, afraid of interrupting, hands twisting round each other in front of her. She stood by the corner of the garage wall and both of them looked up, but he did not take his hand away from Rachel's back nor move away from her.

'People are getting ready to leave, Rachel,' she said softly. 'Are you all right to come and see them out?'

Rachel nodded and touched eyes with Andrews. He took her arm and helped her stand and she leant on him as they followed her mother back across the grass. The wind caught at her hair but she let it fly and his instinct was to smooth it down for her himself. Instead he held tighter to her arm and at the back door she looked up at him and smiled. Grace watched them from the window of the living room and waited.

In the hall the front door was open, a small group of men milling patiently on the drive.

'Take care of yourself, Mrs Lock,' one of them said. 'And if there's anything any of us can do…'

'Thank you.'

'We've left our addresses with your mother.'

'Thank you.'

Kit let go of her arm and she shook hands with them one by one, taking in the details of each man's face, looking for traces of a brutal past, but they seemed to her to be such ordinary men, no signs of what they had seen and done, life going on as if the war had never happened. The men turned away and walked off down the drive as the drizzle hardened again into rain. At her shoulder Kit called out to them and she turned, startled by the closeness of his voice, the touch of it so near.

'Are you going to the station?'

'Yes.'

'I'll give you a lift,' he said. 'It's on our way. As long as you don't mind a bit of a squash.'

They smiled and thanked him and waited on the pavement for him to take his leave. In the hurry there was nothing he could say beyond goodbye but in the look that passed between them a world of words was spoken.

Rachel watched him limping down the drive with his cane, the uneven gait so familiar but out of place next to the figure of his wife. Then he turned away with the huddle of men and was gone. She stood staring after him, oblivious of the rain, until her mother noticed and bustled her back inside.

Chapter Twenty-Four

In the borrowed car on the way home Grace was silent, eyes turned to the window, scanning the changing landscape. Another day he would have asked her what was wrong, the habit of courtesy ingrained, but he had barely even registered her mood: his mind was still with Rachel, the curve of her shoulder under his hand, the weight of her body against him as he helped her to her feet.

Driving was hard in the gusting rain, visibility poor, and by the time they got home he was tired from the concentration, and the awakening of feelings that seeing Rachel had provoked. They sat in the kitchen drinking tea and Grace asked him questions.

'Mrs Lock seemed very upset,' she began.

'Understandably.'

She nodded, fingering the cup in front of her, stirring the tea several times before she spoke again.

'She seemed upset at seeing you.' Grace looked up at him across the table and he observed her, judging her, musing on the possibility of the truth. She had grown harder in their months of marriage, colder, beginning to understand that there was less between them than she had hoped. The once easy friendship had begun to seem demanding, the silences no longer comfortable. Since the news of Danny's death he had not touched her: her obedient acquiescence did not arouse him, and they shared no intimacy in bed, no tangled limbs or whispered secrets in the aftermath. A marriage of duty and habit and politeness. He said nothing.

'You knew her, didn't you?' Grace persisted.

'We'd met. I visited her husband a couple of times.' He lifted one shoulder in a half shrug, as if to dismiss her suspicions as ridiculous.

'It was more than that.'

He grew serious then, aware she would not so lightly be put off. 'What are you saying?'

'I'm not saying anything.' She stared into the half-empty teacup, fingers still rubbing at the handle. 'I just want you to tell me the truth.'

'Are you accusing me of lying?'

She lifted her eyes to his face. 'Yes,' she whispered. 'Yes, I am.'

Kit licked his lips in indecision, touched his fingers to his forehead. He had not thought she would confront him so directly, whatever she suspected; he had thought her less assertive. But seeing Rachel had disturbed the walls he kept around him, marred his judgement, and the moment had been all that he could think of.

'So what do you think the truth is?' he asked.

'I don't know,' she replied. 'All I know is that you've never looked at me the way you looked at her – you almost ran out after her. Everyone was watching, and no one looked at me at all, as if it were obvious what was going on and they were embarrassed. It was humiliating.'

He swallowed, silent, and shifted in his chair, holding the cup between both hands on the table in front of him, searching the tea leaves for an answer. In the pause he drew back inside himself, replaced the accustomed distance between them.

Grace said, 'Tell me the truth, Kit.'

He raised his head and looked at her. 'There's nothing to tell, Grace. She was upset and I went after her to make sure she was all right. It seemed the proper thing to do. That's all there was to it. I stayed with her a few minutes until she recovered and then I helped her back inside. You saw for yourself the state she was in.'

His wife closed her eyes for a moment, and he saw the tightening of her jaw, her lips clenched shut.

'I see,' she managed to say, standing up, taking her teacup to the sink. Then she moved back past the table and out into the hall. He heard her footsteps heavy on the stairs, moving restlessly across the floor of the bedroom above.

It was still early, the light not yet gone from the sky, an underlay of powder blue showing glimpses between the dark and heavy fullness of the clouds. He got up from the table and went to the open door, leant against the painted wood to watch the twilight. Their first proper argument, more passion in her than he suspected. He should have gone up after her, coaxed her downstairs again, tried to make it up to her with more of his lies. He could have made love to her and brought them back together with a touch or a caress, but he could not bring himself to do it. He should not have married her, and now the years stretched loveless out before him, while Rachel was free but still forbidden.

Rachel woke abruptly from deep sleep and the dream that had woken her slipped from her memory. She stared in surprise at the room she still thought of as Kate's, disorientated for a moment, waiting for the racing of her heart to slow.

Behind the curtains the day was bright, later than it should have been, and with a renewed sense of panic she reached out for the clock. It was quarter to ten. She swung herself out of bed, teetered as she shrugged on her dressing gown and hurried, still bleary, downstairs. The house was silent and her mother had left a note on the table.

Rachel,

Thought you needed the sleep so I got the children off to school.

Back at lunchtime,

Mum

Propped next to it, between the salt and pepper pots, was a letter from Kit, the handwriting still so familiar, the writing paper the same pale blue he had always used. The sight of it set her heart into flux again, skin heating with the blush. Trembling, fully awake, she picked it up, running the tips of her fingers across the neat black letters of the address on the envelope, her name spelled out in his hand. There was no return address on the back of it and for a moment she wondered why he had sent it to the house instead of the library. Then she thought that he would not know if she was still working there, and that it no longer mattered, anyway. She held it, savouring the touch of it in her hand, paper that his hands had held, before she coaxed it open and began to read.

She was in tears before she finished it, his loneliness and self-reproach in every line, his regret for his stupidity. She read the last lines over and over, his voice in the words before her.

My darling Rachel, I'm so so sorry. I've been such a fool and because of it I've hurt you.

Forgive me, Rachel, so I may try to forgive myself,

Love always,

Kit x

She had not thought a letter from him could sadden her so much. She had known at the funeral that his marriage was unhappy, that he loved her still, but she had not guessed at the depth of his sorrow: she was sorry she stopped writing to him all those months ago.

A need to see him filled her, a thirst to hold him and soothe his pain away as she knew was in her power to do. For a time she considered it, wondering if there would be a bus that morning, if she could be with him by the afternoon. But he would be at school, in the middle of his life, and to barge in now could only make things worse.

Rachel dragged a hand across the tears that bleared her eyes. She would write to him with all the forgiveness in her heart and just hope that it would help.

She visited Jane. They sat in a patch of sunlight at the open window of Jane's attic bed sitting room, drinking tea and looking out over the road below. It was quiet outside, the lull in the afternoon before school finishes, and there was a cool breeze that made them comfortable in the warmth.

'When are you coming back to work?' Jane wanted to know.

'I don't know,' Rachel said. She was not ready to think about work again. Not yet. Not for a while. She needed to spend some time with the children, and try to make up for all that had gone before.

Jane rested her bare feet on the window sill, tea cup balanced on her thighs. 'And how are you, Rachel? It must have been hard.'

'It was,' Rachel answered, gazing out at the road. A young mother was pushing a pram along the pavement across the street, smiling and cooing at her child as she walked. Rachel followed her with her eyes and smiled at the woman's pleasure: it seemed such a long time ago that her own children were that small.

'And now?' Jane turned to regard her friend.

Rachel took a mouthful of tea as the woman on the pavement retreated out of sight around the corner. She watched the space for a few seconds more.

'Kit came to the funeral,' she said. 'With his wife.'

'Oh no,' Jane sighed in sympathy. 'That can't have been easy. Did you manage to talk?'

'A little.'

'And?'

Rachel looked across at her. She was waiting, eyes vivid with interest and concern. Such a pretty girl, Rachel thought again. Such a shame about her RAF boy.

'He's miserable,' she shrugged. 'He still misses me.'

'Then why doesn't he leave her?'

'He can't.'

Jane rolled her eyes and leant across to put her cup back on the table. 'Why not?' she demanded. 'It's not like it was with you and Danny. She isn't a cripple or anything, is she?'

'She knows.' Rachel ignored the question. 'About us. She suspects. He wrote and told me. He denied everything of course but he said she wasn't fooled.'

'Then you think she'd be pleased to be shot of him.'

'Apparently not.'

'Why can't he just leave her?' Jane asked again.

Rachel hesitated, reluctant to explain, aware that his reasons would make no sense to Jane.

'There'd be a scandal,' she began.

'Do you care?'

'He married her for better or worse. He's a man of his word. I don't like it either, but I do understand.'

'Oh, honestly,' Jane huffed. 'The pair of you need your heads banging together.'

Rachel laughed.

'It isn't funny,' Jane retorted. 'Do you both want to be miserable for the rest of your lives? Divorce isn't the end of the world any more. Lots of people do it.'

'His father's a vicar. And so is his brother.'

'Then they ought to understand about love and forgiveness. And if they don't then that's their problem, not yours and Kit's.'

They stared out at the leaves that flickered on the trees as the sun caught them in the wind. She was doubtful now, Jane's words stirring a hope that she knew to be false.

'She loves him,' she said.

'No she doesn't. Not really. If she really loved him she'd let him go. She'd want for him to be happy.'

'Perhaps.' But Rachel thought that Grace would never let him go. She would keep him until one of them died and in the end he would come to hate her for the cage she put around him.

'Go and see him,' Jane urged. 'Talk to him. Beg him. Go on your hands and knees if you have to.'

'I can't,' Rachel whispered, though the thought of it was all that occupied her waking thoughts. 'I can't do that to him.'

'Do you want to be with him or not?'

'I want to be with him. Of course I do. But he has to come of his own accord. He has to follow his conscience. To go against it would destroy him and I'd rather be without him than do that to him. I could never forgive myself for that.'

Jane shook her head in exasperation and they fell silent again, looking out at the quiet road. A wood pigeon cooed in the peace and the sound brought to mind childhood holidays with her aunt at the cottage near Marlborough. She had always wanted to live there one day, falling in love with the countryside, the river with its swans. She wondered if she had ever come across Kit in those days, unknowing, the back of his head before her at church, a boy playing cricket in a garden as she cycled past. She sniffed and blinked back her tears before they could form and fall.

'Go and talk to him,' her friend said again. 'At least ask him to leave her. He asked you, remember. Several times.'

Rachel said nothing, and the two women sat in silence for a moment before Jane said, 'More tea?' She spoke brightly, trying to dispel the languid mood that had fallen.

'Yes please.' Rachel rubbed her hands across her face, put the mask back in place as Jane got up and went to the stove. She was tired of the drama of her life.

'So how have you been, Jane?

'Fine,' Jane replied. 'Always fine. You know me. But it's very boring at work without you. The new girl's ever so serious all the time. No torrid affairs there to keep me interested.'

Rachel laughed. Her friend turned from the kettle at the sound. 'And…' she began.

'What?' Rachel asked. 'What is it?'

Jane tilted her head, a coy smile, a different mood. 'And, there's this chap I like. He comes into the library. Borrows poetry and classics: he's from Scotland and he's got the loveliest accent.'

'Perhaps you should ask him out.'

'D'you think I should? Really? You don't think he might think me a bit, well, forward?'

Rachel shook her head, thoughtful. 'I don't really know,' she said. 'I don't know what the rules are any more. But I think you ought to take the chance. Don't you?'

'Yes. I think so. I think I will. Next time he comes in.' She smiled again then turned away to make the tea, and their talk moved on to less serious things.

Chapter Twenty-Five

Andrews wandered home from school, all thoughts absorbed by Rachel, preparing in his head the words he would write to her that evening, determined they would start to write again. Not to have her in his life at all when she was all that mattered was no longer possible for him to contemplate. Without her presence in some form or other, he did not think he could survive.

At the door to the cottage it took a moment to understand the scene in front of him. Grace was kneeling on the rug before the unlit fire, letters strewn all round her, the papers messy, out of order, read and carelessly discarded for the next one. Rachel's letters.

She turned to him quickly at the sound of his step on the flagstones of the hall. Her face was red and blotched from weeping and the first thought that came, God help him, was how ugly the tears had made her, how lovely Rachel always seemed when she cried. Carefully he leant his cane against the wall, placed his briefcase on the sofa, aware that she was following each movement with sore and anxious eyes. He breathed deeply, trying to quell the anger, the sense of violation.

He said, 'You went through my desk.'

'You lied to me,' she answered. 'You lied.'

'Yes.'

'Why?'

'What good has it done you to find out the truth?'

Grace sniffed back a sob, cast her eyes across the scattered papers. He followed her gaze, appalled that she had read Rachel's words, disgusted by her intrusion into their private world.

'I want you to burn them,' she said.

'No.'

'Why not?'

'I'm not going to burn them, Grace.'

In the silence he squatted down and began picking up the letters, straightening out the ones she had crumpled, trying to marry the pages of each one together. The papers trembled in his hands and, overwhelmed, he began just to gather them together, to get them away from his wife's prying eyes. He would sort through them later, put them back in order when he could do it properly, with devotion. He should have left them better hidden. She should not have been allowed to find them. Scowling at his own stupidity he thrust them in his briefcase. When the floor was clear, he sank down on the sofa's edge, elbows on his knees, watching his wife still kneeling on the rug, eyes cast down to her hands, clutched together on her lap.

'You were lovers,' she murmured, without lifting her head.

'Yes,' he replied, though it had not been a question.

'For how long?'

'About a year.'

She nodded, taking in the information before she raised her face to look at him. He held her gaze, detached and unashamed. Then he wondered at his own indifference and thought that life had made him cruel.

'She was the wife of one of your men,' Grace said.

'He was no longer one of my men.'

'That's splitting hairs.'

'She used those very words, when we first fell in love, before…' He could remember the exact conversation, his desperation to persuade her, the way his need for her had taken him to pieces.

'Before you seduced her?'

'If you like.'

'Well, she was right,' Grace retorted.

'It isn't splitting hairs,' he said. 'It's an important distinction. If he had still been one of my men I would have left her alone, because I would have needed his trust and respect. Our lives would have depended on it. But neither of us was going to war again, so it didn't matter any more.'

She dropped her eyes. 'I thought you had more integrity.'

There was contempt in her tone but he did not care. 'So did I.'

'Then why? Why did you do it?'

He was silent, waiting for her to look at him again, to see his eyes. Slowly, in the silence, she raised her head and turned her face to his.

'Because I loved her,' he said.

'And you couldn't control yourself?' she sneered.

'I needed her,' he whispered.

'Why? Why did you need her?'

Because I was in pain after Italy, he thought. Because she understood. 'I can't explain it. Not to you.'

'But to her?'

He nodded, remembering his grief and rage, the fear that once had lit his own brutality, the self-disgust, all locked away and festering so that he could not allow himself to feel at all for fear of reigniting uncontrollable emotions. Rachel had taught him how to feel again, taught him how to love. Rachel.

'I want you to burn them,' Grace said again.

Kit shook his head.

'Why not?'

'I don't have to explain.'

'I'm your wife, Kit,' she breathed, the words heavy with anger and emotion. He had never seen her so fervid, so intense. 'And these are love letters from another woman.'

'They were written before I married you. Before I proposed.'

She stared, eyes bright with fury.

'So why do you have to keep them?' she demanded. 'If it's in the past, then you don't need them any more.'

Kit returned the stare. 'For the memory.'

'You're with me now,' she reminded him. 'And you need to forget the past.'

Her breathing was the only sound in the room, shoulders lifting with each laboured breath. He watched her, almost fascinated by this woman he did not know. Outside, across the river, a tractor started up, the sound carrying easily on the warm summer air. Grace got to her feet and stumbled slightly, legs stiff after kneeling for so long. She brushed the creases from her cotton dress and looked down at her husband. There was a tightness to her movements, an assertion of self-control.

'Why didn't she leave him for you, then?' she said. 'If you loved each other so much?'

Kit glanced away to the window. The sky was clear after all the recent rain, and the evening warm and inviting. He was weary of the confrontation, wanting only to go to his study, to write to Rachel.

'Her husband was crippled,' he answered. 'He needed her. He had nowhere else to go.'

'And now that he's gone?'

'I have you.'

Grace was silent, all the anger washing out of her in a wave. She stepped back and lowered herself into the armchair next to the fireplace, where she sat slumped and sad. For the first time Kit was sorry, guilt at what he had done to her swelling through him. Tears fell silent across her cheeks. She wiped at them gently but they were quickly replaced by more.

'I'm sorry, Grace,' he whispered. 'I thought we could be happy together. I really did.'

'Even though you were still in love with her? How on earth did you think we could be happy?'

He shook his head, bewildered by his own stupidity. 'I thought we would be friends, companions. I hoped that we could have children, be a family.'

They stared at each other across the small width of the rug but it felt as though a chasm ran between them.

'I never said that I loved you Grace,' he said.

'But you did marry me. I thought that counted for something.'

'I'm very fond of you,' he said. 'I wouldn't have married you otherwise.'

'Fond of me?' Her voice rose in disbelief, sadness turning angry, the implications sinking in. 'Did you really think that being fond of me would be enough?'

Kit lowered his face into the grasp of one hand, rubbing at his temples, caught and ashamed: no excuse and no escape.

'I thought you felt the same,' he said. 'I thought you felt as I did.'

'Why would you think that?'

'Because…' He had thought it was obvious. 'Because … we've known each other all our lives. Because it's what our parents wanted.'

She stared, incredulous. 'I've always loved you, Kit,' she said. 'Ever since we were children. All these years I've waited for you, getting news from your parents, the odd letter and visit now and then, waiting and hoping. I thought you knew. I thought you knew how much I loved you. I thought you'd always known.'

'I'm so sorry, Grace,' he whispered.

'How could you not have known?'

Tears prickled at the back of his eyes and he screwed up his face to keep them in. He had ruined everything. His life, Grace's, Rachel's. All of them to live in lonely sadness because of his stupidity.

'I didn't know.'

They sat in silence until a knock at the front door disturbed them. Neither of them moved to open it. The visitor knocked again and waited for a moment before turning to walk back down the path. They heard the gate's light click swinging shut, and the muffled tread of footsteps receding in the lane.

'I wonder who it was,' Grace said.

'They'll come back if it was important.'

'Yes. I suppose they will.'

There was another silence. Grace stared at the logs in the fireplace, the fire neat and ready to be lit, and Kit watched her, appalled. In the silence the tick of the clock on the mantelpiece seemed to grow louder, time passing with inexorable finality, the rest of his life measured out in bitter seconds. She did not move, and in her immobility and silence, unreasonably he hated her. He stood up, and stepped across the room towards the window at the back. In the garden a single blackbird hopped across grass grown long with all the rain, and the sun on its feathers gave the black a blue-green sheen. He watched it till it flew away, then turned back towards the room to face his wife.

'What do you want to do now?' he asked.

She looked up, startled. 'What do you mean?'

'I don't love you, Grace. I never have.' Resentment was

making him cruel, but he could not help himself: this woman was all that was keeping him from Rachel. 'Do you think we can go on together, after this?'

She gazed at him, and expressions crossed her face he did not recognise. A harder, colder Grace, a woman capable of cruelties of her own. She observed him for a moment, making a decision, then stood up and tried to keep her dignity.

'I think…' She hesitated, apparently aware her next few words were crucial. She said, 'I think we need some time to think this over. Time to calm down. Both of us. It's all come as rather a shock.'

'Yes,' he agreed. 'Of course.'

They stood facing each other across the rug, and she waited to see if he would say say more, to make some move towards peace, but he was silent, unwilling to bring her back to him. If she would just go, go and leave him be. A long moment passed and when finally she understood he would not try for her forgiveness she spoke again.

'I'm going to go to my parents' house,' she said, blinking back her tears. 'When you're ready to talk to me again that's where I'll be.'

Kit nodded, then turned again towards the window so that he did not see her go, nor notice that she did not take a key.

It took three days of indecision before Kit could force himself to see her, days of agonising, knowing he could coax her back, but knowing he did not want to. He barely slept, conscience struggling with his heart, the argument revolving round in circles that never seemed to change: now he fully understood how Rachel must have felt.

Gossip had already spread, like a virus, house to house, poisonous, and though he cared about the damage to her reputation, the crux was something different. It came down to what was right. He had taken vows to her in church, knowing even then he did not love her, and it seemed a weakness on his part not to honour them. In his own eyes it lessened him, his conscience no longer clear: as Grace had pointed out, he used to have integrity.

Did he still, he wondered, or had his love for Rachel already left it compromised beyond repair? Rachel had been married after all, the wife of one of his men, and despite his neat distinctions he had always known that it was wrong. All the same, he had taken it for granted that she should leave her husband – her love for him enough that nothing else should matter – and he had sworn and cried and cursed to try to make her change her mind. Now the roles had been reversed and it seemed he lacked the grit to do himself what he had asked of her. But now behind these thoughts flickered the hope that had lit when Grace had left the cottage and gone back to her parents. An alternative ending, the possibility of a new path opening up.

He visited Grace on Saturday when school had finished for the morning, striding along the lanes that led from the town to the village, the way well-known, automatic. Cow parsley lined the road, the air heavy with summer. Occasionally he flicked at a fly that buzzed close to his head, but the action was instinctive, his mind on the scene ahead. Even as he walked the decision still vibrated in his mind, the very last moments of a different possibility still clamouring to be heard.

In the lane outside her parents' house he stopped, out of sight behind the hedge, the blackberries just beginning, still small and green and hard. Remembering the kiss that had begun it he closed his eyes against the rising of regret, his future sealed in that single moment of desire. Even then he had known the wrongness of it, and he had not desired her since. But he had married her all the same, finding himself carried along on a road that seemed to have no turnings. How could he have been so stupid?

Two boys from the village cycled past with fishing rods, old bikes rusty and rattling on the uneven road. They exchanged a brief hello and he watched them until they rounded the bend and were lost to sight. He took a deep breath, still lingering, still unwilling. He thought of Rachel, how she had been when they could still make each other happy, her body close to his on the bench at the Green, or lying half undressed before the heater in the hotel room that had always felt like home. For the time they were together he had found his faith anew, a belief in love and hope and goodness. But her loss had stripped him once more and now he lived again behind a wall, a mask in place to face the world.

He balled his fists, searching for the courage to act. Above him wispy clouds were painted in brush strokes across an azure sky, and a wood pigeon cooed from the beech trees along the lane. Staring into the heavens, he called silently to a god he no longer believed in. Then, with a deep breath, he stepped out from the cover of the hedge, pushed open the small wooden gate and strode up the path to the door.

He knocked and there was an answering flurry of yaps from the family's two terriers. He could hear their claws scrabbling against the other side of the door and in the pause he had to quell the urge to turn and walk away, to find a different answer. The door opened, and Grace's mother filled the space. The terriers leapt at his legs and he ignored them.

'Kit.' The greeting was non-committal.

'I've come to see Grace. Is she in?'

Mrs Whitlow stepped back to let him through. 'She's in the

garden,' she told him. 'Weeding the rose beds. You know the way.'

'Thank you.'

He made his way across cream carpets and around rose-covered armchairs towards the French doors at the back. A narrow terrace led to a well-kept lawn, sunlight flickering across it through the branches of an apple tree, and to one side he could see his wife, kneeling amongst the bushes, her hair tied back with a scarf, heavy gardening gloves on her hands. Beside her was a small pile of weeds and, engrossed in her task, she did not notice him. Watching her work, for a breath he felt a rush of sympathy. She was a simple woman, he thought, with modest wants, a woman who had always loved him. And he had ruined her life: whichever path he followed now the damage was done.

He stepped down off the paving and crossed the lawn, feet sinking slightly in the soft spongy grass. Grace caught his movement from the corner of her eye and stood up slowly, taking off the gloves, tossing them carelessly onto the pile of uprooted weeds. She stood and faced him, and he saw the determined calm that crossed her face, the distrust of him in her eyes.

'Kit.'

'Grace.'

She waited as he hesitated, the words hard to find, hard to say, words that could never be unsaid. He swallowed and searched the garden with a glance for help. The silence lingered, and he could not bring himself to break it.

In the end it was Grace who spoke first. 'What is it that you came to say?'

He heard impatience in her tone, irritation, and he realised she had no comprehension of the pain he was in, the sacrifice he was about to make for her.

'Grace, I'm sorry,' he began. 'For all of it.'

'And?' She turned her face back towards him. It was set and firm with a determination not to show him any weakness.

'Come home. Please,' he said.

'Why should I?' she asked. 'When it's her you love.'

'You're my wife, my partner,' he answered softly, shoulders lifting in the slightest of shrugs. 'I made you promises.'

'One of those promises was to love me,' she said.

He gave her rueful smile. 'Yes. It was. I'm sorry.'

They stood in silence for a while, looking everywhere but at each other, and he could think of nothing else to say. She untied the scarf from her head and ran her fingers through her hair. Then she twisted the scarf between her hands distractedly. He watched the movement, searching his mind for words. Then finally, he said, 'Do you want to come home, Grace?'

She sighed, and for a wild moment of hope he thought she might say no and set him free. But instead she asked, 'It's completely over between you? No more letters?'

He swallowed, and thought of the box hidden safely now in his room at the school. But how he would get through his life to come without more of her letters to sustain him, he could not imagine. Thicker walls, he guessed, a more rigid mask. 'No more letters,' he agreed.

She nodded, slowly, still considering. He wondered if she had hoped for a more abject apology, a plea for her forgiveness, and realised he had no idea of what she was thinking: in spite of their friendship through all those years, she was a complete stranger to him.

'You have to forget about her,' she said.

'I know. And I'll try,' he lied.

She lifted her face to look at him then, her eyes searching his for signs of deceit. He met her gaze with a detachment that surprised him: there was now no lingering fondness, and he knew he could never learn to love her. The two of them would go back to the cottage and live all the years of their marriage loveless and alone, and only his memories of Rachel would ever give him joy.

'I'll come home,' Grace said. 'And we won't ever speak of it again.'

In the warmth of the summer day he shivered, aware the ice had cracked and he was falling. But he smiled anyway, and offered Grace his arm to walk together back to the house. After a moment's hesitation she took it, and they walked across the lawn side by side, feet sinking with every step into the soft short grass.

In the end Rachel could not stay away, worn almost to exhaustion by the struggle not to go.

The bus trip took forever, a tortuous journey that seemed to stop at every village. In another time she would have taken pleasure in the trip, a journey out of history, historic pubs and ancient churches, a countryside she had forgotten in the years since she had seen it as a child, beautiful in the early summer sunshine. But impatience dulled her interest and with every village they went through the knot of nerves pulled tighter in her stomach.

It was almost lunchtime when the bus drove past the College on its way into town. She stared from the window, a hand against the glass until the bus turned the corner and the buildings fell away out of sight. She gathered up her bag, slid to the edge of her seat so she was ready to get up and when, finally, the bus pulled up in the High Street, she was first to the door, hurrying back along the uneven pavement the way that they had come. She was afraid she might have missed him, the school year at the private college already finished for the summer. Her heart was beating hard in her chest, the sweat of nerves in the small of her back as she walked beneath the high brick arch across the road and approached the gates.

At the porter's lodge she slowed, unsure again, aware she was intruding, courting danger. The wrought iron gates loomed tall and forbidding, and her breath trembled as the porter came out to meet her. He was a small man, elderly, and in other circumstances he might have been kind, but his first glance appraised her and made a judgement straight away. Rachel tucked a stray strand of hair behind one ear with nervous fingers, and thought she should have stayed away.

'Yes. Can I help you?'

Rachel smoothed perspiring hands across her dress, and struggled to assert herself.

'I'm looking for Capt … that is … Mr Andrews.'

The porter pursed his lips, disapproval in his eyes, shades of Mrs Pitman. The thought made Rachel smile, memories of Kit provoking her.

'School holidays have started, you know.'

'Yes I know. Is he here?'

'I'm not sure.'

'Could you find out?'

The porter sighed and folded his arms. 'Whom shall I say is here?'

'Mrs Lock,' Rachel answered. 'Mrs Rachel Lock.'

'Wait here,' he said, and walked away from her around the courtyard. She stepped forward a few paces from the shadow of the hallowed walls and into the sunlight to cast her eyes across the school; the perfect lawn that lay between the buildings, the ivy clad walls, the statues that stared down from the roof of the chapel, judging her like the eyes of the porter. In the warm morning she shivered and glanced at the clock on the high wall across from her, watching the hands move slowly round, ticking off the moments that her hope had left. It was easy to imagine him here, as a boy and then a teacher, the weight of its tradition heavy in his soul.

Then the porter was approaching, busy and important. Walking at a distance behind him, slower with his cane, was Kit. He still seemed so unfamiliar out of uniform; the image that she carried in her mind of him was in his service dress, or naked by the fire, pale skin reddened by the heat. He was a different person in the jacket and waistcoat, a man she could not have.

Raking jittery fingers through her hair, Rachel checked the straightness of her dress and waited.

'Thank you Luckridge,' Kit said when he reached her, and the porter, disgruntled, retreated back inside the lodge.

'Rachel.'

They stood together for a moment, awkward here where their feelings had no place. He looked as sad as she had seen him.

'This way.'

He took her to a classroom and closed the door. There was an unexpected hush, the sound of a school out of term time. She followed him across the empty room and they stood together at the window. His eyes were restless on the scene outside and he did not turn to look at her. It was painful to be so close to him and she wished she had not come.

'You shouldn't have come,' he said. 'People will talk. Luckridge will talk.'

'He seems as bad as Mrs Pitman.'

The stern face softened and he smiled. 'Yes. He could definitely give her a run for her money.' He turned towards her then, hands in his pockets, out of reach. 'It's lovely to see you, Rachel.'

'You too. I'm sorry for coming, but I had to see you.'

'I understand.'

He reached up a hand to tuck a curl behind her ear. Rachel

moved her head towards his fingers and thought of that first time on the corner by the library steps in the rain. So long ago.

With the touch the awkwardness was broken. They moved together into an embrace, holding close, his cheek against her hair, his hands moving restlessly against her back, her shoulders, and everything about him was exactly as she remembered, the perfect image that filled her dreams.

He ran his fingers through her hair. 'You've had it cut,' he said, and tightened his fingers so that the shortened strands were held between them.

'Yes,' she answered. 'Do you like it?' But she did not lift her face to hear his answer, afraid to break the moment, afraid that they would never be this close again.

'It suits you.' His lips brushed against her temple as he spoke. 'Why have you come?' he whispered. 'Why?'

'I had to. I had to come and ask you to leave her.'

He stepped back, breaking the embrace and she loosed her hold on him unwillingly. But they still stood close, his face only inches from hers. The brightness of his eyes was muted with the pain of seeing her.

'I can't,' he murmured. 'You know I can't.

'Because of what people will say?'

He flinched from her cruelty before he answered. 'Because of what my conscience will say.'

'And what does your conscience say about me? About the pain you're causing me? Why are her feelings more important than mine?'

'It's not about her feelings,' he said, and turned his gaze from Rachel, staring out again across the gardens. She could feel the closeness slipping like water through her fingers even as she tightened her hold on his arm. 'It's about what is right.'

'I should have known better than to fall in love with a vicar's son,' she said.

He looked at her and smiled.

'I'm sorry,' Rachel said. 'But I had to ask you. I had to try. You did the same, remember?'

'I know.'

'And I understand. Your family would be very upset, you might lose your job …'

He shook his head. 'It isn't about those things, Rachel. Not really. They matter, but I could live with all of that. But Grace is my *wife.* I made promises to her when we married knowing full well I didn't love her, and I can't renege on those promises simply because you've become free, because it no longer suits me to be married to her. What kind of man would I be to do that?'

She was silent. His logic was irresistible, his sense of rightness inseparable from the rest of him; without it he would be a different, lesser man.

'Rachel?'

'Not the man that I love,' she murmured and moved away from him, head bowed low to hide her tears. She hated herself for accepting it, wanting to wail and beg and plead with him. Knowing it was in her power to make him give in but, afraid to wield that power and damage him forever, she took another step back before her grief at losing him again could sway her better judgement.

'I'm sorry,' he said. His hand was still on her arm, but the distance between them was growing, impassable. 'I wish I could go back in time and take back the words that I said in that church. But I can't.'

'I know.'

There was a silence and in the distance they heard a car pull up on the drive, the doors slam and voices raised.

'I've got to go and see who that is,' Kit said. 'It's probably a parent to collect one of the boys. There are still a few who haven't gone home yet. Wait here.' He squeezed her arm, took up his cane and moved towards the door. 'Wait here for me,' he said again. 'I won't be long.'

She nodded and followed him to the door to watch him go, the familiar lopsided gait as he walked away from her, the tap of his walking stick growing fainter on the wooden floor. When he was completely out of sight she left the room and went the other way along the corridor until she found a staircase. She hesitated, a backward glance at the empty corridor before she hurried down the stairs and away, outside into a garden behind the school. Through the doorway, she stopped, blinded in the summer sun until her eyes adjusted to the glare. An elderly man in a battered hat was labouring across the grass with a lawn mower. Absorbed in the effort he paid her no attention. A heady scent of new cut grass and roses hung in the afternoon.

She looked around her, the vegetable garden away to her right, the line of trees beyond the lawn and the river, hidden behind them. On her left, the path led through an open gate, out of the school and towards the town. The gardener reached the far edge of the lawn and turned the mower round with difficulty. Rachel swallowed, clutching at her resolve. Then, before she could change her mind, she hurried off along the path, and lost herself in the bustle of the busy marketplace beyond.

Epilogue

The emptiness that was in the room when he came back and found her gone never really left him. He had hurried away from seeing off a boy he barely knew, almost running to get back to her, certainty growing that she would no longer be there, that he had missed the chance to say goodbye. Always he regretted it, that she had come to him and he had left it all unfinished, a farewell never said. Sometimes he would hesitate at the door of that classroom, as though expecting still to find her there, waiting at the window as he had left her. Or he would be sitting at the desk, thoughts far away from her, and suddenly look up as though her movement across the light had caught his eye. She would be greying now, he thought, as he was, losing the soft pliancy of her flesh. He could remember every detail of her body, every mark and curve, the line of her teeth as she looked up at him and smiled, the certain angle of her head when she was shy, and in her vividness she seemed to be more real than the distant cool civility of the woman who was his wife.

A few times in the High Street he saw women from a distance he thought were her, women he would follow until they turned to reveal themselves as someone else, women who were not Rachel. Then he would back away, ashamed of having followed them, and with the disappointment all the locked up memories rose inside. Then he would need to be alone, walking in the quiet by the river or kneeling in the church until the walls were back in place, and the mask he used to face the world repaired.

He wrote letters he never posted, the same kind of letters that he used to write, his own life falling into meaning by sharing it with her. He could see her in her life without him; the house, the library, the children growing into adults, away from her. Then he wondered if without them she was lonely too, or if she had found another man that she could love. It was hard to think of that, his own marriage grown cold and barren, and no children of his own to give his love to.

At night he slept alone, the marriage bed long abandoned for the loneliness of separate rooms, and through the sometimes sleepless nights he would think that he should write to her and post it, that the years of silence were a waste.

One day he would do it, he decided.

One day.

Also by Samantha Grosser

ANOTHER TIME AND PLACE

ENGLAND, 1944. A chance meeting changes two lives for ever. Young American pilot Tom Blake isn't looking for love, but seeing Anna Pilgrim in a tearoom on a cold winter afternoon changes everything. So begins a passionate affair.

Their happiness does not last. Shot down over Europe, wounded, in hiding, Tom has no way of telling Anna he is alive. And Anna, left waiting in England, has no way of finding out. How can she know that Tom is struggling to return to her? Or that the thought of her is all that keeps him going on the long journey home?

Interwoven with the danger of Tom's fight to survive is the story of Anna's own struggle to face the uncertainty of waiting. Set vividly against the hardship of the Second World War, *Another Time and Place* is at once a compelling love story, an enthralling adventure and a moving depiction of the resilience of the human spirit.

Available from all good online bookstores.

Also by Samantha Grosser

THE KING JAMES MEN

England 1604. King James VI of Scotland has ascended the English throne and the future of the realm is uncertain. Religious differences divide the country, and in a bid to pacify them the king commands a new translation of the bible.

Merchant Ben Kemp has already suffered for his faith: three years in prison, and seven more in exile. Now, recently returned to England, he joins a small community of Separatists who have so far escaped persecution. But in an age where non-conformity is a crime, the hunt for dissenters is unrelenting, and the net draws ever closer.

Then his old friend, biblical scholar Richard Clarke, is offered a place on the new translation. For Richard it seems like a gift from God, a way back in from the cold where his friendship with Ben has kept him for many years.

But Richard soon discovers there is a price to pay for his new-found favour, and that price is betrayal. As the conflict escalates, his loyalties are tested. Caught between love for his friend and faith in his church, Richard is faced with a choice that could cost him his soul.

In a rich portrayal of the rivalry and ambitions of Jacobean England, The King James Men is a moving evocation of love, friendship and betrayal.

Available from all good online bookstores.